WANDERER'S JOURNEY

THE FIRST BOOK OF
THE *WANDERER* SAGA

H.A. CAMPBELL

Copyright © 2024 H.A. Campbell
All rights reserved
First Edition

NEWMAN SPRINGS PUBLISHING
320 Broad Street
Red Bank, NJ 07701

First originally published by Newman Springs Publishing 2024

ISBN 979-8-89308-426-9 (Paperback)
ISBN 979-8-89308-427-6 (Digital)

Printed in the United States of America

SHATTERED DREAMS

A single drop of water fell through the still air and bounced off of the stone floor, the only sound besides the frantic racing of Demetrius's heart. Along the wall, a sea of plumed hats and silken garments glared at Demetrius. The tension in the room pressed around him, working its way into each of his limbs. He shifted his weight to his other foot as he waited for the nobles to make up their minds. His eyes roved across the room to the empty throne. The back of his throat began to ache. He clenched his teeth together. He couldn't cry. Not now. His older brother, Dunbar, seemed so happy. How could he be happy with their father gone? It didn't seem right. He looked away, unable to stand the sight of his brother's smiling eyes. Why would the nobles choose Dunbar anyway? They wouldn't, right? He was almost sure he would be chosen, almost sure he, Demetrius, the favorite child of his father, would be made king. But what if he wasn't? The curtain over the door rustled, sending the scent of perfume into the room. Demetrius squeezed his eyes shut. He knew that scent—slightly skunkish and overpowering. His mother, the dowager queen. A different ache in his heart began, the way it always did when she was around. Why couldn't she love him as much as she loved Dunbar? Wasn't he her son too? Jealousy filled his heart. The unfairness of it all. Surely the nobles wouldn't crown little goody-two-boots king.

A sound at the nobles' end of the room caught his attention. The men were standing up. Demetrius bounced on the balls of his feet. This was it. They would say it. They would call his name and place the crown on his head. He couldn't help but feel a little prideful—he was especially good-looking today. He had combed his black-brown hair till it shone, had worn the cape and doublet that best accentuated his muscles, had combed his sideburns till they looked tame, and polished his boots. After all, as king, he had better look the part. The oldest noble in the room stood, the crown in his hands. The seconds seemed to drag by in mute silence, as if the room were suddenly frozen in motion. The crown glinted in the sunlight, enticing. The crown, a promise of being more than the younger son, the extra, the son no one but his father loved. A promise of power, of prestige. No one would look down on Demetrius while that crown sat on his head; no one would call him names or ignore him. The noble opened his mouth. The time between the noble's open mouth and the sound that came out of it seemed slower than a summer day. Finally, a thin, reedy voice crawled through the air.

"*Dunbar*, Fangar of Antike, ruler of the realm, firstborn of the line of Soturant, *step forward.*"

Demetrius stared with empty eyes as his brother approached the throne.

No, it wasn't true. Surely they had just made a mistake. Maybe this was just a nightmare. He pinched himself. The awful scene before him—his brother kneeling before the nobles, Demetrius's crown glistening on Dunbar's head—didn't change. His knees wobbled. The light danced in his eyes, sparkling off the tears building at their corners. How dare they. He had dreamed of the feel of the scepter in his hand, the beautiful weight of the gold pressing down on his forehead, since he was old enough to talk. He was supposed to be king. Wasn't that what his father had raised him to be?

"*Kneel before your king,*" the old man commanded, his eyes piercing Demetrius like twin daggers. Demetrius fell to his knees, tears of rage blinding him. Whatever it took, he would become king. Whatever it took, that crown would sit on his head. And he would punish the nobles. They would be sorry. They would all be sorry.

A COPPER DAGGER

"Boy!" Demetrius's voice sliced through the air. Vayorn winced. *Great. He's in a mood.* Vayorn stood. "Come here, boy," he mimicked. Muttering under his breath, he dragged his aching feet to the doorway. He leaned against the doorframe, his eyes suddenly locked on a pile of knives laid out the table. His fingers twitched. His gaze wandered to the thin man at the table; King Demetrius. He studied the knives again. *One stab…that's all it would take.* He imagined how it would feel, to sink a dagger deep into Demetrius…he shook himself. He could never escape in time. A copper dagger glinted in the light as Demetrius toyed with it; Vayorn gritted his teeth. *No one catches him off guard.* His fingers twitched again. *Still…just one stab…*

"Get…over here." Demetrius said quietly. A chill ran down Vayorn's spine. He forced his feet forward, trying not to stare. *Mama Yanya said he used to be handsome? How?* Somehow, the thing in front of him seemed more monster than human. Demetrius's bones pressed against his gaunt skin, so pale it was almost translucent. The only life in his face was his eyes, burning with hatred and jealousy.

Vayorn caught his reflection in the mirror at the far end of the room. *Can't blame him for being jealous…* He fixed his rumpled hair; it was dark brown, but in this light it looked black. He glared at himself, admiring his reflection. Dark black eyes; stunning, one of the slave girls had called them. *Wish I was taller though.* He lifted his chin and straightened his back. *At least I've got broad shoulders. Makes up for my height.* Someone passed in the hallway behind him. He shot a glance over his shoulder, meeting a girl's eyes for a second. He winked. She blushed and ran past him. Shame hit him for a second. *What would Mama Yanya think?* He shrugged. *She's dead. So, it doesn't matter.* In a way, he was glad she was gone. *It would break her heart to see me now.*

A knife landed in the wood, the blade barely resting against his forehead. He jumped. Heart racing, he tensed up. *Not again*

"If you want to keep your worthless life, get over here!" The man's face flushed a bright red. His hand reached for another knife. Vayorn ran over.

"Yes, Master?" He said with as much fake submission as he could muster. It was never smart to cross Demetrius when he was in one of these moods.

"Pour my wine." His master waved his hand toward a golden goblet. Its jewels shone in the light, and jealousy twinged Vayorn's heart. His glance moved down to his own rough tunic. The color had long since faded, and stains patterned it like patchwork. Without thinking about it, he clenched his fists. The unfairness of it all. His jaw set stubbornly.

"With pleasure, Uncle," he said. Only too late did he realize his mistake—rage darkened Demetrius's face.

"What did you just call me?" His master's voice was dangerously quiet. It reminded Vayorn of the calm before a thunderstorm. The man's hand flew up. A plain copper knife pressed against Vayorn's throat. His stomach churned as a single thought—one he thought every time he saw that knife—flew through his head. *That knife killed my father.* His palms were cold and clammy, and a wave of nausea swept over him. *What kind of monster murders his own brother and makes his nephew a slave?* Painfully aware of the sharp point at his throat, he gulped.

"Master," the bitter word was indistinct through his gritted teeth. Fifteen years of resentment filled him. The knife returned to its sheath. He looked away to hide the hatred in his eyes as he poured the wine and handed it to his uncle. A servant ran in, her eyes carefully averted. She stole a quick glance at Vayorn as she spoke, she smiled at him.

Vayorn nodded at her, holding her gaze for an instant. She looked away, her face bright red.

"Le-letters for Archduke Demetrius Conglar." Her voice quavered. Her hands shook. The papers on her tray bounced. At the top of the pile was a richly decorated scroll. *From his lover probably. Is that his fifth or sixth this month? More importantly, what girl wants to pretend to love that piece of trash?*

Demetrius reached for the tray, his voice strained with eagerness. "Give it here, girl."

Vayorn watched and wished for the millionth time his parents were alive. *Stop hoping. They're dead. Fifteen years dead.* Vayorn wished he had known his father, or at least remembered something about him. Sure, he knew what his father was like; everyone had something to tell Vayorn about him, but that was no substitute for having his own memories of his father. The tales and recollections of the other servants, marketers, and even other nobles painted a picture of his father in Vayorn's mind. The peasants spoke of his justice and fairness. The people in the marketplace said he was kind and gentle. The other slaves claimed he treated them as family. Even Janus said he missed Vayorn's father. The other nobles laughed at how angry he used to get at their "corruption and evil." The old women whispered that he was the only noble who deserved his title. And yet even knowing all that, his father seemed more like some ancient king of legend than an actual person: too good to have been real. "Boy, clear the table." Demetrius sprang from his seat.

A shiver ran down Vayorn's spine; what was in that letter? He wished he could read. Whatever it was, it couldn't be anything good. Demetrius seemed too happy for that. *Why do I feel like that letter was about me?* Vayorn tried to fight back the fear gnawing at his mind. *I'll kill him. Someday he'll pay.* Vayorn glared at Demetrius's back.

He turned and began to slam the dishes into a jumbled heap, cursing Demetrius with each fork, each spoon, each plate he gathered. The plates, made of solid gold, jounced against each other as he carried them through the doorway into the hall. In the silence, the sound seemed unnervingly loud. The stone hallways, so quiet you could hear a drop of water hit the floor, echoed with the clinking of gold against gold. Fine tapestries—garish displays of golds, reds, blues, and purples—covered the bleakness of the stonework but did nothing to dispel the gloom. Gold candles glimmered in deep alcoves, their light dim. The chill of the approaching winter rose from the bare floors, their stone like ice. Vayorn wished Demetrius could have cold feet for once, but Demetrius's wing was padded with the finest Munharibian carpets Vayorn had ever seen. As he descended the steep, winding staircase to the kitchen, he shivered. Water dripped from the roof. The cracked stonework was like an open floodgate, letting in the winter wind. Vayorn paused outside a window. The bleak landscape glared back at him. The fields were bare of the little they grew. It didn't matter where Vayorn looked; the same sickly shade of gray was cast over everything. Clouds hid the sun and crows circled above the town, a rugged square of spiked roofs confined by a line of stone teeth. Vayorn sighed. *It's like my life.* With disgust, he turned away from the window and continued descending.

A rank stench stung Vayorn's nostrils as he entered the noxious atmosphere of the dungeon level. Ghoulish shadows reeled on the walls in the weak flicker of the torches. Vayorn's feet had trodden these steps as long as he could remember, yet a sense of dread came over him every time he descended to the dungeon-level kitchen. Deep groans from the black void of the dungeon rose and fell in tortured agony. At times, it was the shriek of a banshee; at others, it was the anguished outcry of some beast trapped forever in the darkness. It was just the wind, but around the fire on winter nights, the slaves told tales of the dungeon. Tales to make a person's blood run cold. Tales of prisoners who were more dead than alive. Tales of monsters who rose from the depths on winter nights to roam the halls of the castle. Tales of shape-shifters who entered the rooms of unwary sleepers to drag them into the abyss from which the creatures came. During the day, the tales seemed to be merely tales. Everyone knew that the dungeon was no longer in use. It was locked. It had been locked for generations. All the prisoners were sent to the prison in the center of town. But at night, the tales were as real to those who slept near the entrance of the dungeon as the very ground they slept on. At night, the floors creaked and howls flew down the corridors. Screams erupted from sleepers, tormented even in their dreams. Vayorn took a deep breath, tensed, and passed the dungeon gate. It was in the center of the wall, and in order to get to the kitchen, he had to pass it. A shriek erupted from the depths. He jumped. *Sooner I leave, the better.* As he approached the kitchen, the cook's voice became louder.

"Burned! Why you…and the custard! I thought I told you…and where's that lazy, slug-a-bed, good-for-nothing Vayorn?" His shoulders tensed. If only he could be free for five minutes. For five measly minutes. The heat of the stoves and stench of sweat blasted him as he entered the kitchen.

A HUNDRED GOLDS

"I'd pay you to take him, Altan." Demetrius slapped the trader on the back. The trader's vice grip on Vayorn's arm tightened. Vayorn smashed his foot down on the trader's foot and broke loose. He put himself on the other side of the table from the two men. A guard grabbed him and shoved him back toward them. Vayorn stumbled.

"Proklyat!" The trader grabbed his foot and started hopping around. "You, Demetrius of heavy hand, can no control him? Shocking," Altan set his foot down. Suddenly delighted, he began laughing. His immense stomach shook, matching his bulbous nose wiggle for waggle. "Well, I tame him." Altan patted a large club hanging on his hip. The veins in Vayorn's neck throbbed. *Wish I had a knife.* He clenched his fists. *They won't go through with this. I'll make sure they won't.* The trader examined Vayorn's biceps again.

"Yes, vey strong. I give you hundred golds. Deal?" Altan offered his hand to Demetrius.

"Well now, Altan, we may be old friends, but the boy is worth more than that. Worth at the very least fifty and one hundred."

Altan sniffed. "Smeshnoy! At most twenty and one hundred."

"Forty?"

"Thirty. No more."

"Deal." Demetrius shook his hand. *How dare they.* Vayorn's face became hot. *They can't do that. Wish I could get my hands on a knife.*

Demetrius smirked at him, gloating. He glared. His eyes suddenly riveted to the knife at the guard's hip. A muscle in his arm twitched. He forced himself to hold still. *Would he notice if I stole it?*

Demetrius escorted his guest to the door, nodding with pleasure as Altan showered him with flattery. *I vow that after this night, I won't ever be a slave to anyone ever again.*

Vayorn shook the guard off. He swung at the man. The guard threw him to the floor. Vayorn made one more halfhearted attempt at rising. The guard kicked him and walked out. Vayorn waited till the room was empty and rose; the dagger's hilt clenched in his fist. Satisfaction filled him. His ribs throbbed. *Worth it. So worth it.* He concealed the knife under his tunic. *That was almost too easy.* He straightened his shoulders. "Vaaaayooorn! Yooooou laaaazy sluuug-aaaa-beeed! Geeeet dooown heeeere!" He could hear the cook's bellow even from the dining hall. *Sounds like a dying cow.*

He turned and stormed out. *Whatever it takes, I'm getting out of here. Tonight. Won't wait anymore.*

The day seemed to fly by him. When no one was looking, he fingered his knife. At last. *After tonight I'll be a free man. Never have to see Demetrius again. Till I kill him. This will be the night.* He broke dishes as he washed them. The cook loaded his bin with yet more dishes. He carried the steaming breakfast and lunch trays up the stairs, thinking about the first meal he would eat as a free man. The cook had to repeat her commands two or three times before Vayorn realized she was speaking to him. The pale sun rose, hung in the middle of the sky for part of the morning, and sank back into the night. Vayorn carried the supper dishes up the stairs.

He laid them on the table, his excitement mounting.

Demetrius sat down but didn't start eating.

What's he waiting for?

The curtain over the door rustled. Vayorn turned.

A woman stood in the doorway, her willowy silhouette lit gold from the candlelight in the dining hall. *This must be madame number six. Wonder how long it'll take Demetrius to get tired of this one and kill her.* It had only taken Demetrius a week with the last one. The woman in the doorway poised one hand on her hip and took a step forward. She was tall, with strong features and well-sculpted muscles. She gave Vayorn a long glance as she passed him, then sat beside Demetrius. She chatted blithely with Demetrius as Demetrius ate, her lilting Nacionish accent filling her words with color. Despite her accent though, her voice had a harshness and authority that Vayorn found shocking in one of Demetrius's lovers. Typically, they were ornamental beauties with little to no willpower. Vayorn found them disgusting.

But not this one. She seemed stronger than the typical escorts Demetrius picked up. Vayorn waited for them to finish eating.

With every bite Demetrius took, Vayorn's anticipation grew. He tried to not show his impatience, but his foot tapped against the floor as the night wore on. He shifted his weight from one foot to the other, waiting for Demetrius to finish eating. *Can't possibly take this long to eat.*

Finally, Demetrius gave a dismissive wave of his hand. The woman rose and left the room, her perfume lingering on the air behind her.

Vayorn threw the plates into a heap at one end of the table, trying to go slowly. Demetrius watched him, his gaze reminding Vayorn of a cat watching a mouse.

"Boy, remember this. The next master you have won't be so kind as myself." Demetrius chuckled. "I've seen to that. Xira has a rather infamous trade route. Of course, you didn't know that, you poor, simple, undereducated whelp. Oh, but you'll know plenty about it quite soon, yes. But no matter if your mind's not much to mention. You only need brawn to work the quarry mines up in Kharghis."

Just leave already. Vayorn looked away, afraid his eagerness for Demetrius to leave would show in his eyes.

Demetrius chuckled, "Sad, are we? I share your sorrow. It pains me to give you up. It almost strikes me as not worth the gold. I would have so preferred to send you to your father. At the tip of this knife!" With a sudden jerk, the dagger landed, its tip pressing into Vayorn's throat.

Vayorn's heart raced. The dagger gnawed into his consciousness as it hovered under his chin. His breathing quickened. He craned his neck away from the blade.

Demetrius's maniac cackle rang out, and the dagger returned to its sheath. "But no. I do believe a slow death is better. After all, you only die once, and once I've killed you, I can't have that pleasure again." Demetrius tossed his empty wineglass on the table, rose, and stalked to the doorway. As he came to the doorway, he paused. "Sleep well, boy. Our friend will be here at daybreak." Still chuckling, he left the hall.

Good riddance, vulture, Vayorn thought. That night he followed the other slaves to the sleeping quarters, if it could be called that. The kitchen slaves slept on the ground by one of the dungeon's many exits, rolling out their thin mats and drifting off into restless dreams. It was silent now, except for the slaves' exhausted snores floating to the ceiling. Vayorn crept silently from his cot. He chose his steps with care, trying to step over the other slaves. A loose stone bounced off his foot and rolled across the floor. Pressure filled his head as he held his breath, listening for the sounds of someone waking up from a deep sleep. Every muscle in his body was rigid. Statue-like, he stood, waiting in the silence. Nothing. His breath rushed out. He threw his few items of clothing into his bag.

The darkness closed around him as he turned and slipped out. He struck a match, his hand shaking. His small candle flickered to life. The wind rose, carrying the howls with it. Like a hammer on an anvil, he could hear his heart pounding in his head, too loud in the silence. He entered the kitchen and carefully wove his way between the tables. The pantry seemed to swallow his hand as he reached into it. A pile of lumps covered by a rough cloth met his hand. The tangy scent of the bread drifted into his nostrils. With gentle hands, he unwrapped a loaf. His mouth watered. There were only twelve loaves left; it was Demetrius's favorite. *See how he likes not having exactly what he wants for once.* He shoved all twelve loaves into his bag. His attention moved to the shelves near the door. Holding his light close to the shelf nearest him, he examined the rounds of cheese. There it was. His hand shot out. Several rounds disappeared inside his bag.

The strong odor of goat cheese, aged for several months, filled the air. His eyes came to rest on the shelf opposite him. Why not? He grabbed a bottle of wine from the shelf. *Can't see why anyone'd ever drink this stuff. Still, never hurts to have something for trading.* The pack was surprisingly light on his shoulder, even with the wine in it. He took a deep breath, like a diver about to plunge into cold water, and passed under the doorway. Darkness engulfed him. The dungeon howled behind him as he climbed the stairway. The wind reached its crescendo. A banshee scream erupted below him. Vayorn jumped. *Gotta get out of here!* The moon shone through the windows, painting the hallway with her own ghostly paleness. The tapestries hung in the shadows. The candles were extinguished for the night. His feet echoed on the stone as he ran through the hall. He held his wooden shoes in his hand, waiting to wear them till he was in the courtyard.

As he entered the courtyard and approached the gate, he ducked. No sound echoed in the desolate courtyard. No light shone in the buildings. Even the houndry was silent for the night. Staying well in the shadows, Vayorn slunk to a low point in one of the courtyard walls. *Can't let them see me.* Vayorn had seen more than one slave shot where they stood by the guards—at times, not even trying to escape. He took a step. His foot caught on something. He fell. The silence shattered, broken by the baying and howling from the houndry, its occupants roused from their slumber. A lantern burst into flame at the houndry door.

"Get 'im!" The sound of hinges squealed open behind him. Vayorn's heart raced. The bloodhounds were after him. Their paws rang out on the stone ground. They were getting closer. He ran. The stone of the wall met his hands. They were coming. With a final defiant glare at the window of Demetrius's bedchamber, he grabbed the broken edge of the wall and pulled himself up onto it. Teeth snapped at his rising feet. He balanced atop the ridge for an instant, then jumped.

The air rushed around him. His feet landed in the hard earth. Vayorn straightened his shoulders. *I'm free.* He shook his head, almost not daring to believe it. His heart pounded as he turned down an alley and faded into the gloom, leaving the sounds of the hounds trying to scale the wall he had jumped behind him. The streets were dark, the silhouettes of the buildings as dim as the clouds covering the moon. The wind threw itself down the alleys and lanes. The large wooden pig hung above the butcher's swung wildly. The shutters of Bomm's goldsmithery rattled. But the wind was just wind. There were no banshees to scream after him. There were no creatures of the night to moan at him. Vayorn wanted to laugh. The shuttered houses—their shapes obscure in the dim—rose above him. The deserted market stalls—gaping like open mouths, empty of their wares now that night had fallen—sped past Vayorn. The gate loomed into view. Its iron bars were barely discernible in the deep of the night. Vayorn slowed. *I'm only halfway to freedom till I make it past that thing.* More than one escape had ended at that gate. He heard footsteps. His legs bent. Prepared to run if he was discovered, he crouched in the shadows behind a stack of crates. The footsteps grew louder. There were voices.

"So, who is she?" The voice was familiar, barely audible in the furious wind. *If I didn't know better, I'd say that's Demetrius's little foreign lover. Hope she stabs him in his sleep.*

"I heard she is a peasant girl."

"Where does she live? Do you know?"

"Yes madam, but…"

"Kill her. The cheating…" she half-shouted a curse word, "How dare he? I want her dead. Demetrius needs no other than me. If you hear of any other little, distractions, tell me. I'll pay you richly to kill them too."

Chills ran up Vayorn's spine. *She's gonna be busy then. I could give her at least twenty other names.* The footsteps drifted back down the main road. Vayorn breathed a sigh of relief. Chills stopped going up his spine. Time was short.

Vayorn leaped from his hiding place and ran down an alley that followed the wall, into outdweller territory. The stink of refuse and mold wafted into his nostrils. The houses were placed in ramshackle disorder, and the roofs of the shacks bent till they brushed the wall. The disrepair and filth were welcome to Vayorn after years of trudging across the palace's icy floors and gazing out the clear, crystal windows. He had dreamed of this escape for years, had memorized the patrol patterns of the guards, had examined the wall every time he ran the palace errands. Now it was time. Vayorn caught a glimpse of a small form scurrying into one of the shacks. He smiled. *Why's Demetrius kill so many of them? Is he even human??* He couldn't help but love these rough, filthy people. After all, they were the only family he had ever known. He had grown up with their children. *We're alike. Everyone hates us.* He slid behind the houses with the furtive slinking walk the outcast children had taught him—so long ago now, it was almost second nature. He followed the wall, searching for the "gate." *Wonder who's guarding tonight?* He rolled his shoulders. He remembered the first time he had used the "gate." He had been about ten. He chuckled. *Scared me back then.* Anyone of less importance than a peasant was allowed to use the gate, and everyone of less importance than a peasant knew how it worked—one shove, and it went flying. It was only a small gap in the wall, filled with a pile of stones. Vayorn felt along the wall till his fingers brushed a loose section. There it was. Vayorn paused. A small scratching sound came from a corner by the hole. *Scratch, scratch, scratch.* Vayorn set his bag down and returned the sign. *Scratch, scratch, scratch.* He crept to the corner, prepared to spring, and leaped. His watcher fell to the ground under him. They scuffled. A fist met his cheek. He swung the person's arm behind them, pinning it straight. "Righto. You take," the person said. Vayorn let go. The boy turned around.

"Bad'rad! What're you doing here?" Vayorn clapped the boy on the back. Badurad shrugged his bony shoulders. His face was sharp, like a rat's, and his nose stuck out from his face like a beak.

"Swingin' left over the looksie. Ain't no highbrow gonna git past me." He gestured to the hole, then at the knife hung from his belt. Vayorn nodded.

"Trouble tonight?"

"Them soldiers come kickin' by not a few punches ago. Getting harder to dodge out it is. You skippin' out tonight?"

"Perm'nent." Vayorn caught himself slipping into the rough outdweller speech.

"So you're cuttin' out, eh? Fin'ly had 'nough 'a old hang'em? 'Bout time." Vayorn nodded. "Well, may yer clouts land heavy and yer arms be bonebreakers. Best'a luck, Vay'rn."

Vayorn tackled him, just to make sure Badurad knew he was grateful. Badurad rose and caught Vayorn in a headlock on his way up. "Git scramblin'!" Badurad shoved Vayorn toward the hole.

"Can't leave 'ithouten tellin' you goodbye," Vayorn said. His fist swung and met Badurad square in the gut. The air flew out of him as Badurad enthusiastically returned his goodbye. As silent as the rats he lived with, Badurad vanished into the shadows.

Vayorn took a deep breath. He threw himself at the wall. The wall gave way under his weight, disappearing in a cloud of dust and pebbles. He crashed onto his back on the hard, stony ground, the dark sky reeling above him. His lungs refused to breathe. White spots filled his vision. Gasping for breath, he sat up. Pain seared through his shoulder. He reached a tentative hand up. No blood. That was good. His shoulder was numb, but even now he could hear the tramp of the booted patrol. His bag flew from behind the opening and conked him in the head. Badurad was frantically signaling to him. The tramp of metal boots was growing closer. Shadows flitted to and fro as the hole filled with rock again. Badurad waved his arm left and made the signal to run. Vayorn seized his bag and made a wild dash for the woods. His chest rose and fell with rapid breaths. Feeling burned back into his arm. He kept running. *So close. So close. Can't give up now. Won't.*

LIGBIRIA FOREST

The trees loomed overhead. He threw himself into their cover and landed face down on the dead, crumbling leaves like a sack of rocks. He lay on the ground panting. *I did it! I really did it!* Free. His tangled hair caught on his fingers as he raked a hand through it. *I actually did it!* "Free"—the word echoed in his mind like a bell ringing in the change of seasons. Every dream that had ever kept him awake at night, every hope he had ever dared to entertain, every yearning aroused by insults and commands, every pain he had ever felt in his life, embraced by that one word. Exultation filled him like a wildfire, burning into every part of him till he was sure he would explode. Unconsciously, his back straightened, and his fists clenched.

"I'm free! Do you hear me? Free!" The dark sky loomed over him, as if to challenge his words. The moon came out for an instant from the clouds. It glinted off something. Soldiers. The raucous clank of swords against armor approached as the patrol made its rounds. Vayorn's lip curled. *Try to stop me now.* He turned his back on Tarshal and strode into the forest.

The lifeless black claws of the branches dug into the sky. A mist swept through the trees like a grave-shroud. Shadow engulfed Vayorn. An intense awareness of the forest grew on him as his exultation wore off. The forest felt alive, as if it had a mind of its own, in a way that sent ice up Vayorn's spine.

Vayorn tried to ignore the prickly feeling at the back of his neck. He glanced over his shoulder; nothing. He shuddered. There was something out there. He knew it. He wrapped his arms around himself as a chill settled in his bones. *What's in there?* He laid a hand on his knife and drew it out. The wind picked up. His feet plodded through the soft leaves, raking up the scent of decay. *Wish it was daylight.* He tried to keep his mind from wandering. Somehow, he didn't feel as brave now. The smell of rotting flesh drifted into his nostrils. *Don't want to know who that was.* His stomach lurched. One of the slaves disappeared last week; into Ligbiria the others said. *Just like me.* He wrapped his arms around his torso. He had to get out of the forest. *What if I get lost?* He pushed the thought out of his mind. A stick broke behind him. He tensed. Slowly, a large shadow emerged from the night. Its head disappeared high above him. The trees creaked as it pushed its massive legs between them. It grunted.

Giant sloth! Vayorn backed away, trying not to make any noise. A log bumped his leg. He turned. It was hollow. The thing came toward him. He dove into the log. The log shook as the creature came closer. A large, wet snout nosed Vayorn's hair. He held his knife close to it, waiting. A claw came through the side of the log and grazed Vayorn's leg. Vayorn rolled away from it. Suddenly, the log began spinning, rolling downhill. Vayorn tried not to scream. The thing followed, growling. Vayorn slid out of the log and ran. Behind him, he heard the log break apart.

Still running, he sighed with relief. *That was close. Too close.* He hoped it wouldn't follow him.

Something flapped above him. He swung his knife. A bat fell at his feet. He kicked it out of the way and kept running. *Hope I'm going in the right direction.*

The storm picked up around him, throwing down fist-sized hail. The wind threw him to the ground. He pushed himself up and kept running. A branch fell. And another. And another. He held his head low and kept moving.

In front of him, something raced across the forest floor. He stopped. *Terror birds.* He tried to climb a tree. They ran beneath him as his legs swung into the branches. His foot barely brushed one's head. He counted them. E*ight…nine…ten.* The smallest bird was about his height; all the others were far bigger than Vayorn.

The storm intensified. They disappeared. The branch underneath Vayorn fell. He yelped.

Rubbing his leg, he ran again. *Have to get out.* Something grunted behind him. A large snout bumped his back. Slowly, he turned his head.

"Oh, great. You again."

The giant sloth roared. It swiped a paw at Vayorn. Vayorn screamed. It jumped back.

Vayorn sped off. *Have to get out. Have to get out.* He dodged between trees. Over the wind, he heard the trees breaking behind him. He swore. *How hard is it to lose a gachiting sloth?* Suddenly, a cliff rose in front of him. He frantically climbed. Rocks crumbled underneath his feet as the thing clawed at the cliff face behind him. His hands began bleeding. He climbed harder.

He swung his feet onto firm ground, scrambled away from the edge, and ran. *There. Try to follow me up that.* He kept running.

The hail turned to rain. It fell like a million rocks, pounding Vayorn's skin through his thin shirt. Water poured into his eyes, blinding him. A branch hit his face. He ducked. Something tripped him. He staggered to his feet. *Have to get out.* A tree above him moaned. He looked up. Lightning struck the tree, illuminating the night for an instant. A crack split the tree in half. The top began falling. Vayorn tried to run away from it.

The air whistled around it as it fell; Vayorn tripped. The tree landed across his chest. He blacked out.

Vayorn stirred. Light came through his closed eyelids. He tried to move. The tree was gone. Warm air blew in his face. He sat up; his eyes opened. Something snapped shut behind him. He swore and stood.

"Stop following me!" he screamed at the sloth. It swung its head. There was blood along its jaw. Vayorn looked down at his leg. The pants leg was ripped, and a light tooth mark was bleeding down his leg. Vayorn threw a rock at the sloth.

"Deng you!"

The sloth roared and charged him. Vayorn ran, slipping in the mud.

The ground shook. The sloth raised its claw; Vayorn ducked. It landed behind his ankle. Vayorn turned into the trees.

"Just find something else to eat!" He grabbed a branch and swung it into the sloth's face. It growled. The tree crashed to the ground. Vayorn slid down a hillside and jumped a boulder.

A tree flew through the air and landed at his feet. He jumped it and wove into the trees…

A soft shower was falling through the branches, pattering onto the forest floor. A chilly wind swirled around him, and he shivered. He dropped to his knees and tried to steady his breathing. *I'm alive! Can't believe I outran it! I'm alive! I'm alive, but where am I?* His legs shaking, he rose to his feet, steadying himself against a tree. He touched his back. Something sticky covered his hand; he gasped. It was dripping with red. *Can't be bleeding! It doesn't hurt.* His arm hit his bag as he swung around. It sounded like it was full of shards of glass scraping together. Vayorn opened it. Pieces of shattered glass filled the bag, mixed into a pile of mush—the bread, he realized with a sinking feeling in his gut. He shoved his hand into the bag. The soggy mush stuck to his hands as he dug it out, shaking it off his hands with disgust. *I'm an idiot. A complete and total idiot.* His hands hit one of the cheese rounds. Carefully, he pulled it out. The cheese's cloth was still tight around it. He breathed a sigh of relief. He wouldn't go completely hungry. One by one, he removed the rounds from the bag, tightening the waterproof cloths around them. Gingerly, he began picking the shards of glass out of the bag, trying to avoid getting cut. He dumped his clothes out on the ground. His extra shirt was ruined; it had been his favorite shirt. Now the rich green fabric was splotched with brown. His vest still looked decent; the deep brown color hid the stains well. He hung them on a branch and wearily rose. The clothing he was wearing hung on him, dripping like a drenched towel. He grabbed a handful of his shirt and twisted it. The water washed over his foot. He wrung his shirt and trousers out as much as he could. They were damp and numbingly cold. He shivered. His gaze wandered around the clearing he was in. Mist waited around its edges, a mellow gray but growing to a shadowy black color. This was bad. Wishing he hadn't panicked last night, he tried to peer into the mist. *Where am I?* The soft rain was swiftly hardening into ice-cold sleet. His clothing hanging off the branch was waterlogged. He shoved it back into his bag. The wind tore down the valley, stinging his eyes and pelting him with rock-hard drops. There was one hole, he realized, in his grand plan: he had never intended to spend the night in the woods—lost, wet, cold. His survival experience was limited to stealing what he needed from the larder of the castle. His plan had been to stop at an inn down the road. He surveyed the area around him. The trees ahead of him were waning in the wall of fog. He shivered. The wind sawed through his soaking rags. *Have to get out.* He picked a direction and started walking. *Hope this is the right way.* His teeth chattered, matching the uncontrollable shaking of his body. Water poured down on top of him. The wind bent the treetops as if trying to break them in half. *There better be an inn near here.* He staggered onward. The day swept by in an endless blur of misery. Hot flashes of fire flowed through his veins, followed by cold flashes of ice, freezing him to his very bones. He was growing sick—fast. His vision was fuzzy, and the forest stretched out without end. And endlessly there his feet were, going ever onward, till he began to wonder if walking was all there was. Perhaps Tarshal was just a bad dream, and this forest, worse even than Tarshal, was the only thing that existed. His mind was hazy, and the forest whirled in dizzy circles around him.

As night began to fall, coughing racked his wretched frame. *Can't stop. Stop. Stop. Rest. Can't. Need to. Food.* His fevered mind wandered. Howls rose from all around him, but he was deaf to their screaming. Night fell, but he did not notice. He dropped his bag and left it where it landed, completely oblivious to its absence. *Walk. Walk. Can't stop.* The only clear thought amid the clouds in his mind was that he had to create distance between himself and Demetrius. The ice of the wind was indistinguishable from the ice in his veins. He was cold. That was all he knew. He staggered, crashing to the ground over and over again as his legs gave out under him. The world was wavy, as if he were looking through water, and the sounds that filtered into his ears were distant. He crashed to the ground, his strength spent, unable to rise. Someone ran up to him. The voice that shouted, "Boy! Boy! Hey! Are you alright?" was indistinct, as if it was shouted down a long tunnel. He dimly heard, "Get over here! Help me carry him!" Then his eyes closed as he slipped into the warm arms of oblivion.

He was dimly aware of a rough hand on his brow. Something damp and cool gently wiped his forehead. Dim light hammered into his head as his eyes fluttered open. He immediately wished he had stayed asleep. His head pounded as if ten blacksmiths were hammering on anvils inside it. A huge man sat on the edge of the bed, the only clear thing Vayorn could see in the gray fog of his blurry vision.

"Ye're awake. Feelin' better?" The man's hand came into Vayorn's vision, a large, wet cloth dangling from it. The cloth smacked onto Vayorn's forehead. Vayorn tried to speak past his sore throat. His voice came out as a creaking "Fine," cut off by a fit of coughing. Black spots danced before his eyes.

"Don't try to speak. Just rest, laddo." The man slid his arm behind Vayorn and helped him sit up. Vayorn's ears rang as he changed position. Still supporting him, the man held a steaming cup of tea up to Vayorn's lips. Vayorn's hands felt heavy, like lead weights were tied to them, as he tried to lift them to hold the cup. He lifted them a few shaking inches off the bed before they crashed back down onto the blankets. *Where am I? Why am I like this? How did I get here?* He tried to clear his mind but gave up when the last thing he could remember was breaking the wall. There were faint glimpses of something in his memory, something broken. A jar, maybe? He gave up. It was too much work to remember right now. His eyes closed, and he sank into the warmth of the tea washing over his raw throat. The room seemed to rock underneath him, as if the floor was moving. His limbs ached, and his scratches and cuts burned.

"I 'ave to put somethin' on those. Big wounds they are." The man gestured to Vayorn's throbbing back. Vayorn tried to clear his head again. The worst cuts and welts were bandaged. Vayorn tried to make himself nod, but his head refused to move. The man pushed a pillow up behind Vayorn, adjusting it till Vayorn was held securely upright, and rose. Light streamed in as the door opened. Vayorn's head felt airy, and his ears felt like they were full of dandelion fluff.

"Artair! Artair, lad!"

A man rushed in. Vayorn tried to make his vision focus long enough to get a good look at the man in the doorway, but all he saw was a large, talking, blurry blob.

"Aye-aye, Blackie." The blob strode over to Vayorn, becoming a large man with a dirty, unruly beard. He held Vayorn up. The other man, whom Vayorn supposed was "Blackie," slid behind him and began removing bandages.

"This might hurt, it might," Blackie warned. Vayorn winced as a cloth touched the first welt. The salve was cool to the touch, but fire shot through Vayorn's back as it penetrated into the wounds. By the time Blackie was finished, Vayorn was exhausted with pain. Blackie gently bandaged Vayorn's injuries again and sent Artair out.

"Sleep now." Blackie laid Vayorn back down and covered him with a heavy thick blanket. Vayorn closed his eyes and sank into slumber, losing the small control he had had over himself.

GOLD FRAMES

I look up at the mouth of a cave. It's so big it's almost the only thing I can see. A candle's in my hand. A sword's in my other hand. There are gems all over its hilt. Strange square shapes are carved into its blade. The metal looks blue in the light. The shapes are a strange gold color, like the light on Demetrius's wineglass. It's pretty. A blast of hot air hits me all of a sudden. I turn back to the cave. The rotten air coming out of it stings my throat and chokes me. Strange, greenish light glows from somewhere inside it. I shudder. It's getting dark around me, quick. I look down. The candle's gone. This thing with antlers and a woman's face bounds up to me. Her voice rises and falls. Can't hear most of what she says in the wind. "You will...destroy...or be destroyed by..."

"What?" A wind hits me, and I fall. The thing shrieks as it disappears. Reminds me of the moon being swallowed by clouds, or a piece of bread being swallowed by Demetrius. I realize the blackness is smoke.

"Eight days...eight days...eight days...," echoes around me. Can't figure out where it's coming from. Seems like it's coming from everywhere.

"Eight days for what?" A wagon flies at me out of the mist. I scream and duck. It runs over me. I stand again, surprised I'm not hurt. A turquoise blur brushes by me. The wind hits it, and it's gone.

"Vayorn!" I hear it yell my name as it flies into the air.

"Your father," a voice whispers. The sound comes from the cave. Suddenly a woman rises in front of me. Her cheekbones are sharp like Demetrius's. I back away. The wind hits her, and she melts like a candle. A hot breeze hits my face.

"All is not as it seems. Watch…watch…watch…"

"Watch what?"

Something roars. The cave comes alive. I hide on the ground, hoping it won't see me. The dirt around it falls off it. Some of it gets in my eyes, and I can't see. When my eyes clear, I'm face-to-face with this giant black wolf. I scream and run. As it chases me, its roar becomes Demetrius's voice.

"I have a plan…a plan…a plan…a plan…" It's behind me. I can feel its hot breath burning my ankles. I look down. My feet won't move. I try to run, but I can't. It digs its claw into my side. The pain is worse than anything I could've ever imagined. I scream and fall down, groaning, pressing my hands to my side. Suddenly I can't see. There's a red fog in my eyes. Then the only thing I can see is black.

*****

Vayorn woke with a start. The sheets beneath him were soaked, and his face was damp. *Was I sweating that much?* He kept seeing the faces from his dream, so real in the dim half-light he could almost touch them. He realized he was trembling. His throbbing back was painful against the wet sheets beneath it, and a splitting headache blurred his vision. The door opened. Blackie walked in.

"Alright, laddo. Got more fer ye." Blackie sat on the edge of the bed. It creaked under his weight. "Ye look like ye've seen a ghost, ye do." He swung Vayorn up. "Slept fer nigh on twilve hours. Here. This'll stand ye up." He gave Vayorn a drink of the tea. "Can ye move yer 'ands yet?" Vayorn's vision cleared. He tried to shake his head.

"Laddo! Ye moved yer head!" Blackie said. The cheerful sunniness in his voice was almost fake sounding it was so exaggerated. Vayorn was struck by how broad his smile was. Too broad. *What exactly's he trying to get from me?*

"Speak! Say something!" Blackie nodded with an animated grin pasted on his face, but his eyes were cheerless. Vayorn felt himself stiffen. *Didn't leave Tarshal just to have someone else order me around.* Obstinately silent, he looked past Blackie as if Blackie did not exist.

"Surely ye're not still so weak?" Blackie glanced at Vayorn out of the corner of his eye, a scornful expression on his face. *Weak?* Vayorn's face reddened. *Weak?*

Mustering up all his strength, Vayorn asked, "Where…am…I?" Like a rusted wheel on a wagon, the words stuck, and his voice sounded like a dying goose trying to honk. He didn't notice the satisfied grin on Blackie's face. The man ran to the door.

"Ho! Lads! Lads, 'e spoke!"

The sounds of raucous cheering filtered through the walls. Vayorn's eyes widened. *How many men are out there?* Vayorn eyed the doorway. *What're they so excited about? What do they want from me?* As far as Vayorn could see, they had no reason to cheer for him. They didn't know him. *Why'd they save me? They couldn't know who I am, right?* No. That was impossible. They couldn't know who he was because he hadn't told them. That simple. He tried to reassure himself, but the uneasy feeling stayed in his gut. There was something strange about all this.

A shadow appeared in the door. Vayorn squinted, trying to focus his blurry vision. The fuzzy outline of a small boy slowly became clear. The child, about eight years old, trotted over the bed with a bowl. The water sloshed out of it, leaving a trail of wet behind him. Blackie followed the child, his feet spreading the water across the floor.

"Let's 'ave a look at that back now," Blackie said, pulling a chair alongside the bed for the child.

"This be him?" The little boy looked at Vayorn, his eyes round. "But he be young. How he survive? Even big fat you would die there." A mischievous light sprang into the child's eyes with the last remark. His *sss* and *ou* sounded more like *sh* and *a*. *Xíran accent*. There was something else strange about the way he spoke, but Vayorn couldn't quite place his finger on it.

The child slid behind Vayorn to support him while the man doctored him. Steam rose from the brown liquid in the bowl beside them. The rag made a small splash as it dunked into the liquid. Blackie touched it to Vayorn's back and began washing the cuts with the liquid. It was warm on Vayorn's back but stung—in a pleasant warm way, like eating something just spicy enough—as it touched Vayorn's wounds. Vayorn could feel the child's steady stare, even without looking at the boy. The child kept saying "Survived Ligbiria?" over and over again. Vayorn enjoyed it at first, until it became obnoxious. He wanted to say, "Yes, I did survive Ligbiria. Knock it off." But he restrained himself.

He could feel Blackie stiffen behind him at the child's remark on his size, "Firstly, *fat* is not the word. I am not fat. Secondly, think I'm that"—he gestured to Vayorn—"'elpless boy? I tell ye, don't know what stuff ye be made of till ye're tested." He shook his head and spoke to Vayorn, his voice anything but sincere, "And, Laddo, ye be made of some thick stuff alright. Don't know how…" He finished bandaging Vayorn's back.

"Agöri, dismissed."

"Aye sir." The child meandered out of the room reluctantly, craning his neck to stare at Vayorn as he slowly passed through the door. Blackie laid Vayorn down.

"Get some sleep, laddo. 'Eaven knows ye'll be needin' it." He went out, and the door closed. Vayorn could hear a hum coming through the thin wooden walls. There were voices, and Vayorn could have heard what they were saying if he'd tried. Sleep danced at the edges of his consciousness, threatening to bring the nightmare with it. It was waiting like a stalking wolf for him to fall asleep, waiting for its chance to pounce.

Vayorn tried to hold his eyes open and keep his senses alert.

Wish there was something to do.

Time seemed to creep by at an almost unbearably slow rate. He stared at the ceiling, counting the planks of wood above him. *Sick of this.* He turned his attention to the cabin. His eyes landed on the wall opposite him. An uneasy feeling filled him. The golden frames around the paintings looked familiar—too familiar. It dawned on Vayorn. He had seen those same frames every time he entered Demetrius's wing of the palace. He tried to reason the uneasy feeling away. Just a coincidence. It couldn't be anything more than that. Still, it was impossible to not notice the lavish adornment of this room. The porthole was covered with a velvet curtain trimmed with fine lace. He couldn't help but wonder who exactly used this room. *Seems like it could just be coincidence. I'm sure it is.* He found his mind back on Blackie. Blackie had been nice—so nice it was almost like he had been putting on an act. What did he want? Vayorn was sure he wanted something. No one was that nice for no reason. *What game's he playing at?* He tried to keep his mind clear enough to think, but his eyelids kept falling shut. *Don't fall asleep. Stay awake.* The last thing he wanted was to have the nightmare again. His eyes slowly closed. The gentle swaying beneath him rocked his senses into peaceful dullness. *Can't fall asleep.* He exhaled and fell asleep.

A sound came through the thin walls of Vayorn's cabin. The noise began building. His eyes opened. *What's going on?* Blocking everything else out, he closed his eyes and concentrated on the sounds. Slowly, they became clear. He heard men yelling curses at each other, loudly punctuated by thuds and slapping sounds. Vayorn wished he could see through the walls. *Hate being this weak. Have to get well. Soon.*

"Wanna say that again?" someone shouted.

"Coward!" Vayorn couldn't be certain, but it sounded a lot like Agöri's voice.

A huge crash, faintly muffled through the walls, resounded.

"Want to visit Davey Jones's locker? No? Well, that be too bad."

Someone started screaming. Heavy footsteps crashed out of hearing. Vayorn lay tense, wishing the walls would disappear so that he could see. The planks above him stared down at him.

"Stop," a woman's voice rang out. *What's a woman doing on a ship?*

THE FLEET

"Set Agöri down, now," she said. There was a small crash followed by the sound of feet running. They stopped outside his door, making a shadow underneath it. *Common Tongue.* Vayorn realized suddenly that he hadn't heard Antikish since he'd woken. It didn't make much difference to him; everyone he knew spoke at least a little common tongue. Vayorn gritted his teeth. *Sick of Common Tongue.* He had been forced to learn it when he was child; like every other person he knew. At least it was useful. But that didn't make Vayorn any less tired of it.

"Agöri, come back here... Who's telling me what happened here? Did I give you permission to fight? How about shout? Alright, how about leave your work without the first mate's permission? Artair! You watched. What happened?" She had a lilting Nacionish accent, but her voice had a harshness and authority that Vayorn found shocking in a woman' voice. Vayorn strained his ears. There was something familiar about the voice. He wished he could see who was speaking. Light shone through the cracks around the door, interrupted by moving shadows in front of it.

"Well, um, uh, well, you see here, Captain, I...don't know."

"The Sam Hill you don't. Half rations, rest of the month..." Her voice got fainter as footsteps started to fade out of hearing. *Who is she? Funny, the captain must have been out there 'cause Artair called someone captain. How come the captain didn't say anything? Why's he letting her order his men around that? You'd think the captain wouldn't let her…unless she's his lover.* Vayorn's mouth twitched. That had to be it. *What else could it be?*

Slowly, he raised a hand, ignoring the pain in his shoulder. He smiled. *I can move!* He planted his hands firmly on either side of himself. Exhaling sharply, he thrust his weight upward. A few inches appeared between his back and the bed as he lifted himself on shaking arms. His arms slid out from underneath him. He dropped and found himself on his back again, glaring at the ceiling. *I'll be well tomorrow. Have to be.*

Golden light radiated through the window, piercing the gloom of the small cabin. Vayorn struggled and rolled to a half-sitting position. A ray of light blinded him, reflected off a mirror on the other end of the room. He could see his reflection. *Don't look too bad. A little pale, but actually look pretty good. A little rest sure hasn't done harm.* The curtain was drawn open over the porthole, and Black-Eye sat by the bed.

"Ah, ye be awake. Yer back's well." Blackie's voice sounded different. Vayorn realized it was because Blackie's voice was shaking. Blackie looked at the door, rubbed the back of his neck, and coughed. Vayorn followed his gaze to the door. He could hear a cheerful babel through the shut door. *What's bothering him?* Vayorn wished again that he could walk. He was sick of looking at the same things day after day.

"Ye'd be ready fer company, I hope?" A shaky fake cheerfulness coated Blackie's voice. There was a strained note to his jollity, and the sunlight reflected off the sweat on his face. The tray in Blackie's hands shook, sloshing a little tea into his lap. Blackie yelped like a cat with its tail stepped on, jumped, and the cup upended. The floor turned into a lake of amber liquid. Vayorn could hear Blackie muttering curses under his breath as he ripped a filthy rag off his belt and began mopping the mess off the floor. Vayorn's lip curled. *Now who's "weak"? Can't even tolerate a little hot tea.* Vayorn tried to sit up. He expected his arms to give way on him again, but they held firm under his weight. With a grunt, breathing heavily, he swung himself into a sitting position on the edge of his bed. His eyes lit up. How was that for "weak"? He pushed an impending smile into a scowl.

"Laddo! Well, this be pleasant fer sure!" Blackie wore a frown. Suddenly, his eyes owled as if he were remembering something, and his frown became a too-wide grin. Vayorn's eyebrows lowered slightly. *Just stop pretending already.* He crossed his arms.

"I'm thirsty." Vayorn kept his voice flat. Blackie laughed, though it sounded to Vayorn like more of a forced chuckle.

"Aye, I bet ye are." Blackie took the empty cup and left the room, muttering to himself. He returned a few minutes later with a cup of water. His hand shook as he handed it to Vayorn. Disgust filled Vayorn. *Whatever it is, he needs to man up and stop shaking. He's acting like some scared little girl.* Vayorn raised the cup to his lips.

The noise coming from outside intensified as the door opened. A shadow appeared on the floor. Agöri threw himself across the floor, arms and legs flapping like a drunken pelican. He ricocheted off the end of Vayorn's bed. Agöri plopped onto his rear on the floor and sat panting, his cheeks the color of ripe apples. He couldn't be more than eight. What was a little guy like him doing here, on a ship? Small for his age, wasn't he?

Agöri looked up. "Blackie, Captain want you." A strange series of expressions contorted Blackie's face. *Gotta be one of the most ugly things I've ever seen. Looks like he's either choking or dying.* "I replace you to serve him now."

Finally, Blackie's expression settled into a strange look—wild eyes, mouth clamped in a thin line, skin the color of maggot-filled white bread, right eye twitching.

"It's not servin', lad. Some-so-someone has to c-c-c-care for him. Ye're sure C-C-Captain wants me? Maybe it was Artair Captain wanted."

Vayorn gave an exasperated sigh. *Had enough of this.* Vayorn glared at Blackie, wishing Blackie would give him a reason to throw a punch. His eye fell on the chair. *Would it break if I threw it at him?* He set a leg off the bed and put weight on it; it began shaking. Vayorn pulled it back up. *Be realistic. Can't throw a punch, even if I want to. So sick of all this, think I'm gonna burst.*

"Leave. I don't need a caretaker."

Blackie backed away, folded his arms into his armpits and stood in front of the bed sputtering. He turned to the door, back to the bed, then to the door again.

"I. Said. Get. Out." Vayorn narrowed his eyes, hoping Blackie would argue with him.

"Blackie!" the woman's voice came through the wall. Blackie's Adam's apple jerked, and he ran out the door. It slammed behind him. Vayorn rolled his eyes and slouched back to lean against the wall.

"Don't send out. Please? You no need caretaker, but company perhaps?" Agöri smiled hopefully. Vayorn nodded. *Might as well humor him.*

"Great, thanks!" Agöri pulled a chair to the bed and sat.

As much as Vayorn didn't want to admit it, he found Agöri's obvious admiration amusing. *Acts like I'm Soturant himself.*

"Where are we?"

"Oh, is great ship! Is always chasing and looting! Are in the Bay of Raichtum," Agöri gesticulated wildly, his chair tipped backward, and Agöri tumbled into a tangled heap on the floor, legs straight in the air like banner staffs. Vayorn stifled a laugh.

Agöri came back up, red-faced and giggling. "Look! I get whole coin this month!" He pulled a small copper out of one of his numerous pockets. The corner of Vayorn's mouth came up. *A pirate ship. Explains a lot. He's so young. What made him join them? Who takes care of him?* The ragged holes in Agöri's clothing were glaringly obvious to Vayorn. Vayorn's eyes were drawn to the child's hands around the coin grasping it as if it were his greatest treasure.

"How often do you get paid?"

Agöri's antics should have been irritating, but somehow Vayorn found them amusing. *Wish I had a little brother like him.* Agöri sprang up and charged over to a cabinet. He rummaged around in it as he talked, flinging the contents of the cabinet across the room. Vayorn ducked as a barrage of items sailed over his head.

"Four copper a year, and bed with food." Agöri grinned proudly. Another box hit the floor. A candlestick hit the wall behind Vayorn, followed by books and a handful of jewelry that was missing its gems.

"You a cabin boy then?" Vayorn asked. He ducked.

Agöri nodded and tipped forward into the almost-empty cabinet, his top half completely disappearing. His heels and rump stuck up into the air.

"Aha!" Agöri flew right side up with a small wooden box in his hand. He trotted over to the bed.

"Do you like being a cabin boy?"

"Is better than on streets of Zaran. I starve in Zaran. I eat on ship." Agöri shrugged and opened the box. It was a wooden chess set. He began setting it up.

"Where's Zaran?" Vayorn asked. Agöri looked away. In the sudden silence, Vayorn chose a white pawn. They began playing. The only sound was the clinking of chess pieces against the board.

"Where you from?" Agöri's voice was quiet as he abruptly changed the subject. He killed Vayorn's queen. "Check." Sadness filled his voice, like a cold sleet in the winter.

"Never mind that." Vayorn noticed how quickly the word "Zaran" had changed Agöri's mood; the sunny smile was gone, and a sullen frown was in its place. The heavy mood pressed around them.

Vayorn looked out the porthole, his eyes suddenly riveted to the ocean. A long serpentine neck snaked out of the water in an erupting volcano of mist. It's ember-red eyes seemed to fixate on Vayorn, peering from behind a short snout. A giant flipper came out of the water and propelled the thing forward. Vayorn's eyes widened. The sunlight was blocked out as a giant hulk shadowed across the porthole. Its scales, like polished green silver, glistened against the glass. A small moan, almost like that of a low flute note, sounded. Vayorn leaned forward. They did exist! The thing was gone so quickly Vayorn was almost tempted to think he'd imagined it.

Agöri cleared his throat, still unsmiling. Vayorn's eyes focused, and his mind returned to the chess game. *He's still upset. How do I make him smile?*

Vayorn moved his king to safety. "Can you read? I can't," Vayorn finally asked.

Agöri's eyes lit. "What! I teach you then! You speak Xíran?"

"No, I only speak one language."

"Never mind. I write Antikish too. Write letters for Captain all time. Checkmate!" Agöri leaned back and crossed his arms proudly. Vayorn chuckled.

"You win," Vayorn said. Suddenly, the chair in front of the bed was empty. *How does he move so quick?* Whirlwind-like, Agöri spun around the room. He chucked items into the closet, flew over to the bed, swept the pieces into the box, ran over to the cabinet, tossed the box in, and banged the door shut.

"Want to see something?" Without waiting for a response, Agöri ran up to Vayorn. He shoved his nose into Vayorn's face, opened his mouth, and began wiggling one of his front teeth with his tongue. "It's loose! Already lost one"—he pushed his tongue through a gap beside his wiggly tooth—"gonna have big teeth so I can...um..." A mischievous grin pulled his cheeks up. "So I can *bite* Ayras!" His mouth snapped shut, narrowly missing Vayorn's nose. Vayorn fell backward.

Who does he remind me of? Vayorn sat back up. Everything about Agöri—his eyes, even his voice—seemed familiar.

"I teach now!" Agöri opened the drawer of a desk sitting under the porthole. He came back with a stack of scrolls and two quills. They spent the next "what felt like forever" learning the alphabet and practicing holding a quill the right way. Agöri wrote the letters along the top of Vayorn's page. Vayorn tried to copy the letters. *Stupid quill.* The quill fell out of his fingers again. *Stupid scroll!* The page seemed like it was always in the wrong place. Vayorn's hand kept wiping across the page through the wet ink. *Stupid letters!* His lines were squiggly and wobbly, and there were splotches of ink all over the page and up his arm. He eyed Agöri's letters. How did he write so well?

Vayorn tried to concentrate on the lesson, but there were too many questions in his mind. Who and where was the captain? Was the thing he'd seen dangerous? He was almost sure he knew what it was; there were plenty of legends and traveler's tales about Plesiases.

Vayorn just hadn't believed the stories. Was it hungry? Why was Blackie so afraid of the captain? Where were they headed? And most importantly, why was Blackie pretending to be kind to him? The noon bell bonged. Vayorn jumped.

Agöri looked up, his eyebrows raised. "Captain want have talk with you. Forgot," Agöri said. He giggled, and an impish grin spread across his face.

There was noise outside; it sounded like the muffled hum of men talking and shouting. Even through the walls, one sound rang out as clear as a summer sky: the woman's voice.

"Where is the idiot anyway?" The voice was slightly quieter now, but clear enough to understand through the walls. Agöri grinned guiltily.

"Must go." He ran out the door. It shut behind him.

The other voices were bleared through the wall, like the vague lines of a smudged painting. He closed his eyes and concentrated on listening. The voices became clearer.

"I here, Captain."

"Surprisingly enough, I'm not talking about you this time."

Then who is she talking about?

"Artair, signal the other ships. See if he's on one of them."

See if who is on the other ships?

"Agöri! Silence! I'm trying to think. You're sure he's not on this ship?"

"Certain, Captain."

Vayorn's brow furrowed. *Wish I could see through the walls.*

"If he sells us out, we're doomed. This is pirate-hunter territory!" Fear shuddered through Vayorn's spine. He stared at the wall. *Pirate hunters.* Unbidden, visions of being cut to pieces and thrown overboard filled his mind. *Is the thing following us hungry? What if they find us? Will they just kill us, or will they let the thing do their job?*

"You all hear that? Remember the Black skull fleet, the Red Hand fleet, the Bloody Sword fleet?" The room was warm, but suddenly Vayorn felt cold. Who hadn't? "Where are they now? At the bottom of the ocean. They came into pirate-hunter territory, and they were killed. Every man was killed. The Plesiases feasted that day." A tickling sensation prickled the back of Vayorn's neck. He peered out the window, almost expecting to see the thing haunting them, waiting to sate its gluttony on their dead. "Want to feed them another feast? Want that to happen to us? If Blackie gets to the pirate hunters before we get to him, *we are done*! *Find him—*" The rest of her words were drowned out by uproar. Stomping, crashing, and the occasional "Darn it! Agöri!" melded into the hubbub. Vayorn resisted the temptation to lie back down and leaned against the wall along his bed. Pirate hunters. Plesiases. *What if Blackie gets to the pirate hunters? Will they mistake me for a pirate? But what if Blackie doesn't get to the pirate hunters and he gets caught by the men? They won't kill him, will they? Do Plesiases eat you after you've drowned, or do they just catch you in midair and swallow you whole?*

A low flutelike moan resounded by Vayorn's window. A shadow blocked out the light, steeping the room in darkness. Vayorn stiffened. His shoulders tightened, and fear made a knot in his chest. The moments seemed to creep by as the small room was filled with darkness. He waited to hear the screams of the men on deck, but nothing happened. Weren't they afraid of it? Shakily, his chest heaved in and out as he forced himself to breathe.

Then the shadow was gone. Cold sunlight flooded back into the room.

A TALE

Vayorn relaxed. The door opened. A woman stood in the doorway, her willowy silhouette lit gold from the sunlight behind her. One hand was poised on her hip as she took a step forward. She was tall, with strong features and well-sculpted muscles. As she passed Vayorn, she gave him a long glance, then turned, and sat at the desk under the window. Her right leg crossed over her left in an attitude of complete indifference. Songlike, her voice rang out, its lilting Nacionish accent filling her words with color. Despite her accent though, her voice had a harshness and authority that Vayorn found shocking. But nowhere near as shocking as the realization that struck Vayorn the second he saw her—he knew her. He crammed down the panic rising in the back of his throat. Demetrius's lover? But Agöri said the captain… She was the captain! But she was a woman… How could a woman—Demetrius's lover at that—be a captain? *She'll return me to Demetrius! Have to get out of here!*

He struggled to his feet and collapsed on the floor as his legs, unaccustomed to bearing weight after his illness, gave way beneath him. Two booted feet appeared in front of him. A pair of surprisingly strong arms lifted him by the collar and his right arm. The woman heaved him roughly back onto the bed and stood in front of him with her hands on her hips, a scornful smile twisting her lips. He sat on the bed, rubbing his arm. There were red finger marks along his bicep. *How's she so strong?*

"Ah, you stupid...," she began a string of angry gibberish. *Been cussed at enough to know when someone's insulting me. She'd better be glad I can't understand what she's calling me, or she'd have problems.* Vayorn tensed and wiped all expression from his face.

The woman went straight from gibberish to Common Tongue again. "I am Laparlana, terror of the six seas. I have heard much of you."

No doubt. Demetrius complained about me often enough.

"And have reason to believe you are just the man to put my offer to."

Offer? Vayorn watched her out of the corner of his eye as she began to pace.

"You are going to hear a proposition you are lucky to be offered." She paused with one eyebrow dramatically raised.

Vayorn snorted. *Lucky? Sure.*

Laparlana narrowed her eyes, her voice suddenly soft and sad.

"I have a tale to tell you. Once there was a fleet, a great fleet of one hundred fine ships. It was known as the Flaming Skull. Such a fine fleet it was. And unlike the other fleets, its captain was female. The only female captain on the seas. The most feared captain from Nacion to Xira."

An exasperated sigh escaped Vayorn's chest. *Stop trying to be convincing and get to the point already.* Vayorn made a show of leaning against the wall and yawning. He felt a smug warmness in his chest as annoyance crossed Laparlana's face. She changed her voice again. It was hard now, as if she were relating rock-cold facts.

"She did not rise easily from the simple oblivion she had grown up in as a Nacionish country girl. She had to fight, connive, persuade, plot, collaborate, even murder to become the captain of the Flaming Skull. Even after she became captain, she had to fight to gain her crew's respect. She was a landlubber, and the only thing these men look down on more than a landlubber is a woman. She was both. She had to execute and severely punish a whole ship of men before the others would respect her."

Execute. I see.

"Soon, they came to fear her. Soon, every town along the coast came to fear her. Her life was perfect: famous, infamous, dangerous at last, feared and respected as she never was in her simple little village. She drank out of golden goblets, had mirrors framed in gold, made friends in high places."

Vayorn felt a sudden urge to snap at her. *Friends in high places. You mean Demetrius. Don't think for one second you're fooling me. I know where you got all those things.* He restrained himself, sending his anger into twisting the blanket in one hand behind himself. A small ripping sound came from under his fingers; he stopped. The woman was silent now.

Something about the way she was telling her "tale" reminded Vayorn of a young child reciting a carefully learned speech. It felt the same way watching actors in the town square felt—rehearsed. It felt like watching a performance. The pauses, the dramatic tone of her voice, her exaggerated expressions somehow didn't feel sincere to Vayorn.

She paced the cabin floor and stopped at the porthole. "And then, he came and ruined everything. In the short matter of five years, her life was ruined. Ruined by Fangar." Her voice was loud, and her movements aggressive. Her closed fist suddenly came into the air and pounded against the glass of the porthole. "He was a lord in exile who seemed to think that terrorizing the Xirans wasn't enough. He simply had to turn pirate hunter as well. He pirate-hunted with a ferocity and determination no pirate hunter should hunt with. No matter how hard a captain tried to escape him, their fleet was always caught and destroyed. Even if a ship managed to escape the ruin, how can a lone ship defend itself for long? It can't. Eventually, the captain was always caught, always caught just as he was about to make his escape." Vayorn tried to ignore the impatience rising in him. *What am I supposed to do about it, woman?* He laced his fingers behind his head and looked out the porthole. *How much more can she have to say?*

"So many good and worthy captains, captains who were my friends, died at his hand. He was ruthless, heartless. My fleet alone was left. He came in the middle of the night and destroyed my fleet. Out of one hundred ships, only fifty remained." Her voice was quivering with barely controlled fury. *She looks angry enough. Why do I feel like she's faking?*

"He never attacked in the open again. No, he always picked off the ships at the rear, sinking them before they could be helped. He trailed her for months, no matter how hard she tried to escape him. Finally, all he had left her was nine ships. Nine ships where one hundred had once been. People ceased to fear us. Worse, they laughed at us now. We were driven out of our early glory, turned into a laughingstock." Bitterness dripped from her voice like venom drips from the fangs of an adder. Vayorn was almost sure she was telling the truth, but still something didn't feel right. He pushed the feeling away.

"The woman's fleet became poor, and her sailors began deserting, feeling there was nothing left for them in the Flaming Skull. They would seek out the pirate hunters and sell us out. They would place the lives of their crewmates on the line for themselves. The pirate hunters would attack, and though the captain never lost another ship, she lost more than a hundred men."

Her voice was near screaming now. "Finally, she decided that she would do anything, even give up her fleet and all the men in it, to see Fangar brought to justice!" She glared out the window in silence. Vayorn was surprised at how little tension he felt. Somehow, her performance felt fake.

She sighed and continued.

"She was getting tired of pirating anyway," she said, with resignation in her voice. "And there was a certain lord who would willingly marry her if she would give up the fleet and settle down. After all, he had helped her many times, and it was time she repay her debts." As if afraid to let Vayorn see her face, she looked away at the floor when she said "certain lord." There was silence. Water dripped from the roof. A rat scurried under the bed.

"And that's where you come in." She regained her composure and used a businesslike tone." I need an assassin. I don't care how he's killed—although an excruciatingly painful death would be ideal—

but he needs to die. I need an assassin who is stony and unfeeling. Like you. Someone who is remorseless and loveless. I need you." Her steady iron gaze fixed on Vayorn.

Vayorn was quiet. *Let her think that I'm some unfeeling tool. Rather be thought of as remorseless than weak.*

Murder. Even though he had lived in Demetrius's realm his whole life—a place where murder and death were a part of life—the thought turned his stomach. *Can I trust her? If I do accept, can I actually go through with it? Will I get any payment for it?*

He used his most unfeeling voice, "What's in it for me?" The corner of Laparlana's mouth lifted a little, as if amused. *How much has Demetrius told her about me?*

"That's the best part. All nine of my ships, all the men on them. With Fangar gone, you'll be at liberty to do as you please. Does this interest you?" She cocked her head and stared at him. The intensity of her gaze was like looking into the sun. Vayorn looked away and remained silent. *How do I know she'll actually give me the ships? She might kill me when I come back to claim my reward.*

"No need to make up your mind now. I'll give you Tres days. It is Larata. I'll give you till Jeuvaño evening. After that, I'm finding a new assassin. I'm sure if being an assassin is not to your taste, Demetrius will gladly take you back." She rose.

Vayorn's hands curled into fists. His nails dug into his palms. *Never. I'll die before I let that happen. I'll kill before I become a slave again.* The door slammed behind her.

The door swung open a few minutes later and flapped on its hinges behind Agöri, bowling in head over heels.

"Hide me!" He dived under Vayorn's bed. A shadow filled the doorway. Vayorn looked up. An immense man with a scraggly beard and a tattoo-spattered neck stomped into the room. His tattoos stood out against his red face, and his barrel chest heaved. He was noisily chomping on something as he yelled. Tobacco.

"Agöri! Where is he? He came in! I saw him!" the man said. His voice seemed to fill the room and bounce off the walls. Vayorn was tempted to laugh. What could've Agöri done that was that bad? Plenty. He barely kept a chuckle contained as various inklings of what Agöri could've done flew through his head. One look at the man's red face was enough to make him stay quiet though, as much as he wanted to laugh. *Gonna have trouble if I make him any madder.* He pulled his face into a serious expression.

"And?" Vayorn asked. There was a shakiness in his voice that he hoped the man didn't hear. His laughter bounced against the inside of his chest like a trapped frog.

"Ship three got lucky! They tricked us into taking him off their hands! Since Artair was stupid enough to take him, the little villain's been nothing but trouble. Takes nothing seriously! I about got tossed overboard because of the kid's childish antics!"

Vayorn took a deep breath and forced his laughter back down.

"No, you attack floor." Agöri's voice was muffled from under the bed. Vayorn was struck by how funny the situation was. *Can't laugh. Don't laugh. Don't you dare laugh.* He held his breath.

"Backwards?" the man asked. His voice rose.

"You talented," Agöri tentatively offered. The man guffawed, and Vayorn stopped trying to not laugh. The walls rang their noise back at them. Finally, Vayorn ran out of breath and was quiet. The man was still laughing. His roaring slowed to a chuckle and then died out. The mirth in the man's eyes was replaced with the same look he wore in.

"I'll let you off the hook this time, but stay out of my way." He spat on the floor, making a small brownish splotch of tobacco spit by Vayorn's foot. "Worthless trash—both'n ye!" A shadow filled the doorway again, and he was gone.

"Agöri, it's safe to come out now." A sweaty face poked out from beneath Vayorn. An impish grin was spread across Agöri's face from one ear to the other. He slid out from under the bed. As he came up, Vayorn noticed a streak of brown across the child's sleeve. His stomach lurched. Agöri had slid right through the pile of tobacco spit. A frown turned Vayorn's face downward. *Trouble's gonna come to the little guy if he stays here. He's not safe.* Vayorn leaned forward with his elbows on his knees.

"Better come with me when I leave," Vayorn said.

"Where we leave to?" Agöri asked. Eager excitement shone in his eyes when Vayorn said the word *leave*.

"Don't know yet." It depended on whether or not Vayorn turned assassin.

"Agöri! I have a letter to write!" Laparlana shouted. Agöri sprang up and ran to the door. It slammed behind him, and the room was suddenly quiet.

Vayorn lay back. He wasn't even going to try to sleep; there was too much to think about. Absently, he counted the ceiling boards again, rolling Laparlana's offer in his mind. Murder. *Way Demetrius talks about me, I do seem like some dangerous criminal. No wonder she chose me to put her offer to. Least she sees me as that instead of as some soft boy. If I take Agöri with me, can't let him know what my real mission is. Do I accept at all? What if I get caught? Murder's punished with death. But to have a whole fleet. Imagine. Havoc beyond my wildest dreams. Sail down the Laangen, destroy Tarshal, capture Demetrius, hang him from the mast. Murder for it? I don't know...*

*****

A longboat pulled beside the ship. A rope was thrown down. A snakish thin man came up over the edge of the ship. No one cheered. He cut through the crowd like a razor, making a thin line to Laparlana's cabin. The door creaked on its hinges as it opened. A shadow fell across Laparlana, standing with her back to the door. She didn't turn to look at him.

"Have you given him our terms?" the man asked. He came up beside her.

"Yes. I won't actually have to give him the ships, correct? The ship part you never told me of till this morn." Her tone was slightly accusatory.

"Oh, don't worry. A dead man doesn't need a fleet of ships."

ARPLE

The blue sky disappeared overhead, blotted out by a massive wooden monstrosity. Fortresslike, it towered over the dock.

"All aboard!"

A girl sat on the dock, clutching her bag and perched atop a pile of trunks. She seemed to curl into herself, as if she was afraid of being noticed. Her face was framed with turquoise scales, the same tint as her ankle-length hair. In the place of ears, two delicate frills came from the sides of her face. Her skin was paper-white, and her eyes were a strange changing color. She scanned the sea of faces, nervously fiddling with a strand of her hair.

A sailor rose from the ocean of people. He stopped in front of her.

The sailor drew his sword and offered her its hilt. "Sechter. you the passenger for ship three, name of Arple Miska?"

Arple nodded and quickly placed her fist on the hilt, muttering, "Brudder." It was impolite to not return someone's greeting, but she wished she didn't always have to be so polite—the man scared her.

He whistled. A group of men assembled and began lifting her trunks, their unwashed stench wafting over her in the breeze. She knew she should be grateful that her family had found her a means of transport, but she was still frightened by the prospect of traveling alone on a pirate ship.

She separated her trunks by various types and counted them one more time. There were all seven. If it had been up to her, she would have swum across the bay. Several aunts and uncles lived beneath the surface, and they always liked to have her. But after one of her uncles, Uncle Jere, was eaten by a Leviath, the family decided from then on to make the trip over the water instead of in it.

She nodded for the men to begin carrying her luggage on board. As she waited, her gaze shifted across her surroundings. Other ships in the pirate's fleet lined the dock. It was called the Flaming Skull; at least that is what Arple thought she had heard when she asked the name of the ship from a man nearby—it was difficult to hear above the din of men talking and shouting.

The crowd parted for a stretcher. A young boy lay on it, his hair and skin caked with mud. His shirt was in shreds, and even in the coolness of the autumn day, he was shining with sweat. Arple caught her breath. Fever. She backed away. Was it the green death? She could almost smell the stench of vomit, see the rows of graves above her town…but no, they couldn't possibly take a green death victim on board. Green Death spread so quickly. She couldn't die; she was all Mother had left. Maria was married and Aila… Arple pushed the memory of a tiny grave on a hill out of her mind. A sense of relief washed over her as the stretcher was carried to a ship farther down the dock.

There was a crash behind her. She turned. One of the men had dropped her trunk. Her cheeks turned red. The trunk containing her petticoats, underdresses, and stockings no less. She chased a petticoat across the deck as the breeze tried to steal it. Avoiding making eye contact, she shoved the items back into the trunk and stood. She heard laughing around her but refused to look up. She wished she were as brave as Maria. Maria would have done something to make them stop laughing; she would have given the men a sound tongue-lashing about being more careful with her things, hands propped on her hips, giving them the glare no one could meet for long. But Arple simply looked away and followed the men up the gangplank.

As always, her spirits rose. There it was, the sea, sparkling before her like a sheet of polished diamond. Off in the distance, waterspouts rose against the sky like shattered glass. The waves played with the horizon, dancing a delicate dance that could spiral into a vicious fight in a second's time.

Her shoulders straightened as if a great load were suddenly lifted from them. The man with the last of her trunks was far ahead of her now. Arple shifted her sack and ran up behind him. Her eyes shone, and the sun glinted off her jewel-bright scales. She wanted to laugh and dance and sing all at the same time; she was finally going. A fresh breeze stirred her hair. she threw open her arms. A gull flew overhead. The gangplank was raised up from the dock. They were off. She would see Auntie Zara, travel alone, and go to festival all at one time!

She found a coil of rope to sit on and reached into her bag. Mother had told her to keep her dress in the bag till festival lest it get soiled, but she just had to have a look at it again. The dress glimmered in the sun as she drew it out. It was embroidered with bits of glass, jewels, and shells. Dreamily, she ran her hand down the front of it. She might fall in love this time. Her eyes closed. She could see the kind of man she wanted: tall, strong, brave, blond hair and gray eyes, a smooth voice and a ready laugh. Maria just got married. How her eyes had shone on the day of her wedding. Arple could just see herself in a wedding dress, her groom waiting at the center of the circle. He was out there; she just knew it. Her eyes opened. She carefully folded the dress and placed it back in her bag. Delight ran its familiar tingle up her back.

The secret festival.

She had watched as one of the children for as long as she could remember, but now she was sixteen. She could dance in the ring and whirl a scarf. She could tell tales and accept any suitors who followed her.

Maria had gotten her husband at festival, during the Liito ceremony. It had taken him three of the five days to get up enough courage to make entrance. "Hyväksyn. I accept," Maria had said, as was customary. The words in the ancient tongue, against the rough edges of the Common Tongue, sounded even more beautiful.

"Hyväksyn. I accept," Arple tried out the phrase for herself. It rolled off her tongue sweetly. Someday she would say that; all girls did, when the man they wanted finally entered. Warmth rose from her heart into a smile on her face.

Her hero would walk in. The music would stop. The festivalgoers would remain silent, following the ancient engagement tradition, seeing if she would accept this suitor. She would smile a dazzling smile. "Hyväksyn. I accept," she would say, of course. He would be given a seat and gaze at her as she danced. And she would do her best dance for him. How impressed he would be.

She fell back giggling. It was almost too much.

Suddenly, a man came up to her. He was almost what she would call handsome, bar his somewhat sour expression. He stooped and jerked the pile of rope out from underneath Arple, dumping her unceremoniously onto her rump. She glared at him. How dare he affront her dignity so? He nodded at her, turned his back, and walked off. Once again, she wished she were more like Maria. Maria would have at least said something.

ON THE OCEAN

Vayorn slumped against the edge of the ship. His legs ached. *Who would've thought walking ten steps would be so hard?* The deck swayed beneath him, rocking on the waves. Light glinted off something in the crow's nest. *What's it like up there? Wish I could walk. Sick of being useless.*

A dwarf bumbled by, muttering something in a guttural language. He was carrying a large metal ramrod to the cannons, shouting orders to a team of men. *Even a dwarf is more useful than me.*

Vayorn threw his head back and leaned it against the edge of the ship. He idly toyed with the edge of his shirt, feeling the soft fabric catch on his fingers. He had never worn anything as fine as this before. It made him feel almost like royalty. *What's it like to wear stuff like this every day?* He watched the clouds above him dance. They changed shape as quickly as Demetrius changed moods.

Something shot out of the water—a long neck ending at a small head with hot-coal eyes. Vayorn's mouth went dry. His breath stuck in his chest, unwilling to come out. He forced himself to breathe. What if it attacked them? He was too weak to run. Where could he hide? Could he hide in time? Everyone else would be safe; they could run. Vayorn pressed his back against the side of the ship, as far away from the creature as the ship would let him get.

"Ahem."

Vayorn's head snapped around. A man stood to his left, head towering over the others like an oak in the midst of saplings. A kindly smile stretched across his face. *He's huge! Doesn't he see the thing?* Vayorn looked back at the water. The water was clear, without so much as a dolphin in sight. *Where'd it go?*

"Ahoy." The man's voice was harsh and gravelly with a strong accent. *Must be from wherever that Altan trader was from.* The man sat beside Vayorn.

"You can't walk. Do you want something to do? I know mending rope not honorable task, but it pass time when time need passed." He tossed a net to Vayorn. A gaping hole was shredded in the fraying middle of the net. Vayorn, even with the understanding of Common Tongue that he had, had trouble making out the man's words.

Vayorn was tempted to toss the net back at the man. *How do you fix something like that?* He pushed his hand through the hole. A reek of fish came off it. *Smells worse than Demetrius's shoes.* He was embarrassed to be seen doing such an easy task. Mending was for old men and young children. He looked around the deck. *Wish I could walk. I'd show them I'm no weak boy.* He looked back down at the net, weighing his options: mend nets, or stare at the sky. *Least mending nets is something sorta useful.* He took the coil of rope the man offered him.

The man spoke, "Like this."

He wove the fresh rope through a broken patch of net, deftly knotting it around the edges of the hole. Vayorn tried to concentrate, but a voice coming from the captain's cabin arrested his attention. *Where've I heard that voice?*

"See?" the man asked.

Vayorn nodded, only half paying attention to the man's lesson on rope mending. *Who do I know that sounds like that? Why's it so familiar?* He straightened his legs in front of him. They burned slightly as they stretched. *Feels so good.* The voice was silent now, lost in the hubbub of the other men talking. Vayorn turned his attention back to the man, who was still lecturing on "the fine art of net mending." Vayorn reluctantly took his net and tied a few half-hearted knots, all the while watching the crew. The men were assembled in teams of two, each holding a sail rope.

"Heave!" The sail jerked.

"Heave!" Slowly, it began to rise. *What I wouldn't give to be doing that instead of this. Hate being useless. Weak.*

He yanked his rope through a hole and pulled on it. With a rip, the hole spread. A heavy sigh escaped Vayorn. *How hard can this be? If I can't mend a denger net, how can I assassinate someone?* Vayorn threw his net down on the deck and crossed his arms. His companion was silent now and kept working as if he didn't notice Vayorn's frustration. *Wish I could hit something.* He puffed his cheeks out. *Sick of this.* His legs folded crisscross under him as he turned his back on the man. "Name's Ermolai." The man flipped the net and began another hole. Vayorn turned back to Ermolai slightly.

"Vayorn." He watched Ermolai's hands fly over the net. *He's good. Gotta take years to get that fast. Years of being useless.* He turned his gaze across the deck. Two men walked by them. Vayorn thought he heard one of them say "Blackie." Vayorn gulped. *They're talking about pirate hunters! Did he get to them? What if they find us? Can't die! Need to kill Demetrius.* He ran a hand through his hair.

"S-say, haven't seen Blackie." He hoped his voice didn't sound as scared as he felt. Ermolai's head shot up. His hands were still. Vayorn looked away as nonchalantly as he could, trying to not sound terribly interested.

Ermolai was silent.

Finally, he spoke, "You see here, one traitor thread unravels net." He gave his net a pull. It ripped in half. "You have to remove thread and throw it out, or it give way on you." He gave Vayorn a meaningful glance. *Is that good or bad? Does that mean he found the pirate hunters?* Vayorn swallowed hard.

"Where is he?"

"Captain don't give no quarter. You do best to never hornswoggle Captain if you don't want to dance hempen jig." Vayorn's breath whooshed out, and he realized he had been holding it. *So he's dead. He's dead. I'm safe. They won't find us.* His brow furrowed. What was the hempen jig?

"Hempen jig?"

"Hanging. Captain hung him from mast. When he was finished, they dumped him into sea."

The relief that filled Vayorn turned into a sick feeling in the pit of his stomach. A hanging. He closed his eyes, trying to block out memory. But no matter how hard he tried, he saw Adva dangling from a scaffold in the town square, saw Badurad's pain-stricken face as they watched from the edges of the crowd, felt again that awful sense of helplessness as his best friend's sister died—died for simply being an outdweller. A wall came between Badurad and himself that day, a wall Vayorn couldn't jump. He closed his eyes, but the memory stuck to him like tar, enveloping him in its web of despair.

He felt a hand on his arm, and his eyes opened. Ermolai rubbed Vayorn's shoulder and gave him an understanding glance.

"Aye, lad. He was my friend too."

Vayorn looked away. *We weren't friends. He was weak. Can't trust weaklings. Does that mean I can't trust myself? Stupid. I'm the only one I can trust. Not weak. Never weak.*

The silence grew around them, reminding Vayorn of a funeral. *Gotta do something. Gonna go crazy if this goes on much longer.* Vayorn seized his net and began mending it with a fury, doing more harm than good as the hole spread larger.

"So what Captain want?" Ermolai broke the silence. He tossed the finished net aside and started another.

Vayorn shrugged. *Can't trust myself to talk. Can't look like I'm weak. Something else to think about. Anything else.* His mind rested on Laparlana's offer again.

"Ermolai, what do you know about Fangar?"

Ermolai's face reddened. "I'll dance hornpipe o'er his grave, the nattering flea-bitten murderer!" Ermolai pounded his fist on the deck.

Vayorn tried to seem disinterested and casual. "Just curious." He shrugged. The sense of dread over him lifted slightly as he regained control of himself.

"He is evil, I tell you. Know how he kill us?" Ermolai's voice was sad, and his eyes were foggy and distant. As he described in vivid detail the gruesome method used to kill pirates, all the blood drained out of Vayorn's face.

He seized a bucket. His stomach lurched, and he emptied its contents into the bucket. He avoided making eye contact with Ermolai.

"I was seasick," he said before Ermolai could inquire further. *Had enough of death for one day.* His head hurt, and the sun beat down on the back of it. *Can I kill someone? If hearing about death, remembering death does this to me, what will dealing it do? Can't think about this.*

The sound of childish laughter came across the deck. Agöri. He hoped Agöri didn't know what he now knew. His hands tightened on his net, lying in his lap unmended.

"Does Agöri know?" Even against the backdrop of the ship's noises, his voice seemed too loud after the silence—harsh like gravel.

"He more interested in content of pocket than talk. Only talk he hear 'I'm gonna tan your hide' or 'Kitchen unguarded.'" Ermolai let out a rollicking belly laugh.

Vayorn was suddenly angry. *He's laughing? How can he laugh? I didn't even know my father, and I'd never laugh after talking about his death. Doesn't he care?* Vayorn balled his fist, barely restraining himself from punching Ermolai. "Avast ye! Hang jib! Ye look like Davy Jones himself! No need to cleave me to brisket for joke!" Ermolai shook his finger in mock reprimand.

Vayorn coolly disregarded him, staring straight ahead into empty space. *If I look at him, I'll hit him. Control. Control yourself.* Ermolai tried to get Vayorn's attention. Vayorn still ignored him. A hurt expression crossed Ermolai's face. When at length Vayorn looked over, Ermolai was gone.

A million memories rang in Vayorn's ears, clamoring to be heard, begging to be seen, angry at being pushed away for so long—memories of devastation and demise that had lain long dormant, shoved out of mind to a place where they could be effectively forgotten about for days or even weeks at a time. They were awake now, pounding at the inside of Vayorn's head like a hammer on prison bars. He put his head in his hands and groaned as memories swam before his eyes.

Half blind to the men around him, he stumbled to his feet and somehow reached the high deck at the back of the ship. He fell to a sitting position on a barrel, his face to the blustering southern wind. The gusts hurled icelike air around him, stinging his face with salt. He closed his eyes. As the wind rushed around him, the pressure inside him suddenly burst. He exhaled deeply as his memories blew away with the blue sky.

His mind cleared. He felt suddenly quiet. Raw emptiness welled up inside him. He took a deep breath and looked behind their ship.

Black clouds rode the horizon below the gray covering above the ship, gathering into a dark wall speeding toward them. The men look worried. Vayorn propped his elbows on his knees.

He let his mind drift.

*****

I hide in the corner, shaking. Everyone's been yelling all day, crying too. Can't figure out what's wrong. No one'll tell me anything. Even Janus walked right by me, didn't even talk to me. I hear the wind outside. Sounds like dragon wings. Janus says they're not real, but I don't believe him. How could he know for sure? Has he been everywhere? I'll show him; when I catch a dragon tomorrow, he'll have to believe me 'cause I'll show him one. I tried to tell him about it today, all about my traps and ropes and the pit I dug, but he just nodded. He thinks just 'cause I'm little, I don't catch what he's doing: ignoring me. But I'm all of six years old, and I know a lot. I'm waiting for the scary, skinny man to call me. He looks like a skeleton; least I think that's what a skeleton looks like. My hands are cold, and I want to go down to the courtyard. None of the other kids have to stand by a door and wait on a big scary man. They're all by the fire. I tried to tell Janus this. He said he can't change anything, and I can't change anything, so just do it. He's wrong 'cause I'm gonna be a prince one day. I'll have my very own sword, and I'll never have to be hungry. "Boy!"

I jump. All sudden-like, I'm sweaty. He's mad again. I go to the door real slow, tryin' to look small. Maybe he won't notice me as much. I push the curtain away. There are all kinds of candles on the walls and a great big one on the table. There's a big fire in the hearth, and I wish I could stand in front of it, but not while the man is in here. He makes the room feel cold. Not the kind of cold when the fire goes out in winter. I mean, it feels scary. Lots of things are scary here.

"There's a hanging in town today. Dandru tried to escape." Whatever a hanging was, it had to be bad to make the man so happy. What did he mean, Dandru? Not the same Dandru who's my friend, right? I'm more scared now. I want to hide, but I can't. "Yes, child. Dandru is only twelve. Sad waste of money, but it has to be done."

I back up, trying to get away from him. He starts laughing. I hate his laugh. It sounds like the ghosts in the dungeon. Ghosts are real; Janus said so.

The man throws his cup at me. I grab it and run. My feet echo off the walls.

I dodge under someone. Behind me, I can still hear the man's ghost laughs. I close my eyes as I pass the dungeon. I don't want to see it if a ghost gets me. Mama Yanya tells Janus to stop scaring me when he tells me dungeon stories, but I like dungeon stories; being scared is fun. That kind of scared anyway.

I run up to Mama Yanya. She's crying. I've never seen her cry ever. Something must be real wrong to make her cry. I tug on her sleeve. She looks down at me.

"Vayorn." She sinks to the ground and hugs me. I can feel her shoulders shaking. Her breaths are shaky, like she can't breathe.

"Mama Yanya?" I try to say something to her. I'm scared now. She just shakes her head and cries harder.

"He's too much like his father he is…I told him…I told him to just let be and stay…But no, he just had to try to run off…and him not full-grown yet either…I lost enough children to that Demetrius…Dandru's all I got left…" Mama Yanya stops talking and holds me tight. My neck's wet from her tears. I don't understand what she means, but it's gotta be real bad to make her this sad.

My hair gets in my eyes. I try to wipe it off, and it's covered in boogers. I rub my face; it's wet. My throat's all achy, and my eyes are burny. I wish Mama Yanya would tell me what's wrong. I don't like seeing her sad. If I knew what was making her sad, maybe I could make her better. She always makes me better when I scrape my knee or get burned on a pan.

*****

Vayorn rolled his shoulders back and stretched. He realized he was shivering. The black clouds were almost over them, approaching now like a dark army. Why didn't anyone rescue Dandru? Mama Yanya could've poisoned Demetrius if she'd wanted to; she worked in the kitchen. The screams of Demetrius's victims filled his mind. He shuddered. *Why didn't someone fight for them? Couldn't someone have freed them? There had to have been someone who wasn't afraid of Demetrius, right?* A thought struck him. *What if I'm the only one who's willing to kill Demetrius? What if I'm the only one who can free them, give them revenge? Only one problem with that: I need to kill Fangar first. If I get caught, I'll never have the chance to kill Demetrius.*

Vayorn stood and blindly dragged himself on weak legs to his cabin, stopping thirty times along the way to catch his breath. When he finally threw himself onto his bed, all he could see was the memory, replaying itself over and over again in his head.

The next four days went by in a blur, and even though his legs grew strong again, Vayorn didn't care. He couldn't seem to get his mind free of Adva, of Dandru. It seemed like everything he did brought them to mind.

STORM

Vayorn sat on the barrel again, still deep in thought. Badurad's tear-tracked face appeared in his memory again. His fists clenched. *If I have to risk killing Fangar to give Badurad vengeance, I will.* He rose, feeling different, more powerful, dangerous even. His feet didn't shake the way they did earlier. Proudly, he raised his head and squared his shoulders. There was no more doubt in his mind. This was his purpose: to avenge Adva, avenge Dandru, to take the revenge no one else was brave enough to take. Lost in his thoughts, he stumbled to his cabin. Every clap of thunder seemed to call up the cries of men and women, pleading for vengeance but unable to take it. Every flash of lightning lit the grief-stricken face of mothers and little girls, bereft of their husbands, fathers, and sons.

Like a candle being snuffed out, the little light left vanished. Drops of wet rock pounded into Vayorn's back, stinging his face. *Have to get to the cabin.* Like a blind man, Vayorn reeled forward. His foot caught. A hard surface bashed his cheek as he fell. He grabbed onto it and pulled himself to his feet. A barrel. With one hand anchored to the barrel, he reached out for the next. His hand met something. He moved his anchor hand to the next barrel and reached out again. *Wish I had a lantern. Can't see for bloody nothin'.*

The ground beneath Vayorn heaved drunkenly, throwing Vayorn to the ground. The wind rushed in Vayorn's ears, and he heard the creak as the deck threw itself at the sky, sending its lower edge into the darkness. The iron arms of the water washed over the deck and dragged Vayorn down the tilting surface to the sea. Vayorn twisted around, frantic, as the edge of the deck came into his vision. His throat tightened as the sea swallowed the lower ship rail. Something hard rammed into Vayorn's elbow. The shock of the blow traveled up to Vayorn's shoulder as his arm went numb. He realized he was screaming. The water was close now. It seemed like a living creature, tipping the ship into its mouth like a bowl, intent on devouring every living thing on board. Its watery tongue lapped at Vayorn's feet.

A hand seized Vayorn by the collar. His feet dangled over the raging waves as the deck slanted dangerously. Spots swam before Vayorn's eyes. Vayorn tried to breathe past the collar of his shirt, tightening as the deck of the ship rose like a wall beside him.

"Man overboard!"

Someone screamed for help below Vayorn. He looked down. A head of red hair disappeared in the waves below him.

The ship groaned as it righted itself. The deck swung beneath Vayorn's feet. The hand let go. Vayorn grabbed around the mast and pulled himself to his feet, still hardly daring to breathe. The long arm of the sea rushed over the deck again and knocked Vayorn to the ground with icy fingers.

Another wave slammed down on top of Vayorn and forced itself down his throat. Sputtering, he crawled forward. All the feeling fled his fingers. His knees ached against the soaking planks, and his arms shook under his weight. He fell onto his stomach. His arm dropped straight out and hit something. The door.

His hands groped above him till he felt a metal bar. He turned it and fell forward with a cry. Screaming, he tumbled down the stairs end over end. The hard ground of the hull rose to meet him, and he blacked out.

LOVERS

A candle burned on the table, slicing a golden ring of light around itself. Laparlana and a man sat across from each other at the table. A deep hood shadowed the man's face, and his bone-like fingers curled around a golden chalice studded with gems. He leaned forward in his chair with his elbows on the table. Laparlana splayed out over the arms of her chair, her legs draped over one wooden talon and her back across the other, resting her hands on her stomach. They spoke in low voices.

The man's voice was grim. "He's dangerous, dangerous to you, dangerous to me, and certain death to our kinder." Laparlana looked down at her stomach and back at the man. "We in Antike have a stupid method of king-choosing. The nobles, would you believe it, choose which of the Fangar's children will rule. As long as Vayorn is alive, my claim to the throne is in question and the nobles can make the next heir king."

"What would they do to you?"

"Put me in prison and leave me to Vayorn's mercy, if he has any, which I doubt. I am afraid I cannot take the risk of having him decide my fate. I hate him, and he hates me. If he's placed over me, he'll kill me. I can't leave you and the kinder defenseless. I've seen what it did to my brother's brat. I won't let that happen to you. So—"

"He and the other heir must die." Laparlana nodded slowly, her eyes sad.

"Yes, I'm afraid it's the only way. You've suggested imprisoning them, I know, but having them alive at all is dangerous enough." Laparlana sighed and nodded. "The most efficient thing to do is get rid of both heirs without risking one of my own men. So Vayorn kills Fangar, and my man kills him. Clever, am I not?"

He continued in a joking tone, "And so, after we're safe, we announce our official marriage." They burst out laughing. Laparlana reached across the table and laid her hand over the man's hand, still giggling. "And I make you my queen."

"What will the people say to you marrying a woman who is pregnant?" She shook her finger mockingly. "It's a scandal, they'll say."

"How scandalous can it be? We're married, at least, secretly. But ceremony-wed, nonetheless. Nothing scandalous about that, my dear. And when you're queen, I vow, I'll bring your dreams to life. You said when we met—you remember that day, don't you?"

"How could I forget?"

"You said your dream was to be powerful. I shall give you power, my love. You shall have servants and vassals, your own estates and manors, perhaps even palaces in other countries. Our children and our children's children shall be powerful." He placed his other hand over hers.

The wind howled outside, and the ship swung wildly, like a cradle rocked by a madman.

The peace was broken as the floor of the cabin rose and the wall swung below them. The door swung on its hinges, and water gushed in, soaking the couple. Everything that wasn't bolted to the floor came loose and began crashing against the walls. Laparlana screamed. The hood flew off the man's head as he jumped the table and took her in his arms. The floor slid out from underneath them, and they hit a wall. The man shielded Laparlana with himself as the furniture came sliding toward them. The table creaked against its bolts on the floor. The room was dark. There was a dull thud. A man was screaming as he slid past their door.

"Man overboard!"

Laparlana buried her head in the man's neck.

The room tipped again, and they slammed onto the floor. The man ran across the room. The sounds of a drawer being rummaged through came out of the dark. A light flared into being, and the door slammed. The lamp on the table flamed, and the room was lit again. Laparlana sat on the floor, her hair a mess, her eyes wild. The man ran over to her again and lifted her off the floor.

"Are you hurt?" He held her by the arms and peered into her face. She shook her head and touched the side of his face.

"What hit you? You're the one that's hurt." She touched a large cut across his cheek.

"Not bad." The man started laughing softly. "This seems familiar, doesn't it?"

"But the night we met, it was a tree branch. It was storming that night, but the moon shone so brightly. It was a short storm, that one."

"I'll never regret those broken ribs I got. It was worth it. And if I hadn't been injured, you'd have never stayed to talk to me. Remember that conversation?"

"I remember so well. I remember you telling me what your brother and mother and the nobles did to you, how unfairly you were treated."

"Your story wasn't so different. Extra son, extra daughter—there wasn't much difference between how your mother treated you and how my mother treated me." He put his arm around her and guided her to the table with a chair in his hand. He set the chair at the table. "Can I get you anything? A cushion?" Laparlana nodded and sat. "And after I was better, you stayed with me."

"Remember that walk in the moonlight, the night the healer said you could walk?"

"One of the best nights of my life. Can you believe no one caught us?"

"The way you were sneaking between the hedges, yes." She leaned forward, and Demetrius placed a pillow behind her back.

Demetrius brushed her hair out of her eyes. "And our first kiss? Remember that?"

"I still blush when I remember. You said you had a 'business proposition' to offer me. Business indeed." She playfully shook her head.

Demetrius stood behind Laparlana's chair. He put his arms around her shoulders and whispered in her ear, "Ah, I said what I had to. You wouldn't have come if you hadn't thought there was something in it for you."

"I'm glad I came with you that night." Laparlana turned her head and kissed his cheek.

They whispered together softly for a moment. Demetris said something, and Laparlana blushed.

"I wonder what that fat little peaceman who married us is doing. He'd want to see your child, would he not?" Laparlana laid her hands on her stomach.

"Ah yes, our little hero." Demetrius laid his hands over hers.

"What if it's a girl?"

"Our brave little Sabremaiden then."

A concerned expression crossed Laparlana's face. "Will you pick favorites when our other little ones come?"

"No. I won't do what Mother—" He broke off. "You?"

"No. I don't believe in picking favorite niñosos either."

She rose from her chair. Demetrius tilted her chin up with his forefinger.

"I don't deserve you." He laid his hand against her face, brushing her hair out of her eyes.

Laparlana moved her face closer to his. They paused for an instant, looking into each other's eyes, and kissed. She leaned her head against his chest, her silken hair falling across her face.

LOST IN THE MIST

I look up at the mouth of a cave. It's so big it's almost the only thing I can see. A candle's in my hand. A sword's in my other hand. There are gems all over its hilt. Strange square shapes are carved into its blade. The metal looks blue in the light. The shapes are a strange gold color, like the light on Demetrius's wineglass. It's pretty. A blast of hot air hits me all of a sudden. I turn back to the cave. The rotten air coming out of it stings my throat and chokes me. Strange, greenish light glows from somewhere inside it. I shudder. It's getting dark around me, quick. I look down. The candle's gone. This thing with antlers and a woman's face bounds up to me. Her voice rises and falls. Can't hear most of what she says in the wind. "You will…destroy…or be destroyed by…"

"What?" A wind hits me, and I fall. The thing shrieks as it disappears. Reminds me of the moon being swallowed by clouds or a piece of bread being swallowed by Demetrius. I realize the blackness is smoke.

"Eight days…eight days…eight days…," echoes around me. Can't figure out where it's coming from. Seems like it's coming from everywhere.

"Eight days for what?" A wagon flies at me out of the mist. I scream and duck. It runs over me. I stand again, surprised I'm not hurt. A turquoise blur brushes by me. The wind hits it, and it's gone.

"Vayorn!" I hear it yell my name as it flies into the air.

"Your father," a voice whispers. The sound comes from the cave. Suddenly, a woman rises in front of me. Her cheekbones are sharp like Demetrius's. I back away. The wind hits her, and she melts like a candle. A hot breeze hits my face.

"All is not as it seems. Watch…watch…watch…"

"Watch what?"

Something roars. The cave comes alive. I hide on the ground, hoping it won't see me. The dirt around it falls off it. Some of it gets in my eyes, and I can't see. When my eyes clear, I'm face-to-face with this giant black wolf. I scream and run. As it chases me, its roar becomes Demetrius's voice.

"I have a plan…a plan…a plan…a plan…" It's behind me. I can feel its hot breath burning my ankles. I look down. My feet won't move. I try to run, but I can't. It digs its claw into my side. The pain is worse than anything I could've ever imagined. I scream and fall down, groaning, pressing my hands to my side. Suddenly I can't see. There's a red fog in my eyes. Then the only thing I can see is black.

*****

Vayorn's eyes opened. He was looking up a steep flight of stairs, ending under a wooden trapdoor. *How was I stupid enough to fall down the gach stairs? Door's even a trapdoor. If my legs won't hold and I have to spend another useless day sitting around, or worse in bed, I'll go crazy.* Exasperated, he puffed out his cheeks and pulled himself to standing. His legs held him as he rubbed his aching back. A groan escaped him as he laced his fingers behind himself and stretched. *Gach, I'm sore.* He climbed the stairs, the soreness working out of his limbs with each step. His hand rested against the trapdoor for an instant, and he pushed.

A shower of sea spray rushed through the opening, blinding him. He coughed, wiped the water out of his eyes, and stared out the hatchway.

Green mist swallowed the far half of the deck in shadow. The main mast rose into the air, a black shape wheeling upward like a pillar into the haze. The frayed edges of the sails flapped in the air, where not a gust of wind was stirring. Vague shapes passed in front of Vayorn, ghostlike in the murk. A single fire burned through the mist, a weak glimmer in the night-like day.

"Morning." Ermolai's feet appeared in front of Vayorn, rising into the mist that hid his top half.

"If morning still exists." Vayorn looked around, and he was suddenly cold. How could it have been such a nice day yesterday? He shivered and tucked his hands into his armpits. "Aye. If morning still be existing. I don't like smell in wind. Danger be comin'. You mark Ermolai's word. Something be comin'."

The word *danger* echoed in Vayorn's head and twisted his stomach. Something coming? He shivered and managed a shaky chuckle.

"It's just mist Ermolai." Vayorn tried to believe his own words, but the chill up his spine told him Ermolai just might be right. *Don't be ridiculous. You've seen mist before.* He stepped onto the deck, and his feet disappeared in the gray air. *A man could walk right off the edge of the ship without knowing it in this.* As if bound by the mist, Vayorn's feet refused to move.

Ermolai spoke, "You well enough to be useful?" Vayorn stiffened. *Doesn't need to rub the past week in.* His fist balled, then he caught the joking tone of Ermolai's words. He relaxed. "If ye feel like working, we need an extra crew member. Interested?" Ermolai's voice came from somewhere near Vayorn, but the only thing Vayorn could see was fog.

How do you work in this? Vayorn pulled his jacket tighter around himself and gazed upward at the masts.

"S-s-sure." He winced. Weak. Trying to look confident, he squared his shoulders. A hand clapped around his arm, and Ermolai came out of the mist.

"We can see better near fires."

Fires? I only see one. Vayorn stayed close to Ermolai as they made their way across the deck, hoping desperately Ermolai knew where he was going. They came up beside the main mast, and a tiny fire blossomed to Vayorn's right. The mist grew thinner as they stepped into a small ring of light, hemmed all around by small fires burning weakly in their iron pots. Vayorn realized that what he had mistaken for one fire was actually the combined light of all the fires.

"Yo-heave-ho! Yo-heave-ho! Yo-heave-ho!" rang out from just beyond the circle, accompanied by the screech of wheels against the wood. There was a series of small thuds. *They're loading the cannons. Pirate hunters don't hunt in mist, do they?* Vayorn shuddered. He followed Ermolai to one of the fires, where Ermolai sat and motioned for Vayorn to join him. The men sitting around the fire were silent and pale, almost as if the mist had turned them to stone.

Vayorn sat. He turned his hands over the fire and exhaled. Heat. He sighed. The men were talking now, in hushed, quiet tones.

"Can't raise the sails in this. What's Captain thinking? She can't see to navigate. We might blow right into a rocky cliff, or out of the bay and get lost at sea."

"If sea monsters don't get us first."

Vayorn sniffed, "Sea monsters? This isn't the first age."

The men turned dark glares on Vayorn. Vayorn's shoulders curled in. *Sea monsters can't exist, right?* He rubbed the back of his neck and stared into the fire.

"Aye, they exist." The man's voice was low, and the other men nodded slowly.

"Rigging avast!" A shower of ropes snapped through the air from the mainsail, somewhere in the mist. Ermolai silently rose and caught one. He gestured for Vayorn to stand in front of him and grab on.

Vayorn peeled himself from the fire. Icy wind slashed through his body. He shivered and took his place in front of Ermolai.

Is this really such a good idea? The men are right. Anything could happen if a wind caught us in this mist. Who knows where we might end up.

Vayorn looked around at the glum expressions the crew wore. Not a single man spoke louder than a whisper, and Vayorn found himself shaking. *Weak. It's just mist, isn't it?*

He closed his fists around the rope and braced his legs against the deck.

"Pull on my command!"

The man beside Vayorn tensed with his legs braced against the planks. Vayorn exhaled. He could see two shadows, perched atop the sail. They must hook it in place. *Don't envy them.*

"HEAVE HO!"

Vayorn leaned back. The rope tightened. His heels dug into the deck. Ermolai breathed heavily behind him.

"HEAVE HO!"

He leaned further backward. His eyes burned as sweat streamed into them. He took a deep breath.

"HEAVE HO!"

He gritted his teeth and threw his full weight into the rope. His shoulder muscles burned, and his legs ached.

"HEAVE!"

He moved his numb hands up the rope and bent his legs, his back almost parallel to the deck.

"HEAVE!"

"HEAVE!"

"HEAVE!"

"HEAVE HO! AVAST!"

Two men appeared out of the mist, careening downward along the ropes. Vayorn heard a thud, and his arms jarred.

"SECURE IT!"

Vayorn leaned his weight into the rope. Ermolai took the other end and ran into the fog.

"At ease!" Ermolai called back to Vayorn from somewhere in the dim. Vayorn let go. His leg muscles throbbed, and his shirt was drenched. The wind quickly chilled him as his sweat-soaked shirt turned cold against his skin. The icy air stuck in his throat and nose as his chest heaved in and out, and he caught his breath.

"Ye…are strong…," Ermolai said between breaths.

"Yeah…" Vayorn held his arms around himself and made his way to a fire. He tried to stop his shivering as he held his hands over the flames, but the weak fire did nothing to warm him. *Miserable. Wet. cold. Lost in the deng mist. Who wouldn't want to be me?* He sat down heavily.

"How long do these mists last?" Ermolai sat beside him.

"They are never same. They last sometimes three days, sometimes three hours. There is no telling how long we be stuck here."

"Oh." Vayorn stared into the haze around them. *How long will we be stuck here?*

A low flutelike moan came from the edge of the ship.

ON BOARD SHIP THREE

Arple lay curled in a ball on her bed, unable to ignore the sounds of the storm outside her room. She knew it was fortunate that Mother hadn't come, with her health as fragile as it was, but that wasn't a very comforting thought when one was lying on a rock-hard cot with a tempest raging outside. She turned her back to the door and pulled her sheets up under her chin. Her wide eyes seemed to see every detail on the wall in front of her. it was so different from Aunt Eliina's house. She pursed her lips. Why couldn't she have swum? Under the water, a person never heard the noises of the storm. She tossed. The beds were too hard, her stomach was grumbling, and now this. She crossed her arms. This wasn't fair. She was old enough to decide. But of course, everyone made all her decisions for her. She turned and faced the wall again, rigid.

The roar of a million boulders rolled down a hill and smashed against each other, punctuated by bright flashes of white, came from under her door. Her stomach tied itself in a knot, and suddenly she wasn't so sure it was good that Mother hadn't come. If she had to go, why did she have to go alone? She cupped her hands over her ears and put her head under her pillow. The wind howled outside her door, squeezing itself through the cracks between the boards. Her bed rocked along with the drunken swaying of the ship beneath her. Her spine tingled as the candle went out, and darkness fell over the room. Maria should have come. She always came. Being married shouldn't have made her unable to come all of a sudden. Arple pulled her blanket over her head. It wasn't right to send her alone. Nothing was frightening with Maria around. Maria was stupid for not seeing how much Arple needed her.

Men screaming and howling orders came through the dark around her, muffled under the wind and through the walls, "Secure the cannons! Man overboard!" The sound of running feet and screaming joined the noise of the storm. She put a hand up to her face and pulled it back. It was wet. Had she been crying? Well then, it was Mother's fault. She ought to have let her swim or sent Maria with her. Arple threw her blanket off her head. A drop of ice splashed onto Arple's hand. She jerked it back and yanked the blanket over her head again. It would all be over soon. It had too. Maybe she could just swim the rest of the voyage. Mother would never know.

The room pitched. Its walls flew opposite each other and took the place of the floor and ceiling. Arple flew out of her bed and landed in a heap on the wall, now under her feet. A basket slid toward her. Her back hit something as she caught it. The voices of screaming men ripped through the walls of her cabin. As she waited for the room to right itself, she closed her eyes.

The door smashed open with a bang. The wet rushing of waves filled her ears. Her eyes opened and widened, matching the smile on her face, her jaw slightly open. Water rushed against the walls of her room, bouncing off them and smashing into the roof. Her breathing quickened. Her gaze riveted to the water, and her brow furrowed. Through the open door, the sea rushed up to meet her. Her legs tingled as the water neared them. She bit her lip. The green crest of the wave swelled to the roof of her room, destroying all in its path. She leaned forward, and her fists clenched and unclenched loosely. The basket flew out of her hands, and she held her breath. The sides of her face prickled as her frills moved forward and backward, fire consuming them as they waited for water to close around them. Her chest stopped moving as she felt her throat close. Her frills popped metallically, and air rushed down the inside of her jaw to her lungs.

The water lifted her to the top of her room and carried her out the door. Ice stung her legs, chilling them from within. Her frills quickened their movement. She resisted the urge to itch them as she watched her dress dissolve into scales, fading as her legs grew together and sprouted a fin. A shiver ran through her body as she raised her arms upward, allowing scales to grow around her. She moved her frills forward, feeling the water rush into them, then moved them back and expelled it.

She whacked the water with her fin and swam between the wreckage around her. A pile of broken wood flew around her as she ducked. Her reflexes were swift as she wove between and around the loose objects. She seemed to be aware of everything around her, from the ropes dangling in the seafoam to the smallest nail swept away in the tide.

A scream arrested her attention as a man floated by her, clawing desperately at the air around him as he neared the edge of the ship. Shrieking, he disappeared into the waves. Arple's mouth set in a firm line. She dived after him. Her gaze set on him like the gaze of a hunting hawk on a mouse, she spiraled deeper into the glowing water. Surrounding the falling man, she dimly perceived at the edges of her focus an iridescent blue glimmer around her. The man's form flailed as he struggled, fading suddenly out of the light. She dived deeper. The water turned black around her save for the few rays of light filtering from above. Her vision rippled with the currents. She stretched her arms out and barrel-rolled, tilting her head backward to sink deeper. Her eyes squinched shut, and she focused all her senses on the water around her, waiting to sense a disturbance. Her eyes shot open—a blast of water rose upward as something sank. She pinned her arms to her sides and threw herself into a top-like spin, whirling head downward to the seabed. Sand rose around her. She paused again. The water to her left rose in a spray of gravel and debris. There he was. She swung her arm above her head and flew left. Her hands met something. It was the man. She slipped her arms through his armpits and lifted. The water absorbed his weight, and Arple felt as if she were carrying a small child in her arms instead of a grown man.

Blue surface light surrounded her. Arple swam harder, her gaze set on the ceiling of blue above her.

Her head broke through the surface of the water into clear air, illuminated by a full moon. She held the man up so he could breathe. The moonlight against her skin burned like acid. She tried to ignore the increasing pain consuming her scales as a piece of wreckage floated near them. She swam over to it and placed the man on top of it. With one hand on the plank and one hand holding the man in place, she braced her shoulders and shoved against the current, grimacing. Her body heaved with each powerful thrust of her fin. The ship came into sight, upright but barely afloat. Another ship bobbed alongside it, putting out longboats. One longboat was already in the water, picking up survivors. Something crashed. Her eyes widened. The back of the sinking ship reared into the air and hung suspended for what felt like an eternity. Arple frantically swam away from the ship, waiting to feel it fall. Then it happened. An upsurge of water hit Arple and threw her onto its crest. She grabbed the man as the plank beneath him shattered into a million shards. He gasped as his chest rose. She held his head out of the water. The wave slammed them onto the surface again. She had to get the attention of the rescue ship, or the man would die. She could only hold him for so long. Her lungs burned. She placed her head beneath the water and drank another breath through her frills. As her head broke water, she shrieked for help. The wind drowned her voice out. She dunked her head underwater again for another breath. She screamed louder.

A lantern turned toward her, attached to the prow of a longboat. She let in a big breath through her frills and shouted. A pair of large hands seized her, and someone took the man.

She felt the rough wood of the boat beneath her. Dimly, faint voices hummed around her. She tried to speak but couldn't breathe. Fire devoured her. Something like sandpaper filled her throat. Pain blinded her as her frills shriveled into little bits of paper. Her dress faded back into existence around her as her scales burned into her limbs. Through the haze over her mind, a voice echoed from far-off, asking if she was alright. Someone gasped near her, and indistinctly, a fuzzy voice said they should throw her overboard, or she might bring bad luck. A pair of rough hands seized her. She fainted…

WANDERER'S JOURNEY

My dear mother,

I miss you more than words can tell! The festival is hardly worth all this! Of all voyages I've been on, this is the worst!

There was an awful storm last night. Mother, ship three lost twenty men, out of its crew of thirty-six. Among them was the first mate, the only sailor in this whole wretched fleet who had shown me any kindness. I watched ship three sink. You can't imagine my fright. Of the sixteen survivors, not counting myself, I rescued one man. I would never have seen him if the waves had not torn my door out and swept me onto the deck. Such destruction and wreckage I have never in all my days seen. I was trying to avoid getting hit with the ruins of the mast when a man was swept by me. He was screaming for help, Mother, and when he disappeared over the edge of the ship, I couldn't help but pursue him. He sank to the very bottom of the bay, far past where even the strongest man could have swum, all the way to the black water. I found him mostly by feel. When I finally got him to the surface, I saw a longboat rescuing survivors. I hailed it and got the man onto it. You may wonder why I would save a man I do not know, but I have an answer. I saved him because it was right to save him. I know that Father is a peaceman, of the lighter branch, and he has always told me to ease suffering wherever I can. So I tried. But I am afraid I only caused more suffering. Read on. I fainted from the pain of shriveling under a full moon and woke back in my bunk. I had to go check on the man I rescued, to see if he was alright. He was ill but still quite able to speak and, I may add, yell.

He said his name was Janus. Immediately upon my entrance, he began to berate me about saving him! He was angry that I rescued him! He said I ought to have allowed him to die, that he has nothing left to live for. I felt terrible that he was suffering so. He said that his family was sold away to far lands by his master, the Conglar of Antike, after he befriended a slave child. Why being kind to a slave child would enrage his master so, I do not know. He told me that his master has set an awful task to him, and if I hadn't rescued him, he would never have to do the task. His master has commanded him to murder the same slave child he befriended, who is now as old as I, after the slave commits a murder for the captain. It made my stomach turn ill. You and Father have always instilled in me the ways of peace, of harmony and kindness. You have never allowed me to hate anyone, and I must thank you for that. If I hadn't been trained toward pity instead of annoyance, I very well might hate the man. But I pity him, so much.

The man said that he now has two choices: kill the boy, get rewarded with freedom and gold, and go search for his family; or refuse and die in the most excruciating way his master can connive. He has no choice, he said. He was so angry, Mother, and he made terrible threats to me. I shall not even place them on this page; they were so vile. He has to kill the boy now, and he said that he will kill me as well! I can only think that he must not be fully in his mind yet. No sane man would say such things to someone who saved their life.

He struck me as odd in that he both wants the boy's death and is loath to kill the boy at the same time. It is so strange. When he speaks of the boy, his eyes flash and he screams. He frightens me, Mother, so terribly. I am using far more clean language in relating his story than he used.

I will most likely not send this to you. I just need to get my thoughts out, but you would worry so if I sent this to you. This sounds like a rant, I know, but I have dreaded every second on board this contraption of wood and iron. I long to be around our peaceful, wise people and away from these boorish beasts who call themselves men. I am not like Maria; I am not brave. The men frighten me, Mother.

This letter shall never reach you, for I shall never send it.

If only you knew what I am going through.

Your beloved, confused, frightened daughter,
Arple

Dazed, Arple stared at the tear-spattered parchment. The back of her throat began to ache. Arple threw the quill down on the desk and bowed her head into her arms. Her shoulders shook.

She couldn't, try as she might, get the conversation with Janus out of her mind.

After what felt like hours, she lifted her head and wiped her eyes. Slowly, she pulled another parchment to herself and began to write.

My dear mother,

I am having an excellent time! The festival draws nearer by the day, and I can hardly contain my anticipation. I am in excellent health, and the voyage to this point has been uneventful. I find such exhilaration in striking out upon my own, to have adventures. Not that I have had any such thus far. I am on ship three of the Flaming Skull, a jolly ship to ride upon. The sailors are unusually courteous and refrain from swearing in my presence.

How is Da? Is he well? And Maria, are she and Armas getting on well together? Has she moved to Pyhaako Sanctuary yet? Was not it dear of Grandmother to allow them to reside in her reef until they can afford a home of their own?

Your loving daughter,
Arple

Half-heartedly, Arple rolled the parchment. It would have to do. But it sounded so exaggeratedly cheerful; Arple knew her mother would suspect something was wrong. Perhaps she should just send the first letter and be honest. Her mother's drawn, haggard face appeared before her. No, she couldn't send the first letter.

Slowly, she turned her head. The porthole brought in no light today; lovely emerald mist sheltered the ship. Arple sighed. If only she could swim and leave this ship forever. Her eyes closed. She could almost feel the cool jade mist against her skin as she lay on a rock. In the clouds around her, the air wouldn't burn. On a day like this, without any light or heat, she wouldn't shrivel. She shook her head. No one understood how wonderful mist was. The sailors dreaded it. How anyone could hate mist, she didn't know, but somehow the crew was afraid.

With a heavy sigh, she rose from her chair and went across the room to the bed, moving gingerly. If the moon hadn't been full last night, how much better she would feel today. Full moonlight hurt almost as much as full sunlight. She looked down at her red skin, its peeling outer layer still scaly. Even the soft blankets beneath her scratched against her legs. She lowered her back onto the bed, holding her eyes tight shut against the pain. Her head hit the pillow.

OVERBOARD

The mists gave way to yet another storm, destroying all that was left unharmed by the first storm. Hail poured down from the black sky like fist-sized stones, ripping through the sails. Lightning struck the mast again and again, lighting it like a giant candle. The sails fell burning to the deck, where waves the size of mountains extinguished them. The injured men were dragged down to the brig with Agöri, and the trapdoor was shut against the water. The efforts of the men pumping the water off the deck were futile in the face of the storm; many said it was the worst storm they had ever seen. Under the howls of the wind, the first mate's voice was faint.

"Furl the sails!"

Vayorn let his line up, trying to control it. His hand slipped again. The sail jerked. Someone cursed at him. Breathing hard, he wrapped the rope around his hand and raised his hands upward, the slimy fibers sliding through his fingers. He felt something hit him from behind. With Ermolai on top of him, he crumpled to the deck.

"Deng, you bloody...," the men began to mutter as the sail tilted, crooked.

"The two of ye be as useless as a woman!"

Vayorn shoved Ermolai off him and balled his fists. A hand clapped on his shoulder. He turned. Ermolai shook his head and handed the rope to Vayorn again.

Lightning split the sky in white-hot brilliance.

"Secure the cannons!"

"Lower!"

"Lower!"

The sail—or what was left of it—above Vayorn fell into folds upon the bottom bar along the mast. Something snapped behind Vayorn. He ducked as a piece of plank flew through the air. He could feel his heart pounding at the backs of his eyes. Another wave crashed down on the deck, and shards of the wood exploded into the air. The ship tipped again, its back end dipping into the water. Vayorn clung to the mast as his feet hung in the air. As if around ice, his hands began to slip. He tried to tighten his grip. Like a hand wrenching itself out of a vice grip, the mast jerked out of his fingers. The air bore him downward, almost as if it were trying to slow his fall. The water drew closer. A head shot out of it with hot-coal eyes. Vayorn flipped in the air as he fell. He passed Ermolai, securely attached to a cannon. Waves battered the deck.

Wreckage sailed past Vayorn's head. Water sprayed in Vayorn's face. His heart raced. He closed his eyes and waited.

His feet landed on the deck as the ship's back end rose.

"Keep pumping! Bail out the deck! We're taking on water!"

Vayorn ran to the pumps. The two men working the handles collapsed as he and Ermolai took over. Vayorn raised the pump handle and brought it down. With every pump, a memory flashed before his eyes. Up down. Mama Yanya's hands giving him his first set of leather shoes. Up down. He and Badurad wrestling. Up down. Janus telling him stories. Up down. Adva's sixth and last birthday. Up down. Adva's death.

Suddenly, he was angry. His teeth clenched. His knuckles whitened around the handle. His face was hot. He glared at the pump. Up down. Revenge. Up down. His arms burned as he forced them to keep pumping. His shoulders ached. He gritted his teeth together and shoved his air out, grunting with each down. *Won't be weak. I am not weak.*

"Mind yer heads!"

A giant smashing sound, and the creak of something falling. Vayorn looked up. Like a tower collapsing, the mast split the air and hurtled down on top of Vayorn. Frozen, he stood, numbly watching it fall.

Something smashed Vayorn in the gut, and Vayorn skidded across the deck, a heavy weight lying across his stomach.

When his vision cleared, the first thing he saw was Ermolai, peeling his shoulder from Vayorn's middle. Vayorn looked back at the pumps. They were gone, buried under a mountain of wreckage and broken chunks of the mast. Vayorn's jaw fell open. *He saved me. Why would he do that?* He blinked, trying to find a place in his mind to fit the idea of someone risking their life for him. It didn't make sense; Vayorn was sure he'd never do something like that, not for just anybody. A soft smile appeared on Vayorn's face.

"Why did you do it?" He shook his head, not looking at Ermolai. He felt Ermolai's hand on his shoulder.

"I tell you why if we survive this. Look out!"

The deck buckled as the front and back of the ship came together like the covers of a book. Vayorn jumped as a crack spread between his feet and split the ship.

"Clear the brig!"

Vayorn saw Agöri come out, on the other side of the crack from him. A wave smashed the deck.

"Pull to us!"

Vayorn watched the nearest ship, his throat tight. What if they didn't hear the first mate? He tried to force himself to breathe. A ship appeared beside their ship, but no answering call sounded. The ship began to pass out of reach. Vayorn gulped.

"To us!"

The prow of the other ship swung suddenly toward them as an answering call resounded, hardly more than a whisper behind the shrieking storm. Wood scraped on wood, sending pieces of their ship flying as the other ship squeezed itself against them.

Like a stampede of wild animals, the crew charged to the edge of the deck. Agöri's small curly head appeared for an instant, before being lost in the sea of broad shoulders and shoving arms as the crew fought to be the first to get across to the other ship.

The ends of the ship came closer together. The second mast splintered into a thousand pieces and rained down on the men. A sudden sick feeling struck Vayorn in the gut. Somehow, he was sure Agöri was hurt. He scanned the faces around him, hoping he was wrong. The crew was almost across now. Agöri was gone. Laparlana and a man in a cloak pushed past Vayorn. Vayorn never looked at the man's face, or he would have recognized him. They walked across and stood on the other ship, Laparlana's voice yelling to Vayorn across the widening gap between the ships.

"Vayorn! Leave him! Now or never!" Laparlana shouted.

Vayorn's back tensed. *Leave him?* His fists curled. He turned his back on the other ship and screamed, trying to hear an answer over the noise of the wind and his own frantic heartbeats.

"Agöri!" He cupped his hands around his mouth and yelled till his throat was sore. No answer. The ship's halves were almost vertical now. He grabbed onto a rope and slid along the tilting surface, his eyes half blinded in the driving rain.

"Vayorn!" An arm stuck out from under the wreck of the second mast. Vayorn slid down the rope to the pile and began heaving the planks out of the way. The other half of the ship was close enough to touch, rising to meet the other half like two hands clapping together.

"It's sinking! Leave him!" Laparlana's voice wailed across the wind.

Vayorn grabbed another board and threw it. He could see Agöri's top half now, splayed out like one already dead. Vayorn seized Agöri's wrists and pushed against the pile with his feet. The pile remained firmly clamped around Agöri. Agöri began to whimper. Vayorn pulled harder and flew backward as the wreckage released Agöri's legs and plummeted downward through the crack and into the water. Vayorn threw Agöri over his shoulder and ran, dragging himself across the now vertical deck. It began to sink. Vayorn climbed higher as the water below him rose. Agöri's arms around his neck tightened into a choke hold. The edge of the deck was almost touching them. The water rose higher.

Vayorn jumped as the halves of the ship smashed together and exploded in a shower of debris. Like a piece of corn crushed between mortar and pestle and thrown into the air, the pieces flew around Vayorn. Vayorn looked down, and before he could scream, the water rose hungrily to swallow him. Blackness surrounded him. The surface fell away from him as his lungs screamed for air. He tried not to breathe, but his starved lungs heaved out and water rushed into them. He coughed, and more water filled his chest. He realized he still had Agöri in his arms. Something hit him from the side. The last thing he saw was coal-red eyes and stained orange teeth, shining like candles in the murk.

THE SHELL

I look up at the mouth of a cave. It's so big it's almost the only thing I can see. A candle's in my hand. A sword's in my other hand. There are gems all over its hilt. Strange square shapes are carved into its blade. The metal looks blue in the light. The shapes are a strange gold color, like the light on Demetrius's wineglass. It's pretty. A blast of hot air hits me all of a sudden. I turn back to the cave. The rotten air coming out of it stings my throat and chokes me. Strange greenish light glows from somewhere inside it. I shudder. It's getting dark around me, quick. I look down. The candle's gone. This thing with antlers and a woman's face bounds up to me. Her voice rises and falls. Can't hear most of what she says in the wind.

"You will…destroy…or be destroyed by…"

"What?" A wind hits me, and I fall. The thing shrieks as it disappears. Reminds me of the moon being swallowed by clouds, or a piece of bread being swallowed by Demetrius. I realize the blackness is smoke.

"Eight days…eight days…eight days…," echoes around me. Can't figure out where it's coming from. Seems like it's coming from everywhere.

"Eight days for what?" A wagon flies at me out of the mist. I scream and duck. It runs over me. I stand again, surprised I'm not hurt. A turquoise blur brushes by me. The wind hits it, and it's gone.

"Vayorn!" I hear it yell my name as it flies into the air.

"Your father," a voice whispers. The sound comes from the cave. Suddenly a woman rises in front of me. Her cheekbones are sharp like Demetrius's. I back away. The wind hits her, and she melts like a candle. A hot breeze hits my face.

"All is not as it seems. Watch…watch…watch…"

"Watch what?"

Something roars. The cave comes alive. I hide on the ground, hoping it won't see me. The dirt around it falls off it. Some of it gets in my eyes, and I can't see. When my eyes clear, I'm face-to-face with this giant black wolf. I scream and run. As it chases me, its roar becomes Demetrius's voice.

"I have a plan…a plan…a plan…a plan…" It's behind me. I can feel its hot breath burning my ankles. I look down. My feet won't move. I try to run, but I can't. It digs its claw into my side. The pain is worse than anything I could've ever imagined. I scream and fall down, groaning, pressing my hands to my side. Suddenly I can't see. There's a red fog in my eyes. Then the only thing I can see is black.

*****

Vayorn gasped as he sat up, as if awakened from a nightmare. Water coursed into his open mouth and stopped before it could go down his throat. Air filled his lungs. *I'm underwater!* For a second, he stopped breathing. *But it's impossible. There's no way this is possible.* And yet there he was, surrounded by water, breathing.

His head swiveled as he took in his surroundings. A domed roof towered above him, an alabaster-cream color, falling in the shape of an overturned bowl to meet the floor. He looked down. A circular bed lay underneath him, white sheets floating on top of it over his legs. He turned around. Like a spiderweb, circular spirals brought the wall behind him to the inside of a point, the spiral interrupted with straight raisings of shell.

The room darkened. Vayorn tensed. Then suddenly the light returned.

It shone from a small circular opening cut in the roof near the floor. Vayorn's eyebrows raised. *It's like Mama Yanya's story, the one about the prince who was rescued by merfolk.* Curiosity overcame Vayorn. He found himself half hoping he'd find what the prince found in the story. *Stupid. It's just a story. Plus, last thing you need's a woman. Women make men weak.* Vayorn tried to convince himself he wasn't excited about what he might see out the window, but his racing heart told him different. He swiveled his legs to the edge of the bed.

A hesitant breath, and he pushed off the bed with his hands.

He sailed forward, his feet barely touching the floor, his hands flailing as they failed to catch onto anything. A table flew by him. A wardrobe. A door. His feet skidded in front of his head as he tried to use his hands to slow himself. The wall rose in front of him. His eyes squeezed shut, and the next thing he knew, he was floating backward away from the wall. He hit the bed lightly and grabbed onto a table beside it.

An idea hit him. *So then, if I do this...* Resting his hands against the edge of the bed, he pushed off again and put his arms out as if they were open wings. He brought them together as if he were clapping. His movement paused. *How do I move slow?* Like the clumsy stagger of a newborn calf, his legs came out straight behind him, and he pulled his arms over his head while kicking lopsidedly with his feet. He began to move in slow, jerking spurts. *Wish I'd learned to swim.*

"Hahahaha! Hoohoohoohoo! Ooooh!"

Vayorn looked down. A strange creature—almost like a cross between a fish and a man—rolled across the room holding its sides. Its face contorted in mirth, and water streamed from its mouth in a line of bubbles.

"Finding...your sea legs...my friend?"

Hearing Common Tounge from the creature's mouth was the strangest thing Vayorn had ever heard. He stiffened. His face reddened in embarrassment. Lips tight, he stared in silence at the thing. It stopped laughing and passed an appraising glance over Vayorn.

"I have marveled always at the level of stupidity humans show in the water. Will you be desiring to sate your hunger at any time, my guest?"

Vayorn backed away, trying to not stare at his reptilian host. *What do you say to a monster?*

The thing shook its head. "Come." It seized one of Vayorn's ankles and began to swim.

Vayorn's heart leaped into his throat. His stomach fell to his feet. *It's a Saynasaf! They eat people.* The bite marks around old Karl's arm surfaced in his mind. Old Karl said he was captured by Saynasafs. They tried to eat him, or so he said. *Have to get out of here!* Vayorn twisted and writhed like a bird caught in a snare, but the thing didn't let go. Its fingers tightened like a cord around Vayorn's ankle.

The door loomed up over Vayorn, then purple darkness swam around him.

The thing sped down a narrow tunnel lit with glowing flowers, giving off a shivery red-blue light. Vayorn tried to kick, but his foot lost momentum far before it touched the thing, and his foot only tapped the thing. The tunnel spiraled low over them, falling on top of them like a blanket. The rounded walls were lined with misshapen openings, not round and not square, more like holes in a glass window bashed out with a rock than doors. Some of the openings were bright, and some were dark. Vayorn hit the wall, and something burned his arm. He looked down; the flowers were getting crushed under his arm. Vayorn jerked his arm away as a purple stain spread across his arm.

The flowers stung like a thousand thistles made of wool. *What's going on?*

An undulating melody sobbed down the hallway, ripping through the air. As it reached them, the flowers glowed suddenly red. The creature paused for an instant and bowed its head with slumped shoulders. Vayorn thought he saw it wipe at its eyes. An unexplainable feeling of dread came over Vayorn, the way it did when he passed the dungeon in Tarshal. His skin crawled as if an army of ants covered it. Needlelike, his spine prickled. Unbidden visions of war and famine filled his mind. Fire leaped to the sky, consuming the charred remains of what was once a house. A mother was sobbing. She stood, shielding a small figure in her arms, bent over it as if her nearness alone could protect it. The scales framing her face shone like tarnished metal, dirtied with tears, ashes, and smoke. A horse circled them till it was almost trampling them. It reared. Its rider screamed in a language that seemed both foul and fair at the same time. The front hooves of the horse hit the woman. She fell into the dirt. It reared again. A scream pierced the air…

Vayorn's eyes opened. He realized they had been closed.

An opening rose over them and light like that of the sun blinded Vayorn. He blinked hard, holding his eyes shut till the light was no longer painful.

His vision cleared. A vaulted roof, like that of the room he'd woken in but on a far larger scale, let in the light through a row of openings around a single hole at its center. A giant clamshell lay on the floor under the opening, turned onto its front so that the rounded surface made a kind of table. Open oyster shells, large enough to sit in, circled it like chairs.

In one shell sat a second creature, much like a woman. She was rocking Agöri while humming, her face shining as proudly as if she were his mother. Her hair fell down far past her waist. Agöri's fingers were tangled in it. Her eyes glowed, their color a deep ginger. Her hair was like autumn leaves, a confusion of gold, brown, orange, and black. Agöri's eyes were slowly closing as she sang the last lines of her lullaby:

> Oh, my darling,
> Oh, my child,
> Close your eyes, dear,
> Sleep, yes, sleep now,
> Night has fallen,
> Day won't dawn now.

She looked up. Vayorn was struck with the sorrow in her eyes and the sad way she smiled, as if even her joy was tinged with pain. She swam up from her seat, cradling Agöri in her arms like a baby, and met Vayorn and the man-thing.

"I have prepared a meal for you. The tadpole is asleep, sweet child. I must put him to bed." She turned to the other creature. "Oh, is not it sweet to have a little one again? How I have missed those days."

She swam down the hallway, still crooning a lullaby to Agöri, now fast asleep.

What's she going to do to him? Vayorn yanked his ankle out of the creature's hand and tried to follow. A cold hand pulled him back by one shoulder. He turned.

"Let the child rest. He is not well."

Vayorn sucked in his breath, almost without realizing it. The mast. *He must've gotten hurt.* Vayorn coughed and tried to not sound concerned.

"How bad is it?" His voice shook. He winced. Weak.

"We know not. But I assume you have hunger? Come. My wife has laid out sustenance for us." He waved his hand toward the table. Two bowl-like shells lay on the table, green gelatinous mounds of seaweed spilling over the edges.

Small shrimp and strings of yellow covered the mounds like piles of worms.

Vayorn's stomach did a somersault. *Looks like barf.* He felt his stomach heave and shoved down the chunks at the back of his throat trying to erupt out his mouth.

"No."

"What?"

"No, I'm not eating that."

A hurt expression crossed the thing's face. "Is there something amiss with my wife's cooking? Her food is not usually taken in such manner."

"I'm not eating that."

The thing took a deep breath as if he were about to say something, paused, and was silent. Just when the silence was becoming uncomfortable, the woman-thing entered again.

"He is asleep, dear thing." She looked at her husband's face. "Is there ought amiss?"

"No, there is not. Is the child injured badly, do you think?"

"I dosed him with more heal-shell, so we cannot accurately know how bad his pain is right now. But I feel that he may have broken ribs." She turned to Vayorn. "Ah, you must be Vayorn. He speaks quite highly of you, as if you were his older brother. It is obvious he looks up to you."

Vayorn looked away. *Looks up to me? Of all people? I find that hard to believe.* He shrugged.

"How long've we been here?"

"Three days," the woman-thing spoke.

Vayorn's eyes widened. *Three days? I was asleep that long?* His brow furrowed.

"How did you find us?"

The man stiffened. "I alone saved you. They forbade—" He took a sharp breath. "I saved you from the Plesias, or Terapaidis in our tongue. It was an easy act, for you sank near the great corals, and I was able to drag you into them, where the beast could not follow."

"How are we not dead? I was drowning."

The man held up a satchel. "Fire-flower. I had to work quickly to save you. If Lahja," he waved his arm toward the woman, "had not been with me, you would have died indeed. We forced it down the throats of you and the boy and rubbed the two of you with it."

Suddenly a knock echoed down a second tunnel, to the right of the first hallway. The woman's hands flew to her chest, and her scales paled. She laid a hand on the man.

"Ilmari…" Her voice quaked. Ilmari closed his eyes and opened them slowly. He removed Lahja's hand from his arm.

"Hide the boy." His voice held a strange urgency, and his gaze locked with Lahja's. Lahja's lips parted as if to speak, then her mouth closed in a hard, thin line, and she nodded. Ilmari turned and disappeared.

With one hand on Vayorn's collar and the other on his arm, Lahja shoved Vayorn in front of her, down the hallway he and Ilmari had come down. The sounds of hammering filtered in from the other hallway. Vayorn could hear angry voices. *Sounds like the outdwellers after Adva was killed.* Vayorn chuckled; he knew he ought to be disgusted by what they did, but more than anything, he was proud of the outdwellers. He'd never forget that night: screaming, shrieking, filthy people, savage as wild animals. The sounds of the gate to the palace buckling under their attack. The blood on the courtyard ground surrounding dead soldiers. The shame of not being able to help them, being locked on the dungeon level with all the other slaves.

Vayorn tried to speak, but a severe pinch on his arm silenced him. Lahja pushed him into one of the dark openings in the hallway.

"Whatever you do, do not make a sound, and do not leave this room!" She shook him by the shoulders. "Understood?"

"What's going—"

"SILENCE! UNDERSTOOD."

Vayorn nodded slowly. *What was she so afraid of?*

A new voice came from somewhere outside the room. "Alright Ilmari, where are the humans? Show them to us and we shall go easy on you. But I thought the governor himself forbade you to hide them…"

Lahja's head swiveled around, and her eyes widened.

"Oh no…" She shoved him backward into the dark.

When he found his way to the opening again, it was sealed off with what felt like a rock. His heart began to pound as a thought struck him. *What if they find Agöri?* He shoved his weight against it. Nothing happened. He tried again. Again. Again. Panting, he folded his legs beneath himself and sank to the floor. A small pile of sand rose around him. He crossed his arms. The silence seemed to stretch thin across him, as if the darkness were a living blanket. He tried the door again. *How'd a woman get that thing over the door in the first place?* He hit it with his closed fist and winced. "Deng…Bludegem…Gach…," he muttered every curse word in his vocabulary at the door, unwilling to move, blocking his exit. He shook his aching hand.

*****

Light stabbed the backs of Vayorn's eyes. He sat up and held a hand above his eyes, squinting. *Did I fall asleep?* Ilmari's shape appeared in the door. He was shaking as if he could hardly contain his laughter. He swam over to Vayorn and helped Vayorn up.

"The fools got drunk on my store of wine. Promises were made, and even if we were to keep the two of you forever, you would never be…'discovered.'"

"What kind of promises can do that?"

"I make the wine myself. They like it, so as long as I can keep them supplied with it, we are in good order."

"And Agöri?"

"Still asleep. Lahja refuses to hear of giving him up. She claims she shall raise him herself, that he has no need to return to the above world." Ilmari shook his head. "Ah, that woman. It's one of the things that made me love her, her stubbornness. Even the soldiers did not give her enough fright to consider relinquishing the boy."

"Why's she want to keep him?"

Ilmari sighed. His voice choked up as he spoke. He paused often to wipe his eyes. "We had tried and tried to have children. We were never able to for years and years. And then, a miracle happened: we had a child…the most promising son you could imagine. Handsome, sweet, funny…he was the pride of our lives, and we loved him… He was…killed…" Ilmari paused. Vayorn tried to ignore the feeling of pity welling up in him. "Having the boy so near eases the pain in Lahja's heart… We lost our own son nigh on twenty years ago… The child has healed Lahja…more than you can imagine. We cannot give him up… She needs him."

Vayorn sucked his breath in. *Can't give him up?* He crossed his arms.

"She has no right to keep him. He's not property."

"I never said he was."

A strange feeling hit Vayorn in the gut; he'd heard this conversation before. *Mama Yanya's voice rang out in his mind: "You don't own him, Janus." Then Janus's voice: "I never said I did." Mama Yanya again: "He don't belong to you, he don't." Janus's voice was bitter. "You're right. He belongs to the master." Mama Yanya: "And if'n you did own him, I know you wouldn't treat him well as you be doin', stayin' on his good side!" Janus: "Come now, he's a child. What do I care about staying on a child's good side?" Mama Yanya used a caustic tone. "He be useful, that's what. You're a slave with a slave long as 'e likes ye. Don't try to fool me."*

"Don't try to fool me." Vayorn pushed past Ilmari and turned to look at him. "Where is he?" Ilmari hesitated.

"Well?" Vayorn examined Ilmari's face. Suspicion filled him. Exactly where was Agöri? *Do scales hurt more than skin when you punch them?* His fingers curled into his palm.

Ilmari sighed. "Follow me, but I shall warn you, he is not well. Do nothing to," Ilmari looked meaningly down at Vayorn's closed fist, "excite him."

Vayorn clenched his teeth together.

Ilmari turned. Vayorn followed him as quickly as he could.

They came to a large room, ornately decorated with shells made of gold and something like thick pads of lace across the floor. *Is that coral?* Vayorn resisted the temptation to reach down and touch it. *Wonder if it's true that if you touch coral, you'll be unwoundable? If Saynasafs are real, how many more of the old legends are true?*

A large bed sat at the center of the room, ornate strings of pearls falling over it from the roof. A small form lay curled up in the center of the bed. Lahja sat on the edge, smoothing Agöri's hair back from his forehead as she sang. Jealous for an instant, Vayorn looked away. *She acts like she's his mother. Maybe, if we stayed...* Vayorn's head shot up. *Stupid!*

You'd stay here just to have a mother? Idiot. Weak. You don't need parents. His shoulders tensed.

> Kauklia jar maa poist,
> Pakenemmerik, pakenemmerik paivanir tau,
> Paivani miekkana Kutisne se nakymas
> Kutisne yoner mustaanik.
> Afar and off in lands away,
> We flee, we flee the break of day,
> Day's swordlike light,
> We shrink from its sight,
> We shrink into the black of night.

Her song sent a shiver down Vayorn's spine as, before his eyes, hundreds of the creatures fled into the sea, leaving a war-torn land behind them. The day burned upon the lands, and they left their houses and barns empty behind them, escaping into the ocean. They shrank from all light as they traveled, even full moonlight, and only came onto land during the blackest nights, when there was no moon or light of any kind.

He shook himself, and the dream was gone.

The woman was whispering softly to the man. Vayorn closed his eyes and pretended to sleep.

"Ilmari, can't we keep them? You almost died to save them. Why should we give them up? I am certain the governor would understand, and if he did not, we could always move. The ocean is large, and there are many places to go."

"The young one would perhaps adjust to our life well, but the older one…"

"I understand your hesitancy, but surely there is still hope for him?"

"I do not see a gentle heart when I look at him. I see scorn, I see anger, and I see fear."

Vayorn almost sat up. Fear? He dug his nails into his palm. Trying to seem like he was still asleep, he took a deep breath and squeezed his eyes further closed. *Not smart to let them know I'm listening.* His clenched fist tightened.

"I think he's waking up."

"Come, let us allow them to sleep."

Vayorn opened his eyes. The room was empty, and he was alone with his thoughts. Agöri murmured in his sleep. The sounds of void silence filled the room, as if the tables, the bed, the walls, the very ground itself were chanting, "*Fear. Fear. Fear. Fear.*" Vayorn put his head in his hands.

Vayorn looked away, trying to think of something to say.

"We must now return you to your ship," Ilmari was saying. His hands flew as he threw items into a bag. "The child needs to get to one of your human physicians. I have done whatsoever I can, but I fear he is far beyond the injuries we expected. I cannot take him to one of our physicians. Our governor would be angry enough should he learn we harbored humans and took them to the secret village, much less used up valuable medicine on them."

Anger filled Vayorn. *He can't just send us away! Human doctors? What doctors? Besides, Agöri'd never make it to the surface.*

"Oh, so your safety is more important than Agöri's life?"

Vayorn didn't try to keep the acidic tone out of his voice.

Ilmari stiffened. "I did not say that. You deliberately twist my words, young man. You have been a rod of contention since you awoke. I would suggest you behave in a more civil manner while I am your host." He turned his back on Vayorn.

"I have my wife to consider. She must be safe."

A wry smile tried to twist Vayorn's lips. *Women make men weak. As if I needed further proof.*

"What exactly do you think the ship's doctor's gonna be able to do, huh? You'd just abandon Agöri to save your own skin, is that it? Your own life's worth so much more than a child's anyway." Vayorn's voice dripped sarcasm. "So why not, why not just throw him to the wolves and stand back? Sounds pretty safe to me."

Ilmari turned back to Vayorn, his nostrils flared. He pushed Vayorn out of the way and swam out of the room.

"He shall heal. It is well you sent for me. The tadpole wouldn't have survived another night." A wrinkled gray thing swam up from Agöri's bedside, its tentacles waving in the air around it. Vayorn grimaced. *It's disgusting.* The thing had no nose, just a flat scaly surface with two holes in it. One of the holes was its mouth, the other was in the center of its face and was shining with pink light.

What is it?

The thing, as if in answer to his unasked question, said, "I am an Ocatarus. An old one, with no reason to tell the governor—or any other creature—my business. You have no need to worry, Ilmari. But return the lad. You cannot keep him. He must be raised by his own kind."

Lahja nodded sadly and smoothed back Agöri's hair with gentle hands. "I did so hope we could keep him. I have always wanted to raise at least one child to adulthood," she began to sing again. Vayorn settled back in a corner to listen.

BACK TO THE SURFACE

Demetrius rolled his shoulders back and rubbed his temples. The letters on the scroll in front of him blurred. His candle's stub barely lit the page. He went over the figures again. If he paid the generals what they asked, would there be enough left to live on? Twenty thousand golds was more than could be scrapped together in a half decade. As if the gold of foreign cities wasn't enough to pay the commanders. Winter was coming. Laparlana would be large with child. There wasn't much food left—certainly not enough to feed all the palace slaves, guards and keep Laparlana healthy. For the millionth time, Demetrius wished life could be simpler. There was obviously only one option: sell off more slaves. The palace staff was small as it was, so the outdwellers would have to be captured and sold. But no one cared about them anyway; what were they besides rabble-rousers and troublemakers? Suddenly, a small smile appeared on Demetrius's face as a new thought entered his mind: at least he only had to track down one heir to the throne, now that Vayorn was dead. Demetrius had to admit it was brave of Vayorn to jump off the ship in the last storm, but bravery hadn't saved him. A sense of relief filled Demetrius. His child would be safe, now that Demetrius's claim to the throne was unchallenged.

The door opened. Laparlana came in.

"Dear, something is here to speak with you." The disgust in her voice made Demetrius turn his head. A Saynasaf stood in the door.

"Enter." Demetrius didn't stand. What respect did he owe a thing like that?

"I have a message for you, from the captain of the guard of the hidden city."

*****

Demetrius slammed his fist against the table. How much would it take to kill Vayorn? It couldn't possibly be that hard to protect his child's future. Alive? How? And why would anything save Vayorn's life, even if it had a reason? Laparlana laid her hand on his shoulder. Without looking at her, Demetrius waved his hand dismissively. He heard a small, irritated huff from his right. He puffed out his cheeks. Hadn't they argued about this enough already? What more could Laparlana have to say? Two days had passed, and she still wouldn't just drop it.

He heard her footsteps behind him leave the room. His mouth hardened in a determined line. Enough was enough. Strategy was well and good, but if Vayorn ever came to the surface again, he would die—immediately. Enough with secret missions and trickery. And nothing Laparlana said could change that.

The door opened again. Laparlana was back.

Demetrius stiffened, annoyed. Didn't she ever just give up on having her own way?

"I cannot let you kill him. Imprison him, sell him, but don't kill him." Her hand cupped Demetrius's chin, and she turned Demetrius's head so that he was looking her in the eyes. "You are better than this. I cannot believe that this ruthless killer is the man I married. The man I married is funny, sweet, perhaps a little arrogant, but not a murderer. I know you better than to believe that you would do that."

Demetrius closed his eyes. What did she understand of revenge? Nothing.

*****

Vayorn and Agöri stayed with Ilmari and Lahja for three weeks. With each passing day, Vayorn found it harder and harder to seem "strong." After all, how can you fight with someone who won't argue with you? No matter how hard he tried to instigate a fight, Ilmari never took the bait. Vayorn longed more and more for a good argument, a good reason to punch someone, but none of Ilmari's guests argued with him. He tried everything short of attacking someone for no reason, but still no one would fight him. Vayorn began to worry he was becoming weak and withdrew from interacting with Ilmari and Lahja. It was angering how kind they were to him. Didn't they ever get mad?

With each day, Agöri's strength grew. Vayorn had to begrudgingly admit that even though the Ocatarus was repulsive, it was skilled at healing. Agöri's ribs healed rapidly, and his tie with Lahja grew till she referred to him no longer as "the little human" but as "my little boy." Whenever she called Agöri that, Vayorn found himself worrying. What if Agöri wouldn't come back to the surface with him?

Soon, the day came for them to return to the ship.

Ilmari took them to the surface, and after he had pulled Agöri away from Lahja, Vayorn called up to the ship. A rope fell down the side, and they climbed aboard.

Vayorn's feet thudded onto the deck. He looked up. Not a single face around him held even a trace of surprise. Not a voice spoke. Quiet shuffling, like feet slowly walking, slid behind Vayorn. He glanced over his shoulder; the edge of the ship was blocked. The clenched way the men were standing reminded Vayorn of an execution squad.

The screeching sounds of swords being drawn.

They couldn't have known I'd come back to the surface, could they? He tried to ignore the frantic pounding in his chest. *Why do they have swords?*

The creak of a cabin door opening.

His eyes locked with Demetrius's. They stared, one silently daring the other to make the first move. Time seemed to pause. And in that pause, for the fraction of an instant, they understood each other. What was about to be done had to be done; it was too late to turn back time, too late to make amends. A thought flashed through Vayorn's mind, so quickly it was only a half thought; could he and Demetrius have ever been friends? But just as quickly, it was forever gone. A sense, so clear it was almost spoken, almost like the words on a page, passed between them: "It's either you or me. One of us has to die."

Then time caught up with them.

"Bring him to me!" Demetrius shouted.

Vayorn's head snapped around. A pile of planking lay on the deck. A bucket with a mop still in it lay by the mast. A net was splayed across the edge of the ship, drying in the sun. Vayorn bit his lower lip, a plan forming in his mind.

Vayorn bent over and whispered the plan to Agöri.

"Got it?" he mouthed.

Agöri nodded.

"Run."

Agöri was gone.

Vayorn spun around as a fist missed him.

Something flashed to Vayorn's right. He barely had time to see the gloved fist before all the air left his gut. He doubled over, teeth gritted. Out of his peripheral vision, he saw the shine of metal.

A foot slammed him to the ground and pinned him there. Rough hands seized Vayorn's arms and dragged him to standing. The sword hovered over his throat. He struggled as someone began to force him forward.

Each step rang out like the knell of a death drum. *Thud. Thud. Thud.* And with each step, Demetrius was closer and closer and closer.

Vayorn steadied his breathing and managed to turn so he could see the mast out of the corner of his eye. Agöri held the bucket. The time was almost right. Vayorn took a deep breath.

It was time.

"PHASE ONE!" Vayorn sank his teeth into the man pinning his right arm and threw the second man over the sword point. Something warm hit him as he heard the dull sound of metal slicing into flesh.

He ran.

There was a slosh. Water slid across the deck. Men slid and fell, skidding in the soapy water. Vayorn wove around them till he was by the net.

"Phase two!"

Agöri took the mop and threw it at Vayorn. It sailed through the air.

A hand arrested it midair. Vayorn ran his gaze down the massive arm to one of the ugliest faces he'd ever seen. Black spaces made jagged lines in the tobacco-stained grin. Vayorn tried to run as the man advanced toward him.

"Why'd Conglar ever offer that kind'a reward fer a scrawny thing like ye? Ye're as weak as a puppy, or my name don't be Ayras." A hand seized Vayorn by the throat. Vayorn's feet left the ground. He kicked, trying to free himself.

Agöri threw the bucket at him.

It sailed by his head and caught Ayras full in the face. A furious bellow rang out. The hand on Vayorn's throat tightened. Vayorn fought to remain conscious. All the sounds around him faded. When he could see again, he was lying on the ground beneath a raging Ayras—or at least as much of Ayras as Vayorn could see. Somehow, the bucket had gotten stuck, helmetlike, over the man's face. It would have struck Vayorn as funny, except that Ayras was about to get the bucket off. The men were distracted for the moment. There might not be a chance like this again. Vayorn crab-crawled backward, away from Ayras. He looked at the mast. *Will Agöri remember the next part of the plan?*

Someone stepped on Vayorn. Every head turned toward him. Ayras was forgotten. They'd seen him. They charged.

Vayorn curled in a ball under a rain of blows. His whole body throbbed. He threw his arms over his head in a feeble attempt to shield himself. A metallic taste filled his mouth. Was he bleeding? He put a hand up to his lip. It was covered in red. His chest tightened.

Suddenly angry, he rolled to his hands and knees, grabbed the nearest pair of ankles, and jerked. Someone fell. For an instant, the rain of blows paused.

Vayorn peeled himself off the ground. His veins coursed hot.

His face flushed. He ducked and barreled over to the mast.

Agöri handed another bucket to him and ran over to the net.

Vayorn gripped the bucket handle in both his hands and swung. It connected with a head and smashed into fragments. He took what was still left of it and swung again.

Without looking back to see if the bucket worked, he grabbed the mop and began frantically whacking around him. Like wet hair, the ropes on the end of the mop wrapped around a man's face. Vayorn shoved forward. The man fell backward. Cursing rang out, accompanied by a series of thuds as the man knocked others to the deck.

Vayorn turned.

Suddenly, he was trapped. A gapless wall of metal and fists surrounded him. Their drawn swords came closer.

Vayorn took a deep breath and arced the mop over his head. It hit something. Blindly, he hit again. Again. Again.

He spun, not pausing to look at what he was hitting. Someone groaned. He used more force.

Something hard hit him. He dropped the mop. Before he could pick it up again, a foot caught him in the small of the back and he fell to the ground, pinned beneath what felt like a boulder.

He reached out. Something met his hand. The planks. He pretended to give up. His head throbbed as someone grabbed a handful of his hair and yanked him to his feet.

He hooked his foot under a plank.

The men began to pull him away from the pile.

A kick, and the plank rocketed into the air. Vayorn threw his legs out from underneath himself and dropped to the ground.

Startled, the men loosened their grip for a second. "PHASE THREE!"

The net sailed through the air.

Vayorn scrambled out of the way.

The men fell in a tangled heap beneath the net, tightening it around themselves with their writhing and twisting against the cords. Vayorn jutted his chin upward proudly. *It's not over yet. Numbers don't win a fight.*

Vayorn lifted the plank and charged forward, knocking the men aside in front of him. He knew he'd be sore enough when it ended—however it ended—but right now he could feel the battle heat in his veins. There wasn't any room to be sore when you were fighting for real, not when you enjoyed it as much as he did.

Agöri picked up a second net.

Vayorn tried to fight his way across the deck as a group of men charged to the edge of the deck, where the tiny form of Agöri cowered. Vayorn fought down his panic, but his thoughts raced. Agöri was good at sneaking, but what could he do to protect himself without Vayorn's help? Vayorn screamed and attacked with renewed vigor. He had to reach Agöri first; what would happen if he didn't? Vayorn shuddered and pushed away the thought. He wouldn't let that happen.

His board broke. Helpless, he watched the men surround Agöri. Vayorn looked away. There was nothing more he could do.

Suddenly, there was another disturbance. The men around Agöri lay in a pile, their feet caught in the net. Vayorn's jaw dropped. Maybe Agöri was better at taking care of himself than he looked.

Vayorn ducked and made his way to the pile of men. He began shouting and running around, trying to get as much attention as he could. Maybe if the men were paying attention to him, Agöri could escape.

He glared at Agöri. "Run!" Agöri ran.

Vayorn frantically tried to create part two of his plan. There were no buckets left. The nets were out of reach. The planks were out of reach. Panic seized him. There was nothing left to use. He backed up. The tide of swords was coming closer. The copper dagger flashed before Vayorn's mind. No, he couldn't let that happen. He turned and ran.

Someone threw him to the ground. It was over.

A shriek rang out from Ayras.

"The little vermin bit me bottom!" The sounds of a scuffle and Agöri was pinned against the mast.

Vayorn sighed, suddenly so sore he could barely move.

DUNBAR

The woman in the painting seemed alive in the golden firelight. Her eyes glowed with matronly purity; Dunbar knew now how false that glow was. But if she ever came back, he knew he could never turn her away. No matter what she did, she was his, and he loved her. His gaze traveled to her arms. A baby lay in them, his curly brown hair and round pink face shining midgiggle. He blended so perfectly with the other figures in the painting that Dunbar alone could have told he was added in years after the original completion of the picture. A little boy sat in the lap of a young man, his head just tilting against the man's shoulder, his eyes almost asleep. Raw aching filled Dunbar's chest, as far-off laughter filled his ears, coming from a time and place that were dead to him. Without realizing it, Dunbar reached one hand out, as if to grab the memory and hold onto it. His throat ached as tears built at the corners of his eyes.

Someone knocked, and he hastily composed himself.

"Enter," he said. His voice was deep and loud, but just a little shaky. The door opened. A servant came in. Dunbar stood and offered the man a chair.

The man shook his head. "You're my master. You should be sitting and I should—"

Dunbar took the man's arm and sat him down. "What did you need to tell me?" He began pouring a glass of ale. "He's found you. You need to run." A sudden urgency came to the man's voice. His eyes were wide with fear. "Nowhere's safe. All of our forts, all of our hideouts, Cragcliff, Darkmoor, Tintgold Gulch—Demetrius knows where they all are! All except for Canjon. That's the only place you can run. You can't hide here."

Dunbar's eyes owled. It was impossible. The castles were so well hidden. The only way Demetrius could know where they were was—Dunbar closed his eyes against the thought, but he already knew what had happened. The only way Demetrius could know was if one of Dunbar's men turned traitor. Dunbar lost all pretense of calmness. Who? And why? He'd been safe. So close to reclaiming his throne. And now this.

He slid the glass to the servant and rose. His feet pounded on the wood slats as he paced back and forth in front of the fire, his hands clasped behind his back. Six years of worry, of walking to and fro, lay underneath his feet in a deep groove where the boards were worn away in a line.

"Tell me more." His voice quavered.

The servant downed the ale as he spoke, dribbling it off his chin and down his shirt front. Sweat streamed off his face and shirt, discoloring the rips in the shredded fabric. The last time Dunbar had seen him, he'd been a young boy, raw, skinny, lighthearted. Now, he was a man. No longer young-looking, a full beard hid his once-childish features. His muscles rippled, and Dunbar could swear he'd grown three inches. The lightness of old in his eyes was replaced with a grim seriousness; six months of scouting will do that to you, so Dunbar had found. The man (Aurel was his name) had spent his mission in the mountains, alone. Dunbar hadn't wanted to let him go, but he'd been the only volunteer. There were times when Dunbar wanted to order men to scout, but he never did. Scouting promised enough risk it was nigh on murder to force a man to do it; many scouts never returned.

Aurel was speaking in between gulps.

"You know the man named Geoff. His wife died when the enemies attacked Crimson Gulch." Dunbar winced. Crimson Gulch. If he could choose to erase one memory from his mind, it would be that place. His chest tightened; those words would always call to his mind the smell of smoke, the screams of women and children, the dead lying on the ground like fallen leaves. He didn't try to reason away the vague sense of guilt weighing on him. Maybe if he'd prepared better, Crimson Gulch would never have happened. Even in his sleep, he saw the faces of men—men who in the worst pain would never shed a tear—red from crying till they nearly unrecognizable.

"Caught him about a month ago with a band of soldiers." Aurel's voice was angry. "They had his children they did, so the only way to save the little'uns is to tell everything he knows. They was Antikish soldiers too."

Aurel pounded his cup on the table. "I tried to stop 'im, but I couldn't afore he'd told everything." He sighed. "They let his chil'runs go they did, then they catches me listnin' and tries to get me 'afore I can warn you. I leads us on a merry chase and loses 'em finally."

He wiped his mouth, set the empty cup on the table, and leaned in on his elbows. "Get while the gettins good. I took the liberty I did to order your horse saddled and food packed. Sent a messenger to Antarulra too. She'll be expectin' you now, she will. Don't thank me. I owe it to ye."

Dunbar nodded wearily. He rubbed his temples. "Thank you, Aurel. Get some rest. We'll have little enough of that in coming days."

"Yes, sir." Aurel bowed and left.

Dunbar waited till the door latched then threw himself into a chair. His shoulders slumped as if a heavy weight were slung across them. He slowly raised his head to stare at the ornate carvings above him. Each one seemed to say, "Mistakes…mistakes…mistakes." Dunbar sighed. Mistakes was right. Hadn't he been living a mistake for the past six years? Guilt filled him again. Just that morning, news had come to him that his older son was lost, disappeared into the Grenzewood. If only he'd acted sooner, if only he'd rescued him while he could. But it was too late. A year too late to prevent Crimson Gulch. Fifteen years too late to prevent that fight with Demetrius, so long ago. It had cost him everything, his throne, his family, and he couldn't place all the blame on Demetrius either. Perhaps if he'd been kinder to his brother, Demetrius would never have felt the need to take the throne from him. Blind, that was what he'd been. About everything.

Perhaps if he'd noticed Marliesel was lonely, he would have given her more attention and she wouldn't have had to seek it from someone else. It was too late to go back now. He could only go forward.

Dunbar rose and stretched his limbs. He sighed. Forward. What exactly did forward have in store? It couldn't be worse than what had already happened. His gaze roved the room. He could abandon almost everything, but there were a few things he refused to leave behind for thieves or vagabonds. A dry smile appeared on his face. There were so many times when he'd been the vagabond himself, benefiting from stolen loot.

He walked across the room to a table where a map lay spread out, red and blue dots speckling it from the east to the west. A small town lay outside Grenzewood, a star beside it. If only he'd acted sooner. There were so many times he could have rescued the boy. Now it was too late. He rolled the map up and shoved it into a metal canister. Not that he needed a map. He'd lived for so long in these mountains there wasn't a trail he couldn't find. But these lands could be treacherous; even his best scouts could get lost and die, and it didn't matter how well they thought they knew the land.

He walked to the wall opposite the door, where a chest lay in the shadows. He rifled through it till he came to the bottom. The bottom of the chest was rough against his hands as he swept them along its empty bottom. So many times his men had ridiculed him for carrying an empty chest with him, but it wasn't truly empty. The wood rose underneath his hands. With one hand on the spot, he drew his knife out of his belt. The blade slid under a small crack in the wood. He pushed the blade down and wiggled it back and forth.

Snap. He pulled up, and the bottom of the chest lifted out.

There it was. The hilt shone in the light, inlaid with precious gems and runes along the blade. The firelight traveled around its edge to glint at its point. His sword. Once a source of joy to him, now it seemed only to epitomize his mistakes; by now, the sword should have been passed down.

Passed down to his son, who was dead.

Dunbar sighed. If only. That seemed to be the resounding longing of his life. If only.

He buckled the sheath around his waist and slid the sword into it, wrapping a cloth around the hilt to keep the gems from being damaged.

He strode to a bookshelf and ran his hands along it till they brushed the spine of a wooden book. He pulled. A creak, a clang, and the shelf swung out to reveal row upon row of bottles and packets. The overpowering odor of krydderurt wafted out from a shelf covered in rocks. They were split open to reveal small piles of golden powder at their centers. He carefully filled a bag with the powder and tied it to his belt.

The door flew open. His head turned. Soldiers. An arrow zipped past his ear. He ran to the window. Too late, always too late. He jumped. A sword sliced the air behind him.

THE BRIG

The chains clanked together as Vayorn moved. He winced. A small ring of blood appeared around the edge of the chain on his right wrist. *They'd better not have done this to Agöri.* Even with his arms wrapped around himself, he was cold. *Wish I'd just stayed with Ilmari.* Above him, he could hear the tramp of booted feet and hear the first mate hollering orders. He shifted his position, trying to keep the irons from scratching him. The hold was dark, and beyond the bars obscuring his vision, he could see the shadowy shapes of barrels and rats. He shuddered. Rats. If there was one creature he hated more than any other creature, it was rats. His skin crawled. *Why'd I have to be so stupid? Couldn't just have been content. Just had to go back to the surface. No wonder that woman's offer seemed too good to be true. It was.* He gritted his teeth. *Is Agöri even alive? Wouldn't put it past Demetrius to kill him.* He tried to ignore the icy fear in his chest.

Thud. Clomp. Thud. Clomp.

Vayorn looked up. An old man with one peg leg stomped down the stairs. In one hand, he held a bowl of gray slush, and in his other, he held a ring of keys.

The door grated open on its hinges. The man passed the bowl to Vayorn, as wordless as if he were simply dumping slop to a hog. The bowl was cold. Chunks of hard potato and watery gray stuff sloshed over into Vayorn's lap. He shivered. *Hope Agöri's faring better than this. If he's still alive.* Vayorn tried to push away the gnawing anxiety at the back of his mind.

He lifted the spoon slowly to his lips and gagged. The mush tasted the way rotting garbage smells. He set the spoon back in the bowl.

"Not hungry." He held it out to the man. As the man's hands closed around it, Vayorn tipped it. Mush plopped onto the man's shirt.

"Ach! You…," the man began swearing roundly while scrubbing at his shirt. Vayorn looked away. Somehow it wasn't as funny as he'd thought it would be.

Something flew down the stairs and charged toward Vayorn.

Vayorn's eyes widened. Agöri. *He's alive!*

The man screamed as Agöri knocked him to the ground. *Snap.*

Vayorn chuckled. The peg leg lay on the ground, unhooked from the end of the man's leg. Agöri dived into Vayorn's lap.

Ignoring his wrists, Vayorn pulled Agöri into a bear hug. "You've got no idea how much you scared me tadpole!" Agöri nodded. "Scared me too. They was talking about making you dead."

Vayorn's smile upended. *Dead?* Suddenly, he realized just how weak he looked, hugging Agöri like some soft old lady. *Stupid.* He dumped Agöri on the ground. His heart began to race. In his mind, the copper dagger hovered over his throat again. No. *Demetrius can't win.*

"You don't look fine. Look scared," Agöri observed.

Vayorn stared straight ahead. *He can't kill me. I was so close to getting away from him.*

The old man got himself off the ground and clicked his leg back on. "Now, come out of there." He tried to grab Agöri. Agöri bit him. "Fine, have it your way. Worthless trash, ye deserve each other." He swung the door shut and locked it. His footsteps tramped away across the brig.

Sunlight flooded in as he opened the trapdoor. Then darkness descended, and the brig was empty, except for the rats and Vayorn and Agöri.

"Mice in here?" Agöri spoke. His grin spread from ear to ear. "Never been keyholed before. Would be scared, but you with me." He turned the bucket over and sat on it, resting his feet on Vayorn's lap. A rank smell wafted out from it to fill the cramped space. Vayorn's eyebrows rose to meet. *Of all things, of course, he would dump the chamber pot. It's not like he could just sit on the floor.*

"Really?" *With everything he does to annoy people, she's never put him in the brig?*

"Really. One time, Captain say she lock me in brig, but she no do it." Agöri started giggling uncontrollably. "I takes something she wants, I no give back if put in brig. Is long, flower, love paper."

"I see." *They were talking about killing me?* He tried to ignore the word echoing in his mind, but over and over he heard it, "death...," over and over till he thought he might go crazy. Vayorn pretended to be listening to Agöri's prattle, but his mind was on the copper dagger and the gallows in Tarshal Square.

"She deserve it. I give, and she not let me write papers to him again." He looked down at Vayorn's wrists. They were bleeding all over Vayorn's pants where he'd been resting them on his knees. "Does hurt?"

Vayorn shrugged... *Death. No. Can't die. Need to kill Demetrius. Can't die...*

Agöri clapped his hands together. "Hey! Listen to me! Asked a question!"

Vayorn jerked. "What?" His voice held traces of annoyance. *Why's he have to be so bludegem curious?*

"Does wrists hurt?"

"No. Not really," Vayorn lied. *Already been weak enough today.*

Agöri looked up at the ceiling. "Is like time I get arrested!" He fell off the bucket giggling and landed on Vayorn.

Vayorn shoved him off, and Agöri got enough control of himself to say in between giggles, "I...about to get punished by master...he say he gonna have me sold...I in dungeon...servant escapes me...I run! Old fisherman wife, she hide me in shed. I leave – next day!" He collapsed, laughing still.

Vayorn stared in stunned silence. *He thinks that's funny? That's gotta be the worst funny story I've ever heard.*

He sighed. Agöri was still talking. Now he was describing in vivid detail what biting Ayras on the hind end was like. He was using a dramatic tone and making it sound like the greatest battle ever fought.

His voice began to slow, and he began to yawn. "Bited Ayras… Wanted bite Ayras long time…" He yawned again and said in a sleepy voice, "Had big day. Didn't sleep night back." His eyelids were half closed.

Vayorn moved the bucket out of the way, and Agöri curled into a ball in the corner. His breathing slowed to a steady rhythm, and he snored quietly.

"Sleep." Vayorn looked away. *He trusts me too much. When's he gonna learn? Only person can take care of you is yourself. How doesn't he see this?* Even years later, Vayorn could set his finger on the day—no, the minute—he learned that trust only hurt you.

The ship rocked underneath him. His thoughts began to wander.

*****

"Me? Take care of you?" Janus is laughing. I don't get it. He always took care of me. What's different now? He looks mean—meaner than I've ever seen him. I back up. I don't like this. Not one bit. He's still laughing. It's making me mad. I want to bite him. I wiggle my new tooth with my tongue. He deserves to get bit. I don't like it when he's mean.

"You tell me, why do you think it's no one what's gonna want to take care of you?"

I shake my head. I'm confused now. Why's he acting like this?

"I'll tell you. Our beloved master is your uncle." He's saying *beloved* sarcastically. What's he mean? He's not talking about the skinny man, is he? But all the uncles I've seen are nice. Really nice. He's not an uncle, not an uncle to me. I don't even look like him. Janus is crazy. Why'd he say something like that anyway? I shake my head. He's been mean all week; that's why. He didn't even look at my dragon trap, and he's been yelling at me. I want to yell at him, but he's always too loud to hear me, even if I did yell.

Janus looks at me, and I'm scared all of a sudden. His eyes are all mad-like, like he wants to hit me or something.

"You don't believe me, do you? You little scar-cheek vermin! Can't you see! Because of you, because of your uncle, I've lost everything! And all you can do is just stand there and suck your thumb like some weak baby!" He's screaming real loud.

I run. I can't see all sudden-like. There's something wet on my face. Am I crying? I huff out. Snot comes out of my nose and drips down my face. I blow my nose on my shirt. I need to think. There's only one place that's good for it: my thinking bush.

The grown-ups say I'm ten years old now, and that's too old to hide under the rosebush and think, but I don't believe them. There's not a better place for organizing my mind than the bush.

I run to the corner of the courtyard by the gate and crawl under the bush. I'm big enough now; I get scratched, but I don't care. Why'd Janus say those things? He's never done that to me before. We're supposed to be friends. I cross my arms. Even when I'm mad, I don't say poky things to Janus. He's supposed to be nice to me. He's my friend. Or that's what I thought. I shake my head. Lose everything? How much could I take from Janus? Most days he didn't even have to share his food with me. I don't want to believe him, that the skinny man is my uncle. But I have to. Janus is a grown-up.

He knows about grown-up things. At least he could've explained more. He didn't have to just yell it at me and not explain anything. My mind feels like the vegetable garden before we plant it: all full of weedy weird things that I can't sort out. Usually it's so easy to organize my mind. Why's it so hard right now? Usually when I can't sort something out, Janus helps me, but it's him that's got my mind muddled. Plus, he's mad. He won't help me when he's mad. I don't think he even wants to be my friend anymore. Friends don't treat friends that way. He won't talk to me, except to yell. I cry harder. Why doesn't he want to be my friend?

Suddenly, I get an idea. Mama Yanya. She'll explain. I run back through the doors to find the kitchen…

Mama Yanya tries to give me a hug. I push her away. Why'd I think she could help? Now I'm even more muddled. She says that our master is my uncle too. So it must be true. She said that he killed my parents for the throne. Why would anyone kill someone else just for a big chair? She said that he hates me 'cause I'm the heir, whatever that is. She says I'm lucky to still be alive. I don't understand, and I don't want to understand. I always knew I didn't have a mommy or a daddy like the other kids, but I didn't know that master killed them. If he didn't kill them, I'd have parents. Parents couldn't ever hurt you; Janus wasn't actually my daddy, so it all makes sense now. I get a feeling all at once: I don't want to ever trust a grown-up again. I can't trust Janus. Guess I couldn't trust my parents to not die either. And I can't never trust Demetrius. I look at Mama Yanya. She's a grown-up. Can I trust her? If she made me even more confused? I'm not so sure now. She tries to hug me again. I push her away. No. I can't trust her. She's a grown-up. I run out of the kitchen.

MIASTO PORT

Laparlana's hands toyed with the curtain, her fingers showing through the pink mound of lace. She gently tugged and adjusted its edges, pulling first one side, then the other, then fanning the bow, her fingers lightly playing against its surface. Demetrius shook his head; no matter how hard she tried to seem tough and loud, nothing could take the sweet charm of a country girl out of her, the gentle ways of a housewife. He watched her move around the cabin, adjusting first one item, then another, trying to make her surroundings pretty. The rough items of metal and glass seemed a crude imitation of a real home to Demetrius, decorated with true treasures. He knew that to Laparlana, they were pretty, but he imagined how delighted she would be when she was mistress of the fine wealth of Tarshal. All the jewels and gold in the castle were to be hers, to rearrange and decorate with as much as she wanted. Demetrius saw past the façade of strength she pretended to have. She was tired. She wanted a home. She wanted power without the strain of making decisions.

"No, I won't kill him," Demetrius lied.

He watched her with admiring eyes. He'd known plenty of women, but never a woman like her. Her silhouette, black against the sunlight, promised something to Demetrius no other woman had ever promised: a future. Three months had already gone by, each month growing Demetrius's anticipation and anxiety. How would he protect the child? There was so much he could protect the child from, but could he protect him from the Green Death? Heartbreak? Raising him wouldn't be a problem; Demetrius's father had been an excellent man, and an exemplary father. But teaching him? Tutors were hard to come by, as no native Antiken—aside from members of the House of Historians—wanted anything to do with learning. He couldn't be expected to teach the child himself. When before in the history of Antike had a king ever played tutor? Never.

"Thank you." Laparlana smiled, her eyes beaming on Demetrius with favor for the first time since he'd captured the boy. Demetrius smiled. He would never admit it; he needed her approval. He needed her love.

He felt guilty for an instant. Maybe he shouldn't have lied to her. Then it passed. After all, selling the boy to dwarves wasn't directly a murder. Sure, no one survived for long if a dwarf owned them. It was said dwarves hauled their prisoners over the edge of the world into a place no human has ever seen, across a land of fire into Dwarvendale. But those were only myths. It was common knowledge that dwarves were notorious for beating their slaves to death. Nothing mysterious about that.

"LOAD OFF THE CARGO!"

Laparlana's face brightened. "Dear, is this a good time to ask for something?"

"What?" Demetrius chuckled. She was finally asking things from him again. He always found her requests amusing; the last thing she'd asked for was a pair of satin shoes with gold lacing.

"A pet Saynasaf. Such intelligent creatures, why, I've heard they even turn into fish if you want them to. Can you imagine how entertaining one would be? Oh, and female preferably."

What next, Demetrius thought. He nodded. There was no question about it; she'd get her wish, but Saynasafs were expensive. Why couldn't she have asked for a Varul puppy or a miniature horse?

The door flew open. A man ran in. Demetrius and Laparlana turned.

"The boy…he escaped!"

Demetrius's face turned red. "WHAT!"

*****

Splat. Arple jumped back, her nose wrinkling at a pile of stinking donkey dung, just touching her feet. Her teeth gritted against the bile trying to rise from her stomach into her throat. A million vomity smells accosted her nostrils, so long accustomed now to the clean sea air it had forgotten how foul-smelling human cities were.

A chill breeze danced around her cheeks. She sighed. If the air weren't so dirty, it might actually be refreshing. Why did humans never understand the value of good, clean air? The filth they tolerated was shocking sometimes. Even now, Arple could feel every piece of dirt, every blade of straw in the wind. And not just that, but the invisible things like illness and rot. Yet the crowd went about its business as if it were the finest day ever.

Bright flags waved in the breeze, fluttering from poles over carts and wagons, marking the only option for people traveling with more than a single bag and no cart of their own. Arple looked for the driver her family used last year. He had a green flag the last time she'd seen him. But not a single flag was even close to green. She strained her ears, trying to pick out his bawling voice from among the drivers' banter. They spoke in Common Tongue, a strange language that came from no country in particular and was made of words from all languages. Most children, Safl or not, rich or poor, knew enough Common Tongue to rent a cart or buy a loaf of bread in nearly any country in the lower continent.

"Take my cart!"

"No, mine!"

"His has splinters! Take mine!"

"Mine is cheapest!"

"Your horse is old! Mine is fastest!"

"Don't believe him! My cart is largest!"

"This one!"

"No, this one!"

Arple's brow furrowed. There was too much noise. And they all sounded alike. She listened again. No, his voice wasn't there. She would have heard him by now if he was. That meant she would have to approach a stranger. No, it didn't. The last thing she could do was talk to a stranger. What was she even supposed to say? Maria was so much better at this than she was.

A man walked up to her. Arple's eyes widened. What if he asked a question? She would have to answer.

"Understand Common Tongue? These your trunks? Looks like you need some help."

Arple's tongue froze to the roof of her mouth. Her mind raced for something to say. Anything. She gulped. If she spoke, she might say all the wrong things. If only mother were here. She always knew what to say. Or Maria. Oh, why couldn't she be brave like Maria? She looked down.

The man asked again.

Arple nodded quickly, her gaze firmly attached to the patch of ground between her feet. She was suddenly aware of how small she was, how insignificant. Her shoulders tensed and curled inward. As if to shield herself, she hugged her arms to her chest. She followed the man, puppylike, to a cart—his own cart, she realized, where an orange flag flapped overhead.

The man held out his hand. She fumbled with the strings of her bag, trying to shove her clumsy fingers into it and make her hands stop shaking long enough to pay the man. Finally, she placed a small pile of coins in his hand.

The toe of her shoe dug into the dirt as the man began lifting her things into the cart. She listened to the boxes and bags hitting the floor. Time seemed to crawl by unbearably slowly. The hole at her toe deepened. This was going to take a long time.

She turned and began to take quick, lurching steps along the side of the wagon.

Her hands curled around the edge of the seat as she settled in the front of the wagon, high above the people. It seemed to her as if every person who passed her was staring straight through her, judging her for being awkward. With slumped shoulders, knees hugged into her chest, she felt more unlike Maria than ever. Maria would be chatting with the driver right now, laughing and jesting as if she didn't have a care in the world, checking that everything was just so, making sure the man didn't steal anything.

Arple knew what Mother would say to her if she were here. "Are you alright?" And that would make her feel worse, because it was obvious she didn't look alright, or Mother wouldn't ask. The last thing she wanted was to worry her mother or anyone else. She didn't want to give anyone a reason to ask the dreaded question, "Is something wrong?" And that was inevitably the next question. "Is there something wrong?" And she would say no and act so exaggeratedly alright Mother would know for sure something was wrong. Then Mother would say, "Just be yourself," and Arple would try even harder and seem even less like herself.

Coarse jesting grated Arple's ears. Her head turned. A line of guards swaggered along the dock, swords drawn, helmets covering most of their faces. Arple drew into herself yet tighter. Mercenaries. The very word sent a chill down her spine. Everyone knew how evil they were, and worse yet, they were Antikish. If there was one thing Arple knew, it was that any man from Antike was two things: wicked and militant. Anyone who was unfortunate enough to fall in the company of a person from Antike was lucky to be alive at the end of the trip. Arple had never spoken to anyone from Antike, and she was glad.

One of them made a joke and pointed at her. Arple flinched. How they butchered the sounds of Common Tongue. Of course, no matter what language they spoke, it was impossible for it to sound even remotely refined coming off Antikish tongues.

A mob of children converged over a merchant. The purse he held in his hands fell to the ground. He picked it up and tied it to his belt, screaming at the children. Howling like a pack of little wolves, they dumped his cart and began shoving items in their pockets. Two little boys rolled across the road locked together kicking and biting, the mirror they were fighting over long before now smashed to bits underneath their feet. A group of little girls threw themselves at the man and dragged him to the ground.

"Get the purse!" one of them shouted.

He was immediately buried below a dogpile of children, his shrieks drowned out by theirs. Arple winced; he had to be in pain.

His purse flew in the air. The children stampeded after it, pushing, shoving, biting. One child had it, then he was on the ground crying and someone else had it, then the child with the purse screamed as the other children buried him beneath their weight. Arple looked away. How could children so small be so cruel to each other? One of the children cried out in pain. Then the purse flew in the air again, and the children followed. Except for the child at the bottom of the pile. He lay curled in a ball as the people walked over him, too busy to help him. Arple covered her eyes. Had the port always been like this and she hadn't noticed? It must have been so.

Finally, a small girl (she couldn't have been more than three) sped into the crowd, the purse held tight in her little fists. The others ran after her.

Arple held her bag tighter. Where were their parents? Did they even have parents? And such small children too. She shook her head. It was dire straits indeed that would compel children so young to do that.

Arple closed her eyes. Her chest felt empty and heavy. Father had always spoken of the good in the world. She sighed. What good? It was all lies. She sighed, almost ready to ask—no, beg—the driver to hurry up. If only she were more like Maria.

The driver was almost done loading her trunks. He was tying them off with a rope. She rested her chin on her knees, trying to get her queasy stomach to calm down. Where was Maria when she needed her? At Pyhaako Sanctuary, happy, safe. Arple blew out her cheeks. Mother should have come. Didn't they see? She was too young to do this on her own.

"Alright, done. Where to?" The man jumped into the driver's seat beside her.

"Twenty miles north," Arple mumbled. The man nodded.

"Hyah!" The wagon lurched and began a slow crawl through the crowd.

Arple slowly relaxed. When the people were farther away from her, they were quite interesting. A group of dwarves caught her eye and her ear too. They were screaming curses at a cart-driver over his prices. Arple chuckled; the scene was familiar. The man tried to cheat them; that much she could guess. Dwarves were dangerous to cheat. One of Arple's uncles almost died when he tried to make a profit off them. Uncle Ilmari. He was a wine seller, renowned for his coral wines and cordials. Coral wine was far sweeter and stronger than plain wine and so expensive on its own it was hard to tell when one was being cheated, if the swindler did it right. Uncle Ilmari did it wrong.

Arple would never admit it out loud, but the vile creatures interested her. All her childhood, she'd heard myths about them. She wanted to believe that all the stories were true, that they actually did come from a land so far south you fell off the edge of the world unless you were careful. That they were guarded by the fire-lands, inhabited with dragons. That they lived in a magnificent world called Dwarven-dale.

All the young Saynasafs she knew called the stories "children's tales," but Arple didn't care. She had memorized nearly every story her people told, whether about the icedrakes above the world, giants to the east, dwarves and dragons to the south, or her own fabled ancestral home.

Her people were supposed to come from a place called Saflhome, where both Saynasafs and Fiynesafs lived in peace with each other and the animals. The eyes of the old ones grew misty when that land was named. Arple's own grandfather claimed to have come from there, but Arple was the only one who truly believed him. Although she didn't think she would ever see Safl-home with her own two eyes, her fondest dream was of her child or child's child returning home, somewhere past the western edge of the world.

A sound caught her attention.

"Run! Agöri, run!"

A small child sped past the wagon and slid through the crowd like an eel, quickly disappearing in the people.

A young man shoved past her cart, his broad shoulders pushing through the crowd as if they were no more than stalks of wheat. Arple's eyes widened; how was it possible for a man to be so handsome? The fire in his eyes, so brown they were almost black, drew Arple like a magnet. His hair, so long it was almost to his chin and as unkept and tangled as a wild horse's mane, whipped in his face as he ran. Unconsciously, Arple let out a longing sigh. Her heart fluttered like a caged bird in her chest. Those eyes. She could stare into those eyes forever and never tire of them. A scar ran along his right cheek, making him seem almost dangerous. The thought of a tall blond hero fled her mind. Who wanted that anyway? She far preferred dark eyes and hair. Who wanted a prince when one could have a warrior?

A cart flew by. Perched atop a pile of cushions in the back, a man in colorful robes and pompous jewelry reclined. A woman shrieked as the cart ran over her; the driver never even tried to avoid her. The man in the cart screamed at the driver to go faster.

It was speeding toward the young man. He needed to move. He wasn't moving. It was going to hit him. Arple cried out slightly as it came upon him. Didn't the driver watch where he was going? She stared, horrified, as the cart passed over the boy.

Her horror turned to fascination as the boy came up unscathed from between the wheels, grabbed onto the back of the cart, and stood on the loading board, perched precariously between being crushed and keeping his footing.

Such daring. Was he engaged? Arple's smile faded. Surely, he wasn't. He just had to be single. So that she could fall in love with him. So that he could fall in love with her.

Then reality struck her.

The chances of ever meeting him again were small. It was nigh on impossible. Why torture herself with a foolish hope like that? After all, she did prefer blond hair, or so she tried to convince herself.

But still, that face…those eyes…

She tried to make herself stop thinking about him. She couldn't.

THE ROAD

Vayorn's heart raced. He dodged through the crowd.
His feet drummed a tempo on the ground, singing "Runrunrun-run." His ankles burned. He gritted his teeth. His breath rang in his ears, matching the frantic rhythm of his feet.

He ran through a flock of geese. Something hit him. he fell rump-first. A sharp beak goosed him in the back of the neck and hissed. He crawled away and staggered to his feet.

Run. Faster. Can't get caught. Vayorn squeezed between carts and slid around people. How long would it be till the soldiers came after him? His ankles throbbed. He pushed himself harder.

Vayorn could see Agöri ahead of him for a split second. A wheelbarrow caught Vayorn in the shins. He went flying. Peeling himself from the road, he looked back. An old woman was trying to right gather her things and tip the wheelbarrow back to standing. She pleaded for someone to help her.

Vayorn ran.

The crowd pressed tight around him. Vayorn put his arms out and shoved people aside. His lungs burned.

The sound of wheels behind him. He turned. A pair of wild manes and frothing muzzles bore down on top of him. He closed his eyes. They opened; he was on the ground between the wheels of the cart, somehow unhurt. A sudden idea hit him; he readied his hands.

The cart was almost done passing over him. The front wheels... The back wheels...

Vayorn threw his hands up. They latched onto the back of the cart. Its momentum swung his legs up onto the loading board.

The crowd parted in front of it. Vayorn kept his head down. *Last thing I need's that noble to see me.*

The cart hit a rock. He swayed. His grip tightened. *Should have passed Agöri by now. Where is he?* Vayorn ran his gaze across the bobbing heads around him again.

It landed on the edge of the forest, bordering the road from a short distance. A familiar, curly head poked through the branches of a tree. Vayorn's eyes widened. What if soldiers caught Agöri? They'd send him to Demetrius. There was no escaping a second time. Vayorn had to get him back in the crowd, where they could hide.

"Hey, you! Get your sorry hind end off my cart!" A large head with bulbous cheeks and a reek of old cheese stuck into Vayorn's face.

Vayorn screamed and jumped.

He landed on someone. Vayorn shook himself as his vision cleared. Whoever was under him didn't try to move. Vayorn leaped up. He elbowed to the edge of the road and ran.

His feet skidded on the hard ground. Frost slid under his feet as the trees neared. *Once I catch him, not letting him out of my sight. Have to stay together now.*

He stopped below Agöri.

"Get...down...here...now." He gasped.

Agöri laughed.

"Was fun. Do again?" Agöri hooked his legs around the branch and hung upside down. Vayorn glared at him. Agöri began swinging.

"Get down." Vayorn crossed his arms.

Agöri began whistling a tune, blatantly ignoring Vayorn. Vayorn closed his eyes and tried to curb his frustration. *Yell and I'm not gonna get anywhere with him.* He tried again, asking in a nicer tone. Agöri began humming. Vayorn groaned.

"Come down or else!"

Agöri dropped from the tree, landed in front of Vayorn, and ran toward the trees. "Catch me!" he called over his shoulder.

Vayorn tackled Agöri and grabbed him around the arm.

"*No*," Vayorn secured a grip on Agöri's collar, "stay with me." Vayorn dragged Agöri back into the crowd.

They began walking. Vayorn noticed with satisfaction that they seemed no different from any of the people around them. *Maybe the soldiers won't even notice us.* A wild goose flew overhead.

"We go west like goose."

"Yeah." *What if they find us?* Vayorn looked at his raw wrists. *Would they give me away?* It was hard to hide the fact that he'd been in chains. And soldiers weren't dumb. "Always wanted see mountains. Dragon in mountains."

"Yeah." *We're far enough into the crowd now, right?*

"Look. Lady." Agöri pointed and waggled his eyebrows. Vayorn looked where Agöri was pointing. Not long before, the "lady" Agöri was talking about would never have elicited a second look from Vayorn, but after meeting Ilmari, there was something interesting about Saynasafs to Vayorn. And the one Agöri was pointing at was enchanting, Vayorn had to admit that much. But "lady" didn't quite describe her. She was hardly more than a child.

"What about the lady?" The terseness in his own voice surprised Vayorn.

"Lady for Vayorn. Yes?"

"No. I don't even know her."

"I introduce." Agöri tried to run to the girl.

Vayorn pulled Agöri back. *Women make men weak.* He caught himself looking at her again. *Stupid. You don't need her.* He jerked his head away from her, determined to not look at her. But she was different. The turquoise scales around her slim face and her ankle-length hair were striking, but more than anything, Vayorn noticed the way she curled into herself, the fear in her gaze as it darted over the crowd. She rode in a cart, so rigid she bounced with every stone it hit. *For all I know, she's a thief.* The more Vayorn entertained the idea of her running from something, the more plausible it seemed. After all, only a thief had a reason to be afraid. And even then, it was stupid to be so obviously troubled. *She's weak.* Vayorn looked away, trying to feel disgust.

"Kock it off." Vayorn grabbed Agöri again.

At the end of what felt like an hour, Vayorn found himself looking for a roof or a town. Preferably an inn. Even during planting season, his feet hadn't hurt this much. But there was nothing. Agöri was bored; after about the tenth complaint, Vayorn stopped listening. His ears strained for the tramp of soldier's boots. Nothing but the clanking of pots and screech of cart wheels. But he didn't allow himself to relax.

This couldn't last. It had taken almost dying more times than Vayorn wanted to think about to get here. Freedom was expensive. And he wasn't safe, not yet. He couldn't let his guard down.

"Feet tired." Agöri slid the ground and sat with his arms crossed. His bottom lip stuck out, and his brow furrowed. His shoulders slumped. Vayorn sighed. *Have to keep moving. Can't pause like this.* He shook his head.

"Want me to carry you?" Vayorn asked. Agöri's face brightened.

"Shoulder ride!" Agöri sprang to his feet. His eyes brightened.

Thought you were "tired." Vayorn shook his head, bent down, and swept Agöri up onto his shoulders. He gripped Agöri's ankles and adjusted Agöri's position till he felt balanced. *How is he so heavy?* He began walking forward with Agöri's merry, distracted chatter over his head.

"Did you know merchant has baby?" Agöri bent his head down to talk into Vayorn's ear.

Vayorn nodded.

"Goldfish!"

"Ouch! Don't yell in my ear." Vayorn let his breath out slowly. *How can one little kid make so much noise?*

"I buy one? Please?" Agöri tipped off to the right to gaze into the bowl of fish. Vayorn's top half swung out of balance. He swayed, bounced on one foot, spun a little, jerked Agöri's left leg, and slammed both feet back onto the ground. He exhaled slowly, trying to keep his patience. *How much longer can this Bludegem day last?*

"*No.*" Vayorn braced his legs and waved the merchant off.

Agöri sighed and began muttering. Every now and then he would fold his arms and slump over Vayorn's head, the seeming spirit of dejection. "No goldfish," he repeated while shaking his head sadly, suspiciously close to Vayorn's ear.

Vayorn's mouth formed a firm line. He walked rigidly, trying to keep himself from yelling at Agöri. "LOOK! LADY AGAIN! HI, LADY!"

Vayorn held in a groan. *My ears.*

The girl giggled and waved. Agöri waved back, and Vayorn almost dropped him.

"If you don't want dropped, hold on," he said through gritted teeth. He jogged along the side of the road, where there were less people, trying not to spill Agöri off. He moved a safe distance from the lady and goldfish man then slowed down.

"Again!" Agöri bounced up and down. "Was fun! Faster this time?"

"STOP BOUNCING!" Vayorn shouted. "No."

"Pleeeeease?" Agöri whined.

Vayorn growled. *He'd better be glad I'm not meaner than I am.* He stopped walking.

"Walk." He dumped Agöri on the ground and started walking. A few steps later, he looked back.

Agöri was on the ground pouting again.

"Agöri, please." Vayorn thought for a minute. An idea struck him. "I'll buy you something at the end of today, before supper, if you walk. Deal?" Agöri's face brightened immediately.

"Deal!" He flew up and ran to Vayorn.

They began walking again. Agöri was still talking. *Does he know how to shut up and keep his thoughts to his little self? Can't possibly have this many things to say.*

"Had a pet goose once…" The air began to chill. Vayorn ignored Agöri. By his reckoning, only an hour or so had passed. Vayorn's feet ached, but he didn't stop. *Still not safe. Need more time behind us…*

"Ate a mouse once. Puked…" *Where do we hide if soldiers come?* He looked back. The port was hours away on foot, but horses traveled so fast. *What if the soldiers caught up?* Vayorn's feet had long grown numb to pain. He'd lost track of how long they'd been walking for.

"Climbed tallest tree in the world…" All around Vayorn, people were walking slowly, shoulders bent under their bags, silent. The sun was more than halfway through the sky. Even the travelers in carts looked tired. Time seemed to drag by at the pace of a snail.

"Met a queen…" *Need to rest.* The sun was sinking below the mountains now. Several families were making camp off the road. Vayorn kept walking. *Have to put as much distance behind me as I possibly can.*

"Bit a camel—"

Vayorn interrupted him, "Want to play a game?"

"What game?"

"See how long you can be quiet for." Vayorn tried to keep his voice from sounding annoyed, but it was still anything but kind.

"You grouchy. Very, veeeery grumpy."

You don't know the half of it.

Agöri kept talking.

Vayorn rubbed his temples. This was going to be a long night.

THE VANHEN

Arple dropped her bag. "Uncle Ilmari!"

She threw herself at her uncle. He lifted her off the ground and swung her through the air.

"I could not bear to let my favorite niece go without her coming of age."

"You are going to stand in for Father! Thank you! Is Auntie here?"

Uncle Ilmari nodded and set her down.

A sweet voice spoke behind her, "My child, come here." Arple turned. Aunt Lahja opened her arms. Arple ran into her arms and buried her head in Lahja's shoulder. She felt her aunt's hands gently stroking her hair. "Oh, little one, did you think I would miss your coming of age? After all, someone needs to stand in for your mother. Poor child. You've been through so much this year. What an awful way to spend the last year of your childhood. Oh, little one…"

A firm hand rubbed Arple's shoulders. Arple realized she was crying.

*****

The firelight flickered off the painted walls of the carts. Arple leaned her back against a wheel. She could hardly believe three days had already passed. How was tonight the night already?

Arple licked her lips nervously. Now that it was time, she wasn't so sure she could go through with this. Could she really leave her childhood forever?

She looked around. At least ten youths her own age were sitting around the circle. She'd seen one of them earlier, so nervous he was puking. At least she hadn't puked—yet. Her stomach burbled. She'd already made at least twenty trips to the outhouse that evening. Now that it was truly time, she didn't want to grow up. Mother wasn't there to watch. Father wasn't there to cheer her on, to say the right words to calm her. Worse, she would become an adult, and they would never be able to share that moment with her.

Uncle Ilmari waved to her. Arple spread a thin grimace across her face that she hoped looked like a smile.

She could just imagine herself tripping, right as Uncle Ilmari said Father's line, or worse, as Auntie Lahja said Mother's line. She couldn't take care of herself. Everyone would see the truth; she wasn't ready. Why did everyone think she was? She didn't know how to be an adult, to go into the world alone. Maybe she shouldn't go up for the ceremony. She didn't have to. She could always wait another year.

She sighed. If only she were more like Maria. Maria was ready for the ceremony years before she was sixteen. She already knew what she wanted from life, was already working to get it. Arple rubbed her temples. Her stomach growled. She pressed an arm against it.

Oh no. They were emptying the ring. Arple's hands began shaking. She began sweating. A sick feeling filled her stomach. Her throat ached. Suddenly the corners of her eyes were wet. Visions of her childhood filled her mind—playing with her siblings. Running through the field outside her house. Being so young she didn't know what "slavery" meant. Not understanding what "death" was. Freedom to do whatever she wanted, no responsibilities. Never having to make tough decisions, always having Mother with her to tell her what to say or do. She couldn't walk away from all that. She couldn't change that much. How would she know what to do without Mother there to guide her? What if she made all the wrong decisions?

The old ones rose. Their papery scales were dull in the firelight, their shine rubbed off by years of toil and hardship. It was difficult to tell scale from hair or skin; all were the same washed-out milk color. But their eyes were still beautiful. Arple looked into them and saw wisdom.

She looked into herself and saw fear.

"The Vanhen has begun!" the old one spoke in the Ancient tongue, the beauty of the words falling like rain over Arple's ears.

A hush fell over the crowd. Arple toyed with the hem of her dress. Her heart pounded. She heard his words as if in a daze. She wasn't ready. She wasn't ready. She let her breath out in small jerks.

"Each year we celebrate Vanhen to commemorate the coming of age of our newest adults! They are young, but the work of their parents has made them ready to take on this challenge, to cut the ties of their dependence upon their elders and forge their own way in this world! They are ready, and they are unafraid!"

Arple groaned. The woman beside her rubbed her arm sympathetically. Arple heard her whisper, "You'll do fine."

Arple nodded quickly. If only she actually believed that.

"Rise!"

Arple staggered to her feet. The parents and stand-ins stood. A small group of children raced one another to the center. Arple remembered when she was their age; the Vanhen never seemed so daunting when she was little. The part of the children had always been fun. Now, Arple was sure she would give anything to stay their age forever, to never have to participate in the coming-of-age part of the Vanhen.

Even that morning, it hadn't seemed so serious or so final as it did now. After she was an adult, she could never go back. The words echoed in her mind: never go back. Arple wrapped her arms around herself. She had rehearsed the ceremony that morning, but now the full seriousness of it struck her. She couldn't do this. Somehow, she found her feet moving to join the crowd. Uncle Ilmari came to stand by her. No turning back. It was time.

"These youths stand between two things: childhood and adulthood. The small children who have so generously volunteered represent the childhoods of these young men and women. But they cannot become healthy adults without letting go of their childhood and stepping into adulthood, into the world of their parents. You see here young men with young boys and their fathers. Young women with young girls and their mothers. Each one will let go of the child when they are ready, but it must be done. They cannot continue to hold on to acting and thinking like a child. They are adults now."

Arple placed her hand in Auntie Lahjah's. A little girl grabbed her other hand. Half the parents and all the children formed a circle. The extra parents made a circle around their circle.

Slowly, solemnly, they began to move around, a giant wheel within a wheel. Arple gulped back the ache in her throat. They began to move faster. Faster. Arple squeezed her eyes shut. How had Maria's smile been so big at this part? She wished she were more like Maria.

A flute shrilled a single high note.

The inside circle split into small circles. Arple, Lahja, and the little girl spun. In the corners of her eyes, Arple watched other groups spin. The boy she'd seen puking looked as close to crying as she was. Somehow, the thought was comforting. She wasn't the only one this was hard for. Aunt Lahja let go of the little girl's hand. Arple forced herself to breathe slowly. Arple looked down at the little girl, blurry through her tears.

The drum struck a solitary beat. Arple let go of the little girl.

The child flew backward, laughing as if it was all a game. Arple felt Aunt Lahja squeeze her hand. Arple looked into her eyes. Lahja nodded encouragingly.

Arple let go of Lahja's hand and spun to the middle of the circle. All the young adults grabbed hands. They whirled in a dizzy circle. Some of the faces shone with joy; others were as teary-eyed as Arple's. The parents and stand-ins circled around the circle of the young men and women. Arple watched her aunt and uncle whiz by, their faces as proud as if Arple were their own child.

The music came to an abrupt stop. The dancers stopped. Arple let go of the hands beside her. The new adults fell to sitting crosslegged in a circle. Arple craned her neck to watch the adults sit in a line in front of them. Uncle Ilmari rose. Her stomach fell to her feet. It was her turn first.

Aunt Lahja followed Ilmari. Arple looked away, feeling sick. She would have to go up in front of all those people.

"Have the parents of the child anything to say?" the old one asked. It wasn't actually a question, just a tradition. All the parents had prepared a short speech to give about their child. Arple wished her mother and father could give her speeches. It was good of her uncle and aunt to stand in, but there was no replacement for her real parents.

Uncle Ilmari spoke, "We have." He turned and addressed the assembled crowd. Arple avoided making eye contact with the people around her, but she felt their eyes burning holes in her back. She was glad she didn't have to sit facing them; she didn't know how Uncle Ilmari did it, speaking in front of so many people. And his voice didn't shake.

"I address this speech to you, the assembled Saynasafs of the Lower Continent. It is not usual to address the Vanhenia, but I also address you, my sweet, gentle niece." Arple's head shot up.

"I want all assembled to know three things about my little Arple, who is not so little anymore. Firstly, she is kind. It has never been in her nature to turn her back to the poor, the needy. She will give of herself time and again, just to ease suffering or bring joy. She aches when others ache, laughs when others laugh. She has more kindness in her heart than any other maiden I know.

"Secondly, she is stronger than she believes herself to be. She is brave. When lives are at stake, she spares no expense, fears no danger, to save others, to love others. She is kind to people others are afraid to go near, such as the poor and the ill. She is a woman of action, and I am so proud to stand in for her father and speak these words, to you, and to her.

"Thirdly, she has a strong sense of justice and fairness. Her heart is noble, and her world is black-and-white. She sees things as either right or wrong, but never neither. She rescues the wronged and seeks to vindicate those who have not been fully heard."

He turned his back to the people and bent down to speak to Arple. His stare held Arple's gaze firmly. She forgot that she was being watched by people.

"To you, my niece: remember your strengths. Your kind heart is not a weakness. You are not weak. You are not helpless. You are strong. Hold to your values. Never compromise. Do what is right, stand by what is right. More important than any of these: you are loved. Your entire family loves you and would die a million deaths for you. Hold on to that, even when you don't have anything else to hold on to. I release you into adulthood without any fear for you. I trust you, and I know what I hope you know: you are strong."

Arple looked down, realizing she'd been holding her breath. She tried to believe Uncle's words. He really saw all that in her? A smile played on her lips. Maybe, just maybe, she could make it. Maybe they were right; maybe she was ready.

Aunt Lahja took Ilmari's place. "Darling child," she gave Arple a hug, "your mother should be telling you this, but she is not here, so I hope I am an adequate substitute. This is entirely addressed to you. I remember the day you were born. Your mother was staying with me and your uncle. Your father had gone hunting in the corals. It was sunset, and your mother wasn't hungry. I thought it strange and ordered her to bed. We summoned a healer, and late that night, your mother brought the most beautiful child into the world. She called you Arple, which means *sun*. And that was exactly what we all thought, the second you made your first sound. Most babies' first sound is crying, but your first sound was laughter. It was as if you were as happy to see us as we were to see you. Since then, you have brought light into all our lives. Your sweetness, your gentle heart, your loving nature has all been like sunlight to us. Precious, as your aunt, I do not want to relinquish you to the world. And I know your mother feels this way too. We wish you could remain a child forever. But that would be cheating you of the wonderful, rich life you have ahead. It would not be fair to keep you in childhood, for that would be selfish. You are a light, and we know we must share you with the world. If we keep you a child, you cannot bring joy to anyone else.

"You cannot find the splendid man you were born to marry if you never grow up. You can never hold your children someday and sing to them, tell them stories if you never grow up. You can never have adventures and discover who you are meant to be if you never grow up. So we, your family, let you go. I know that we cannot even begin to comprehend the joy you will bring to others as you live your adult life, but I know this: as an adult, you will bless many more people than you could ever have blessed as a child. Live well, live without fear. Live, and, darling, never be afraid to love. Love will hurt at times, but it hurts far more to never have loved in the first place than to love and lose. So never be afraid. I love you, and because I love you, I give you your freedom."

Arple smiled. Salt water and snot ran down her face. Her shoulders shook. She wiped her eyes. Someone handed her a cloth. She blew her nose and dried her face. Suddenly, she felt completely ready. It made sense. She couldn't stay a little girl. And she didn't want to anymore.

"Arple Miska, rise."

She got to her feet. Surprisingly, her legs were no longer shaky. The old one handed a scarf to Uncle Ilmari. He passed it to Arple. She tied the middle to her wrist. Her uncle tied one end to his wrist, and Lahja tied the other end to her own wrist.

"The scarf shows the ties of child to its parents, unable to feed itself, provide clothing for itself, or protect itself. Its parents must do everything for it, as is right. It would be evil for parents to delegate these tasks to any other person, for no person is as suited as the parents to care for their child and educate their child. But this dependence cannot continue into adulthood. As an adult, the man or woman must provide for themselves and make their own choices. Till the rope of dependence is severed, the young one cannot live a healthy adulthood. They cannot live as an adult if they still rely on their parents like a child. The child will always fall back on them, afraid to make her own decisions, afraid to trust herself, afraid to reap her own consequences, afraid to no longer rely on her elders for all her needs to be met, if the rope of dependence remains unsevered." The elder passed a silver pair of shears to Uncle Ilmari.

"With the severance of the scarf, her parents and guardians release her to the world and to her own independence. From the time of severing the scarf onward, she is free to make her own decisions and to have her own opinions. She is an adult. She is sovereign in her right to rule herself and reap the consequences if she rules amiss. The parents hereby let go of her and show their trust in her by cutting their right to command her as one commands a small child. They may advise, as an older adult to a younger, but they may not make her decisions for her. She is an adult now."

Arple locked eyes with Uncle Ilmari. The sounds around them faded. Uncle Ilmari blinked hard. A tear trickled down his cheek. He nodded. Arple nodded.

"I proclaim this woman to be strong and prepared to face the challenges of the world. I give Arple Miska independence as a full adult." His voice shook he as cut his end of the scarf.

Arple looked at Aunt Lahja. Lahja smiled, her eyes shining with tears.

"This woman is mature and wise in her decisions. I grant Arple Miska full independence as an adult." Lahja cut her end of the scarf.

Arple looked down at her wrist. Suddenly, she was excited. She was a woman. She was free.

The old one lifted her wrist into the air. Loud cheering and applause rang out. Arple heaved a heavy breath. It was over. Uncle Ilmari and Aunt Lahja pulled her into a hug.

"I never thought I would see the day when little Arple became a woman. I'm so proud of you." Lahja kissed the top of Arple's head. Uncle Ilmari nodded.

"Thank you, Arple, for not allowing fear to stop you from doing this."

At the front of the ring, the next set of parents were speaking.

Arple followed her aunt and uncle to the edge of the ring. She sat, her eyes shining with excitement. She knew now why Maria had been so happy at her Vanhen. She was her own. She owned herself. She was in charge. As she looked around the circle, she felt no fear. Her back straightened. She looked the old one in the eye. There was no fear.

THE SAYNASAF GIRL

When midnight lingered black over the land, Vayorn finally stopped. In the cavern-like valley, howls rose to the air from somewhere beyond a curve in the hills. Vayorn had stolen a knife earlier that evening, but for some reason, the thought wasn't very comforting. It was one thing in broad daylight to have a knife, but at night, if you couldn't see, what use was it?

Vayorn found a sheltered spot under the sweeping branches of a pine, and Agöri fell asleep within two breaths. But not Vayorn. His heart hammered in his temples. His palms sweated. Whenever he was just about to drift off, fear would overtake him, and he would sit up and lay his hand on his knife. At some point, after what felt like hours, his frayed nerves gave out, and he fell into restless dreaming.

*****

I look up at the mouth of a cave. It's so big it's almost the only thing I can see. A candle's in my hand. A sword's in my other hand. There are gems all over its hilt. Strange square shapes are carved into its blade. The metal looks blue in the light. The shapes are a strange gold color, like the light on Demetrius's wineglass. It's pretty. A blast of hot air hits me all of a sudden. I turn back to the cave. The rotten air coming out of it stings my throat and chokes me. Strange greenish light glows from somewhere inside it. I shudder. It's getting dark around me, quick. I look down. The candle's gone. This thing with antlers and a woman's face bounds up to me. Her voice rises and falls. Can't hear most of what she says in the wind.

"You will…destroy…or be destroyed by…"

"What?" A wind hits me, and I fall. The thing shrieks as it disappears. Reminds me of the moon being swallowed by clouds, or a piece of bread being swallowed by Demetrius. I realize the blackness is smoke.

"Eight days…eight days…eight days…," echoes around me. Can't figure out where it's coming from. Seems like it's coming from everywhere.

"Eight days for what?" A wagon flies at me out of the mist. I scream and duck. It runs over me. I stand again, surprised I'm not hurt. A turquoise blur brushes by me. The wind hits it, and it's gone.

"Vayorn!" I hear it yell my name as it flies into the air.

"Your father," a voice whispers. The sound comes from the cave. Suddenly a woman rises in front of me. Her cheekbones are sharp like Demetrius's. I back away. The wind hits her, and she melts like a candle. A hot breeze hits my face.

"All is not as it seems. Watch…watch…watch…"

"Watch what?"

Something roars. The cave comes alive. I hide on the ground, hoping it won't see me. The dirt around it falls off it. Some of it gets in my eyes, and I can't see. When my eyes clear, I'm face-to-face with this giant black wolf. I scream and run. As it chases me, its roar becomes Demetrius's voice.

"I have a plan…a plan…a plan…a plan…" It's behind me. I can feel its hot breath burning my ankles. I look down. My feet won't move. I try to run, but I can't. It digs its claw into my side. The pain is worse than anything I could've ever imagined. I scream and fall down, groaning, pressing my hands to my side. Suddenly I can't see. There's a red fog in my eyes. Then the only thing I can see is black.

*****

Vayorn sat up. Yellow light seared his vision. The silence buzzed in his ears. Not a bird sang; not a crow cawed. There wasn't even wind. No sounds of voices, no laughter, just empty silence. Vayorn fought down the panic rising in his mind. Where was Agöri?

There was nothing but a circle of smashed-down pine needles where Agöri had slept. Vayorn turned his gaze into the trees around him.

He tried to convince himself that the woods was just like any other woods. But it wasn't. It was hiding something, deep in its shadowy heart. What, Vayorn didn't know. But nothing good; that much was certain. Under the trees it was dark, as if even the sunlight were afraid to enter. It felt almost alive, almost as if it was daring Vayorn to enter and waiting to swallow him.

"Agöri!" He cupped his hands around his mouth and yelled. Silence.

"Gach." He ran his fingers through his hair. *If I were Agöri, where would I go?* Somewhere stupid.

A stick broke above him. He jumped. Another. Another. The hair on the back of his neck rose. The thing got closer. He could hear its breathing. Now he could see it. A black shape, crawling head downward toward him, spiderlike. It hissed. His heart raced.

A head swung down into his face. Its teeth snapped together and nicked his nose. He screamed. It screamed then laughed.

"Scared you!" Agöri pointed at Vayorn and began laughing.

He fell out of the tree and rolled on the ground.

"Scared…you…so FUNNY!" He kicked his legs in the air.

Vayorn gritted his teeth. "You little…" He bit his tongue and grabbed Agöri by the collar. "Let's go."

*****

They traveled slowly now, and four long days passed even slower than their shuffling feet. Each night was like the first night, but worse with each setting of the sun.

On their fourth night of travel, the sun began to set again.

A captivating melody danced across the air. Its deep strains, almost as if echoing from some distant land, rang through the trees. The mellow lilting of flutes blended with the rhythmic beating of drums and the discordant jangle of tambourines. The powerful poetry of notes and harmonies was almost hypnotic. Even Vayorn found himself tapping a foot along with the rhythm. The darkness under the trees melted, or so it seemed to Vayorn's eyes. He held up a hand. Agöri stopped talking. A breeze carried a faint savory scent into Vayorn's nostrils. His mouth watered. His right foot stepped forward.

"Hungry." Agöri pulled on Vayorn's hand.

"Yeah." Something told him it was a bad idea to leave the road. *Soldiers? Don't be stupid. Since when can soldiers make anything beautiful, much less music like that?* He paused, undecided. *Can't let my guard down.* Vayorn looked at his crusted-over wrists. His fingers curled into fists. He looked away. That's what happens when I let my guard down. He turned his back on the scent and tried to take a step, away from the sounds.

The music welled up to a crescendo and filled his ears. Slowly, he turned back toward it again. The wind blew harder, hitting him in the face with the tantalizing smell. His stomach growled.

Can't risk it. His left foot stepped forward. *Even if I don't eat, Agöri needs food.* Vayorn took another step toward the music. *But I can't pay them.*

"That smells so good." He shook his head, realizing he'd spoken his thoughts out loud. He turned his head and looked behind himself. *What if it's a trap?* He turned back toward the music, his mind made up. "Come on." He gestured for Agöri to follow him. Agöri trotted along beside him.

"Carry again? Feet tired." Agöri grabbed Vayorn's arm.

Vayorn nodded. He bent down and swung Agöri onto his back. Vayorn's arms weakened. He set Agöri down.

He began walking. The night deepened around him, but he didn't notice. The music was getting louder. If he'd been listening, he would have heard howling behind him, but all he heard was the music. Sticks broke behind him, and red eyes shone from the gathering mist, but Vayorn's eyes were glued in front of him, on a small orange spark growing steadily brighter as he neared it. He heard voices laughing and singing strange words to the melody, words in a language Vayorn recognized—the language Ilmari's wife sang in. A shiver went up Vayorn's spine.

Suddenly he broke into a clearing. The music stopped. Ilmari rose from beside the fire.

"Vayorn?" Ilmari's eyes were wide.

"Agori!" Lahja flew past Vayorn and lifted Agöri off the ground.

Vayorn's head snapped back and forth, from one edge of the creatures to the other. *What the gach?* Every stare that met his was framed in scales, with frills emerging from the seaweed-like hair frizzing in the breeze. *On land?* His jaw hung slack. He tried to say something and realized his mouth was open. Weak. He slammed it shut. Below their expressionless faces, weapons hung at their hips. Vayorn's hand strayed to his knife.

The smell drifted into his nostrils. From the center of a half circle of wagons, a large pot sat bubbling over a roaring fire. Now even Agöri and Lahja were wordless. As if the whole world were turned to stone, not a sound, not even the shuffling of feet, came from the clearing. He looked back at Ilmari. *Someone say something.* Silence. The conspicuous whoosh of the wind in the pine trees bounced off the tomb-like atmosphere. A creature stood. Vayorn recoiled and tried not to grimace. *Looks like a dead fish.* He gulped. *That's not its skin, right?* Shriveled white stuff covered the creature's face, peeling like the bark off of a dead tree. Something came up beside the thing.

It was the girl from the road. Vayorn stared as every other living creature became blurry, as if blotted out by the glow around her. What was changed about her? She seemed different. Suddenly, it hit Vayorn; for some reason, she was attractive. That was what was different. *Look away. You don't need her. You don't want her. Look away.* As if they had minds of their own, Vayorn's feet stepped toward the girl. She seemed grown-up for some reason, changed somehow. Maybe it was the way she held herself, so much more relaxed now. Maybe it was her dress, a sparkly, shiny thing that glowed in the firelight. Maybe it was her hair, now intricately braided with shells and glass woven into it. But whatever it was, she was pretty. Women make men weak, he reminded himself.

Vayorn found his face about to smile. He scowled. She was hardly better than an animal. Just a half fish.

The old creature said something to the girl. Vayorn blinked, feeling suddenly like a small child who doesn't understand what the "grown-ups" are saying.

"Kuka tama on, Arple?"

The girl hesitated for a second. "Han on talla minulle."

The white thing nodded. It said something to the crowd, and the sounds of music and laughter rang out again. The girl placed her hand on Vayorn's arm. Vayorn jerked his arm away and stepped back.

"Understand Common Tongue?" he asked.

An understanding look crossed her face. "Yes, I do. It is well you came tonight."

"Why, might I ask of thee, is that so?" Vayorn mocked her. *Talks so proper. Who else talks like that? No one.*

She shook her head, took a breath, and her shoulders slumped. Vayorn tried not to feel guilty. *It's just a fish thing.* He looked away. *Why'd I say that? Of all the stupid things to say.*

She laid her hand on his arm again. "Please, be my guest tonight?"

"So, you can talk." Vayorn winced. *What's wrong with me?* He looked at her face. Suddenly he realized something: Saynasafs were no less intelligent than Antikish. They weren't animals.

The girl sighed and looked away. She was pretty, he had to admit. He smiled. "Didn't I see you on the road?"

The girl's head shot up. She straightened. "Yes, you did."

"And yes. I'll be your guest. But you've gotta translate the gibberish they're speaking."

The girl's brow furrowed. "Gibberish?"

Vayorn rolled his eyes. *How's she this hard to not offend? Most girls ain't this sensitive.* He didn't say anything.

The girl set a hand on his shoulder. "Sit, it's about to begin." She led him to a place against a wagon wheel. *What's everyone doing?* The middle of the ring was empty. Vayorn tensed. *What's going on?*

He laid a hand casually against his knife hilt. *If things get weird...* He loosened it in its sheath.

The old thing stood. It began to speak.

"What's your name?" Vayorn whispered.

"Arple. Shh." The girl laid a finger against her lips.

The white thing stood in the center. "Liito-seremonia symboloi miehen ja naisen välisiä lupauksia. Liito viitoittaa tietä heidän yhteiselle elämälleen…"

Vayorn threw his head back against the wheel. The old thing's words faded to a low drone in his ears. *Rather listen to Demetrius rant. Doesn't anyone speak Common Tongue here besides the girl?* He crossed his arms. A fly buzzed across the circle and landed on Vayorn's knee.

"Tässä näet Sulhasen, keiton, joka symboloi heidän suhteensa eri puolia, heidän rakkautensa suloisuutta, heidän konfliktiensa katkeruutta…"

Vayorn tried to have patience. *Just don't walk out. Last thing I need's to leave Agöri alone here.* He puffed out his cheeks. *How much longer can this take?* His foot tapped against the ground. *Just shut up already. Can't we just eat? No, it has to give an oration in gibberish. Have half a mind to run up there and—*

Arple started whispering, "The Liito ceremony symbolizes the vows between a man and a woman. The Liito sets the path for their life together. You see here the Sulhanen, the soup which symbolizes the diverse aspects of their relationship, the sweetness of their love, the bitterness of their conflicts."

Vayorn tried not to laugh. Ridiculous. Since when were soup and marriage the same thing?

"Perheen tyytyväisyyttä ja yhteistä elämää. Makujen sekoittuminen symboloi toivoa siitä, että he jonain päivänä menevät naimisiin ja tulevat yhdeksi."

"The satisfaction of a family and a life together. The blendedness of the flavors symbolizes the hope of them someday marrying and becoming one family."

One? How deluded is the old thing? Gotta be going crazy if he thinks vows mean anything. Show me one place, just one, where anyone's ever kept a vow. Every one of Demetrius's wives? Sure, they made vows to Demetrius, and he made vows to them—and Demetrius broke every one; husbands and wives argued, fought, and left each other all the time in Tarshal. He's an idiot if he thinks anything good lasts.

"Neidot, neuska."

"He's asking all the unmarried women to rise." Arple stood, smiled at Vayorn for a long instant, and joined the circle.

Vayorn let out one scornful half laugh. *Know what the way she stares at me means. She likes me. Poor girl.*

The maidens in the center began to whirl. Vayorn's scorn faded as Arple spiraled past him.

A length of sheer cloth shimmered like butterfly wings made of sunset, loosely attached to delicate bracelets around her wrists, seeming to change color in the firelight. A tragic melody soared to the sky as the light twinkle of harps jarred against the solemn time of the drum. Vayorn leaned forward. His eyes widened. Like a surgeon's tool prying into an open abscess, the music stabbed deep into the recesses of Vayorn's heart, digging out all the loneliness and pain he ignored or forgot. He held his breath. The music built till it came out of the invisible realm of sound and flashed around the circle, blinding. The prance of the harps and Arple's feet became one, beating out time with the melody in intricate, complex patterns. Suddenly, the pounding of the drums was Vayorn's life, and the only thing he wanted was for the sweet harp music to be his. The girl's dress caught the light and threw it back into Vayorn's eyes. Her arms were mere silhouettes behind the blaze around her. Vayorn sighed. His heart pounded a counter melody to the dazzle of her dance.

Slowly, the harp music and the drums blended together, jarring contrasts no more. Vayorn stared, seeing nothing but the sunlight in front of him, bouncing off diamonds and flashing into the air.

The music stopped.

The glen was silent. Vayorn shook himself. His eyes came into focus. *What's wrong with me? What if someone had tried to attack me? I wasn't paying attention.* He looked at Arple, now coming toward him. *That's what's wrong.* His smile left his face. *Women make men weak.*

She sat down beside him. He stared straight ahead, acting as if she didn't exist. She cleared her throat. Vayorn pretended he didn't hear her.

"Boy?"

Vayorn tensed. *Boy?* His shoulders tightened. His jaw set.

She tried again, "What is amiss?"

Vayorn ignored her. She huffed. *Don't look at her. Weak! She made me weak.*

A hand grabbed his arm. He jerked and turned his head. His eyes met Arple's.

"I never asked your name of you." She cocked her head.

Vayorn shrugged her hand off his arm. "Vayorn," he mumbled.

"Vayorn," the girl mused, "I do not recall ever hearing a name like that, even after living in Antike for such a long time. You are Antikish, are you not?"

"Yeah."

"You had a child with you. What was his name?"

Vayorn gritted his teeth. *Why's she have to ask so many deng questions?* "Agori."

"A sweet name. Is he your brother?"

"Nope."

"Oh."

She stopped talking. Vayorn sighed. *Finally. Never met a woman who asks so many questions. She's almost as bad as agori.*

The papery creature stood. *Again?*

It began speaking, "Se, että nainen hyväksyy miehen, on ratkaisevan tärkeää, sillä sillä sillä hetkellä kaikki näkevät heidät toistensa omistamina."

Vayorn rubbed his temples. *Can't anyone just use Common Tongue? It's really not this difficult to use something everyone can understand.*

Arple translated, "The acceptance of the man by the woman is crucial, for it is in that moment they are seen by all to be owned by one another."

Owned? Not by one another. Immediately, Vayorn thought of Demetrius and his wives. *Women are stupid, like children. He really is* nuts *if he thinks they should be taken seriously. Plus, what man wants his wife to own him?*

"Neidot, neuska."

What's he want this time? They already danced. Arple rose and stood facing Vayorn. Unconsciously, Vayorn angled his body toward her. *What's going on?* He lowered his gaze. *Remember? You can't trust her.* His hand rested on his knife again.

The old thing nodded to Arple. She smiled and took a deep breath. "I speak for all the young women of marriage age. We each are prepared to accept a suitor in betrothal. He that stands signifies his desire to plight his troth with a woman present."

Men around the circle began standing and taking the hands of the girls. Vayorn looked down and realized he was getting to his feet. *What's wrong with me?* He tried to sit, but his eyes landed on Arple's hand. He tried to make himself back up, but he couldn't. His gaze rose to meet Arple's. *How'd I never notice those eyes? Never seen eyes that pretty.* Arple entwined her fingers with his.

She turned and held their hands up. "Hyväksyn! I accept!"

Polite applause.

Then cries of "She chose him? but, he's Antikish! He's dangerous! Ilmari, do something! She can't marry him! Don't let her do this! It's not right! Don't you care about her? She didn't even know his name till a moment—"

Ilmari held up a hand. "Silence. It is Arple's choice."

Marry? Vayorn tried to convince himself it was a bad idea. *Stupid! You don't need a wife.* They sat. *Idiot! Why'd I do that? Last thing I need's a permanent girl.* He looked down at Arple's hand. *It's just the right size. How's it fit so exactly in mine?* He shook himself. Weak. But his fingers remained locked in Arple's. *What's wrong with me tonight?* Now older couples were passing around bowls of the soup. Vayorn remembered he was hungry.

There was no spoon. *Never mind. Hungry enough, I don't need one.* He lifted it up to take a sip. Arple elbowed him. He lowered the bowl. *Come on! How long do I have to wait to eat?*

The old thing stood again. Vayorn groaned. The girl giggled. Vayorn tensed. Weak. He removed his hand from hers and folded his arms.

"It's almost over, don't worry," Arple whispered. *Don't worry? I'm hungry, not worried. And annoyed. And I thought Agori's chatter was annoying. Rather take that than this any day.*

"Sulhasen juominen on lupaus; Jos mies juo ensin, hän lupaa suojella naista. Jos hän juo toisena, hän lupaa kunnioittaa häntä ja hänen toiveitaan."

"The drinking of the Sulhanen is a pledge. If the man drinks first, he pledges to protect the woman. If he drinks second, he vows to respect her and her wishes."

Vayorn tried to pay attention. *How much longer's it gonna be till he finally lets us eat? What's he want to do? Starve us?*

The old thing raised its hand. Finally. He looked at Arple, then back at the soup. *Oh great. Have to eat, but no matter when I eat, I'm sealing this engagement thing. Why'd I go up in the first place?*

Arple looked at him, waiting. *Great. At least promises don't mean anything.* He nodded. She took a sip. Then Vayorn took a sip.

A contented smile spread across his face. It was good. Savory, spicy, each sip sent warmth through his body. When it was gone, he looked at the empty dish regretfully. *Wish there was more.*

Arple tapped him and offered to take his bowl. "May I get you more?"

Vayorn nodded. She stood in the line around the pot. Vayorn sighed happily. *What's wrong with me? Don't let your guard down.* He shook his head.

THE LETTERS

Demetrius rubbed his temples. Raucous cheering grated against his ears. He squeezed his eyes shut, ignoring the dull throb as the lids met. How long had it been since the letters came? Was it already a full day ago? How long had it been since he'd slept? Too long. They'd run—what, two?—days ago, but Demetrius couldn't remember sleeping at all.

Demetrius gazed across the room at Laparlana. She lay on the only piece of furniture in the shabby room, a hard couch, curled in a kitten-like ball. He looked back at the letter in his shaking hand. What did it mean for her future? Their child's future? Demetrius tried to force himself to think calmly, a hard thing to do with crude drinking songs coming up from below his feet. Downstairs, footsteps and violin music screeched like the noise of seagulls along a cliff.

He read the last line again.

"Bring the boy to us. He is the rightful king. Perhaps we shall be lenient upon you then. Do not think to trick us. We know who the true heir is. If he were dead, as you told us he was, we would have no choice but to seek out his father, the firstborn. But he is alive, and the throne is his. Bring him to us or your head is forfeit. We grow weary of your incompetence. It is time for a new ruler."

A threat. The letter was left unsigned. In his other hand, a second letter lay. He read it again.

"You know our reasons. You know the lives you have ended, the families you have torn apart. The hammer which swings upward must come down, and we intend to see to it that it does. You have sent many, many innocents to the infamous gallows of Tarshal square. It is your turn. You are never safe. We are everywhere. We are watching. You think you have the upper hand. You don't. Our master escaped you. He is out there, waiting. You know him. He knows you. Beware the arrow in the woods, the poison in the cup, the knife in the night. We will win. Try and stop us." A fine scrawl, and two "s" runes, one inside the other. Demetrius gritted his teeth.

The Sons of Soturant, Dunbar's men.

He knelt on the ground beside Laparlana for a moment. "I won't let them win. For you, I have to live. I won't let them find us," he whispered. She stirred slightly, but the peace of deep sleep stayed in her face. He took a deep breath. There was only one choice: hunt down the boy, hunt down Dunbar, kill them both. He should have killed the boy years ago. But it was too late to go back now.

He crept across the room, careful not to wake Laparlana, and opened the door.

The smoky atmosphere of the lower room enveloped him. The lanterns cast their glow down into the room, lit although there was still golden light pouring through the windows. The tavern was shaped like two rectangles, joined together to make an *L* shape. The outside edge of one rectangle was framed by stairs, winding up to a balcony outside the one bedroom the tavern possessed. On the inside of the rectangle, beside the stairs, was a bar, now so full of soldiers not a seat was open. The worn floors were covered with spilled drinks and food, from how long ago Demetrius didn't even want to imagine. The pockmarked oak tables were spread across the room with the same carelessness with which the rest of the building was kept. In various attitudes of restlessness, men sat sprawled along the bar and the tables, talking to each other in a low murmur. Far back around the bend, in the hidden corner of the second rectangle, a small group spoke in tentative, hushed voices. Near the center of the room, a trio stood singing and casting vulgar remarks at the serving maid, who blankly ignored them. An old soldier sat at a table spinning yarns from some campaign long ago, in far-off lands.

A hush fell across the room as Demetrius stepped out onto the balcony and looked down.

He took a deep breath, suddenly conscious of his haggard appearance. Long ago, he would never have let himself get like this. He would have at least bathed. But that was long ago. Added, it was the ruthless man who gained the respect of soldiers, not the polished one.

He began to speak. The men sat in silence as he outlined his plan.

MARLIESEL

Dunbar ran his hand along a tall pine. Deep in the wood, a worn carving still showed. A heart and, inside the heart, four initials. Dunbar's and hers. He leaned against the tree, letting his fingers play along the shape in the wood. The river rushed behind him, almost soundless. He kept his back to it. He'd seen rivers before. It wasn't worth looking at. Besides, that wasn't what he came here to see. His fingers caressed her initials, the only letter still mostly legible in the peeling bark. Her voice rang out inside his head. He could almost see her hand again, carving the *M* with his knife. *M* for Marliesel, the most beautiful woman in the world. His hand at his side was cold now, a reminder that she was gone. He leaned his forehead against the carving. His eyes closed.

"Dunbar, don't ask me again. We've discussed this."

"Please, Liesel, I need you. Antike's not pretty, but we only have to live there a few months of the year."

"But it's your home."

"Yes. Even if we stay away, it's my home. But we can live here most of the time, so you aren't homesick—"

"Hah. Funny. Me? Homesick? Home doesn't exist. Not anymore. Not for me," she snapped, suddenly bitter. Dunbar laid a hand on the small of her back.

"Liesel. Stop wandering. I'll be a good home, a real home. I'll love your boys. I'll help raise them. Please, trust me." She looked up at him,

her beautiful eyes wary. Dunbar wished there were something he could say, something he could do, to prove to her she could trust him. But all he could do was talk.

So he talked. They wandered the woods together the entire day, Dunbar pleading with her to trust him, to let him love her. The rock in her eyes slowly softened under Dunbar's entreaties. Finally, she broke down crying. She'd always avoided talking about her past to Dunbar. Now she told him everything. How she had lived as a slave till she was twelve, when she escaped. How after her escape, she lived a loose lifestyle in a feeble attempt to drown her past. How afraid she was of commitment, of being used. So she didn't trust. Not anyone. How long they sat there, beside the river, Dunbar could never remember, but when they finally set out for home, Marliesel had agreed to marry him. She was convinced she could trust him.

"Or so I thought…" Dunbar picked up a rock and weighed it in his hand. Now she was gone. But perhaps it was for the better. After all, she was probably happier with whoever she was with now than she would be with Dunbar, running for her life. At least she was probably safe. But perhaps it was Dunbar's fault she left. He hated that thought. Or worse, perhaps she had never trusted him in the first place. And that thought hurt worst of all. Perhaps, even after giving birth to their two children, she thought of Dunbar as a danger. If only Dunbar had seen, if only he'd done something. He was sure she loved him, at some point. Where was she now? Where were her other children? The last time Dunbar had seen them, the boys had been so little. Nitard had only been four when Dunbar married Marliesel. And Raivo had been, what, two? Dunbar threw the rock. It dropped into the waves. He threw another. If only. Another. If only. Dunbar rubbed his temples. If only he'd seen. Mother was right; you didn't know what you had till you lost it.

If only he'd been kind to poor Demetrius. It was so easy to make fun of Demetrius; everyone did. If only Dunbar had seen how much his words hurt Demetrius, before it was too late. If only. His mind wandered to that fateful argument, the one that would forever change his life. The little boys had just come in from playing.

Marliesel was a few months pregnant. Demetrius was sitting at the fountain with Marliesel's nanny, Antarulra.

Antarulra was a Fiynesaf. Fiynesafs were said to just be freaks of nature, much the same as Saynasafs. But even if that was true, Antarulra was no animal. She was clever and could even be called beautiful, if you were attracted to antlers and wings. Demetrius was. Even now, Dunbar could see the animated glow in his brother's eyes as he talked with Antarulra. Dunbar could hear the peals of laughter and good-natured banter. He could see Antarulra whack Demetrius lightly with a wing and Demetrius catch her by the wrist and splash her. If only. If only Dunbar had left Demetrius with the illusion Antarulra could love him. Back then, Demetrius looked healthy, young, and handsome. But not after the argument.

It seemed almost as if the change began instantaneously. Demetrius stopped sleeping. He stopped eating. Dark circles appeared around his eyes. His cheeks sank in. The bones of his face, his ribs, his shoulders stuck out like wire underneath thin sacking. He no longer laughed. He took lovers, the worst women in Tarshal.

Dunbar sent Antarulra away with Marliesel's two sons, hoping to get her off Demetrius's mind. But it only made things worse. Demetrius became vengeful, wicked even, and almost intolerable to be around. It all came to a head one day, the day before Demetrius's betrayal.

Dunbar shook himself. If only he'd been kinder to the boy. Maybe they would even have been friends now, if Dunbar hadn't said what he said. His hand strayed to a chain around his neck. Father's ring was cold in his hand. He toyed with it, allowing numbness to sink into his veins. Father had been so wise. He would never have said what Dunbar said. How could Dunbar say that and still call himself a good king? "A good king holds his tongue until it is utterly necessary to speak," Father would always say. Dunbar could almost hear father scolding him, could almost see the hand wearing that ring waving in the air, punctuating the lesson with a pointed finger, shaming Dunbar into doing his duty.

He struggled to his feet. Mechanically, almost like he was sleepwalking, he plodded along the river's edge. His back bent as if his bag were ten times heavier than it was. The words *if only* hung around the ring on his neck like a weight and dragged his head to his chest. He didn't want to look up. There was nothing to see. If only.

    He sighed.

DARKNESS

D arkness fell over the camp, prowling just beyond the glow of the fire. Shadows flickered back and forth against the wagons, almost warlike in their wild dance.

"No! Don't go!"

"Agöri! Don't leave!"

Agöri's small head disappeared behind the other children. Vayorn tapped his toe against the ground. *One hug's enough.* He pushed them out of the way and began pulling Agöri behind him. A little girl sat on Vayorn's foot and grabbed his leg.

"Can't leave." She stuck her lip out.

Vayorn kicked her off. Arple stood near him, hands folded over her chest, heartbroken. Her eyes were dim and beginning to get red, asking the question the children were already demanding answers to. Why did they have to leave? Couldn't they just stay? She came up beside Vayorn.

"You stayed last night. Was our hospitality amiss? Look, we gave you our best beds and placed them by the fire. The blankets are yours to keep. What then is your reason for leaving? Stay? Please?" Her voice began to quiver.

Vayorn turned his back to her.

Persistent, Arple grabbed his arm. "I'll see you again, won't I?"

Vayorn shut his mouth in a tight line. *Don't say it. Don't say you'll stay.* Arple opened her eyes wider. The corners shone with tears.

Vayorn's resolution faltered. *She's beautiful.* He tensed. *What's wrong with me? Can't stay. Not around her.*

"Have to go. Wasted enough time." Vayorn threw Agöri his shoulder. Ilmari stopped him.

"You are free to stay with us, if you wish."

"I don't wish." Vayorn hoped he didn't sound as hesitant as he felt.

"Don't be mean!" Agöri squirmed. "Want to stay."

Vayorn jolted Agöri roughly; the protests paused for a minute. Then Agöri tried a new tactic: whining, "Don't like walking! Feet always hurt! You stink when we walk! Your armpits smell like garlic when you make me walk! Never get clean! Make holes in my shoes! Hurts my head to walk! You listening? You, you, ilithio, megala, tsimpima!"

Vayorn paused. "What did you call me?"

"Not telling," Agöri muttered.

Making me look so stupid. Vayorn dropped Agöri, yanked the child's arm up, and half dragged him to the edge of the clearing.

"But, Vayorn, it is unsafe at night! You would do best to wait till daylight!" Arple placed herself in front of Vayorn, hands on her hips.

Vayorn bit back the words, "Fine, we'll stay," burning on the tip of his tongue. *Get out. Weak.* He shoved her hand off his shoulder, pushed her aside, and ran.

"Slow down! Can't keep up! Hey! Listen up," Agöri protested as he trotted beside Vayorn.

For an instant, it was like being underwater, wrapped in black nothingness. Vayorn ignored the frantic beating of his heart. *Just have to wait for my eyes to adjust.* Like stone pillars, almost dreamlike, the limbs of trees became clear. Gray and black, with all the color washed out of them in the dull-blue light of the dying moon, they stood erect. In the still air, not a twig moved. Vayorn found himself almost missing the wind. *Least if there was wind, there'd be something to listen to. Take giant sloths over this.* It was almost like he and Agöri were the only creatures still alive. The smell of rotting leaves wafted up as his feet squished into the soft ground. *Thud-thud. Thud-thud.* Vayorn strained his ears. *What's that?* He laid his hand on his chest. *Thud-*

thud. *Thud-thud. That's not me, is it?* Vayorn held his breath, longing to hear anything but the hammer inside his chest. But there was nothing. Not a sound. The dead flapping of an owl's wings passed above them. Something about it reminded Vayorn of the old castle.

He could almost feel the broken stone against his fingers, hear the childish voices telling ghost stories, feel the scream of silence against his ears.

He closed his mind to the memory of the girl dancing beside the fire and resisted the temptation to turn back. *Hate this time of year. Days are too short. Almost makes a person want to move north.* He swung Agöri onto his back again. *He'll die if he runs off this time. Who knows what's out there.* Everything, even the dirt seemed to unsettle Vayorn. He tightened his grip around Agöri's legs.

"Ow. You hold tight," Agöri complained. Vayorn kept walking.

What's out there? Wish things were more like home. Terror Birds're bad, but at least I knew to expect them. What do I even look for out here? The breeze was strangely warm. Almost like the breath of a dragon. Or a giant black wolf. Vayorn's mouth went dry. He shivered and looked back. Nothing. Weak. *Knock it off. We're fine. No, we're not.* His eyes widened. *Where's the road?*

He turned in a circle. As far he could see were trees and night. The road was gone, as if it had never been.

"Oh gach," he muttered. *How are we lost? I went the same way I came.* Did they get turned around in the dark? Maybe the road was just in front of them, and all they had to do was keep walking. *But we should have reached it by now. Should've stayed.* He shook himself. *Weak. Gach, you even survived deng near drowning to death. What's this compared to that?* But the bravery he tried to force himself to feel evaded him.

A twig snapped. He jumped. *Just my imagination. There's nothing. We're safe. Right?*

"We're fine. It's nothing," he said, more to himself than Agöri.

Two red eyes, pale lanterns glimmering almost ghostlike, glowed to life in front of them. Vayorn's breaths rang out, entirely too loud in his ears. Agöri yelped.

"What behind us?" He buried his face in Vayorn's neck. Vayorn swung around. All around them, red eyes held them in like an invisible cage.

Vayorn dropped Agöri. A small, icy hand slid into his. He looked down at the child's face. Terror froze its tiny features in a mute expression of horror. The little mouth hung open, a scream building in tiny whimpers.

Vayorn's mind raced back to the woods outside Tarshal. Janus's voice seemed to come out of the night, out of Vayorn's memories. "They can see, yes, but they are predators. It is their instinct to kill when something screams or runs. So don't scream, don't run. Don't rouse their hunting blood." Janus had been talking about Terror Birds, but anything was worth trying.

Can't let Agöri scream. He screams and we're dead. Vayorn looked for something, a hollow log, an outcropping of rock, a tree with low branches, anything to hide Agöri under. *Have to get him out of here.*

Agöri began screaming.

Vayorn clapped his hand over the child's mouth, "Knock it off! Wanna get us killed?" He shook Agöri by the shoulders. Agöri started crying, but he was quiet. Vayorn let go.

The creatures chattered, almost like the crowds around the gallows on execution day, splitting up the belongings of the condemned among themselves. *What are they?* Shadowlike, serpentine shapes darted back and forth in front of them, their long tails and claws dragging on the stony ground. They paused, and it seemed to Vayorn as if they were unsure of which creature to send in first. A small thing finally sped up to Vayorn, claws and teeth bared. It paused just shy of Vayorn's knifepoint; its small head whipped back and forth, the furred outline blurring into the dark.

It jumped. Vayorn threw Agöri to the ground. Something wet and warm washed over his hand. If there had been light, he would have seen the greenish tinge spreading rapidly over his arm. A cloud fell over his mind. His senses dulled. The only thing he felt was throbbing in his right shoulder. His small control over himself snapped; Agöri told him after the fact that he'd been screaming swear words and yelling about someone named Demetrius. But it was as if someone else were screaming, from somewhere so far away the words were merely sounds, all meaning lost. He stared, blind, oblivious to the eyes, the fangs, the claws, getting closer and closer. But shining in front of him, searing his vision, torturing his mind, was a copper dagger. *No! Can't die!* He began to back up, away from the dagger. But it followed him. He never felt Agöri grab his leg. He never heard the squawk behind him. He never felt the knife fall from his hand. He never heard Agöri's pleas for help. *Can't die!* Vayorn turned to run. Something hit him in the back, and the ground rose to meet him. A rock bashed his forehead as he fell. His eyes closed.

Searing pain woke him. Not thinking, he screamed and reached into his sheath; his hand met air where the hilt of his knife should have been. Gach. He rolled out of the way and swung his fist. If it hit anything, he didn't feel it.

"Help! Vayorn! It has me!"

Vayorn snapped out of the trance; his pupils dilated. His vision cleared. One of the creatures had Agöri by the shirt and was dragging him into the woods. Vayorn's feet paused, as if iced over. *What if I die?* Ilmari's words rang out in Vayorn's mind: "I see fear."

"No! I'm not afraid!" Vayorn kicked, dived for his knife, and ran after Agöri.

He wove through the trees. Ahead of him the quick legs of the thing carried Agöri out of his reach. *Can't keep up.* Vayorn's lungs burned in protest. Spots swam before his eyes. He staggered. Agöri was out of sight, his faint screams far-off.

"No…" A hazy film fell over the woods around Vayorn. His temples throbbed. "No…" His eyes landed on a gush of blood, pouring out of a deep gash on the inside of his knee. *Where'd that come from?* His shirt dripped with something. *That's not sweat…* He felt sick as his hands landed in a deep wound just below his throat, between his collarbone and his jugular. His knees buckled. "No…" Then merciful darkness dealt the final blow to his consciousness.

A VARUL

"*Help!*" *Vayorn fell to the ground. Arple tried to go to him. As if she were turned to stone, she couldn't move. She watched helpless as madaraks surrounded him. One of them leaned its head over his arm and ripped into his shoulder. A faint cry reached Arple's ears. Vayorn's lips parted as sickly green tinged his pale cheeks and lips. He made a final attempt to rise, then collapsed. Arple screamed.*

*****

Arple sat up. Where was she? Her heart pounded in her temples. She leaned back. Chills ran down her spine. Somehow, she knew her dream wasn't a dream. Vayorn was lost somewhere, hurt perhaps. She swung her legs off the bed. The awful screams in her dream echoed batlike around her room. She shook her head. This was silly. Nothing was wrong. But now she wasn't so sure. The dream, the screams—it all seemed so real. She closed her eyes. The vision of Vayorn's arm, green venom spreading through its veins, flashed before her eyes. She shuddered. What if Vayorn was already… No. She couldn't let herself think that. He was strong. But what if he was in trouble?

She curled into a ball. Should she go after him? But what could she do? If only she were more like Maria. Maria would already be out in the woods, following Vayorn's trail with the best Varuls in the camp. Maria would never have hesitated. Oh, why couldn't Arple be more like Maria? Small help she'd be to Vayorn. But on the other hand, didn't Uncle Ilmari call her brave? Didn't he call her strong?

She looked at her hand. It still seemed to burn with the delight of Vayorn's touch. Her conscience began to wake. He was her fiancé. It would be like murdering him herself if she didn't at least try to help him. How could she hesitate?

She stood. Her mind was made up. She would go after him. Tonight. Right now, his trail was only hours old. She began dressing and packing her bag, her mind racing. Uncle Ilmari had a Varul he kept on dry land. She was sure she could borrow it. And think of how safe she would be! A web-spinning, fire-breathing, waist-high Varul. Just think.

She turned and ran out the door.

*****

The wind whipped her face. Thunder rang out from under her horse's hooves. An excited bark ahead of her; Apran found the trail. Her lips parted as her chest heaved. She leaned forward in the saddle. Not long now. She was close. The scene from her dream played out in her mind again. She steeled herself, prepared for whatever she was about to see. Whatever happened, she must be strong. The trees reached out fingers to curl around her hair, her dress, trying to hold her back, keep her from him. Apran's turtle shell and peacock crest blended into the night till he was just a shadow. Only the *whoosh-whoosh* of his wings and the wind. Arple closed her eyes; the horse knew what it was doing. It was a hunting mare. Wherever the Varul led, it would follow. Uncle Ilmari once said he had a horse that followed a Varul off a cliff, griffon hunting. Arple took a deep breath. The soft air was almost like water, cool and gentle, like the kiss of a loved one. But it didn't hold the comfort of water; it was raw, almost as if even for its good intentions, it still failed compassion. Her frills tingled, sorting the sounds pouring into them. The closest sounds were the clearest, but if she concentrated, truly concentrated, she could hear another set of hooves pounding the ground. But they were at least a mile off; if they were closer, Arple would feel them.

She placed a hand in the air. Through its currents, she could feel the trees, breaking the stream of air like the rudders of a ship. Something was breathing, and it was getting closer. Arple felt the warmth of its breaths in the breeze. Now she felt it tossing and turning. Her eyes shot open. Was it… Yes, it had to be. She kicked her horse and tried to turn it to the right, toward the sounds. It dug its hooves in. She kicked it again and yanked the right reign. Something dive-bombed her.

"Mistress get much-killed! Smell not over there!" Apran seized the hem of her dress.

"Apran, stop! I feel something! It's him!" She shook Apran off. It just had to be him. She had to get there in time. She had to save him.

"Not good idea! Smell this way!"

"We're going this way!" Arple sped off.

Apran kept up with her. As they disappeared into the trees, he muttered, "Apran have bad feeling about this."

*****

"Track him, I said! How hard is that!" Demetrius screamed. The soldier backed away from him. Demetrius advanced. The men around him stood as close to the walls as they could. One of them held a handkerchief to his head, where a red stain was quickly appearing. Demetrius screamed again, wordless. His chest tightened. *How could they lose the boy already? How hard was it?* He clenched his fist and struck the man across the face. One of the men inched toward the open door. Demetrius slammed it shut. His eyes burned. The sharp lines of his face darkened. The man in front of him stuttered and held his hands up, his eyes darting warily to Demetrius's fists and sword. One of the men lay on the floor, his eyes closed, long past help, his hands pressed to his side. Demetrius's sword point was still warm.

Demetrius threw one of the men to the ground. "I order your execution!" He shoved a captain. "Drown him, poison him, stab him, I don't care! Kill him!"

The man on the floor tried to protest. Demetrius kicked him. The captain opened his mouth, about to speak. Demetrius swung his sword tip around to the man's throat. The captain backed up. His mouth closed. In the corner of the room, Janus leaned against a wall, half hidden in the shadows.

"Anything you wanted to say, Captain?" Demetrius stared at the captain, challenging him to speak. One word, just one, that was all it took. The captain shook his head. Demetrius went to sheath his sword.

Suddenly, he paused and drew it again. He stared at it, for an instant oblivious to the room around him. The sword weighed heavy in his hand, plain, like that of an ordinary soldier. The sword Dunbar should have. The sword of an underling. Demetrius gritted his teeth. Always second. Always lesser. His lungs screamed. His veins burst into flame. How dare he. The one thing, the one thing father promised him. Father's sword, the sword that had belonged to father's father, and his father before that. The only thing of father's Demetrius had left. And Dunbar took it, just like he took everything else. A reminder that Demetrius was worthless, would always be worthless. As long as Dunbar was alive, Demetrius would always be second-best. Always second pick, always the extra, the spare, the replacement. Not worthy of his father's sword, not worthy of his father's power. As long as Dunbar was alive, Demetrius was just the fill-in. Not to be taken seriously, to be laughed at, ridiculed. The jeers of Sverin and Severn, the sons of high noble Rodmerigan rang out. "You'll never be loved," that's what they said. "You'll never be powerful," they rubbed that in Demetrius's face every day after Dunbar was made king. They each went on to have families. Every time they saw Demetrius, they teased him about not having a wife. Well, where were they now? Dead. After Demetrius took the throne, they were the first to go. And where was Demetrius? Feared ruler of the most powerful nation in the lower continent. Husband of the most wonderful woman in the world. They were wrong. But so quickly, so quickly things could change. What if the nobles found Vayorn? What if they found Dunbar? Demetrius would be killed. He would be stripped of the throne. Laparlana and the baby would be widowed and fatherless. Why hadn't Demetrius killed Vayorn all those years ago? Why hadn't he ordered Dunbar's execution?

Demetrius threw his sword to the ground. "I should have killed him! Killed them both! It's mine! The throne's mine! Do you hear me? Mine! Mine!" He took it! He took the sword! He took the crown! "I hate him! I should have killed him! Killed him! I'll kill him!" He paused. Had he said all that out loud? He hadn't meant to. But it was true, wasn't it? He should have secured the throne while he could. His screams died in his throat. The stares of the men around him said everything: they were scared of him, maybe even thought he was insane. His mouth shut. He forced composure back into himself.

"Janus, it seems these little meedchens"—one of the captains winced—"cannot handle a real job. You find him. Take whoever you want. I want the boy dead. Don't bother to capture him. If you come across my dear brother, give him this, just a little token of my affection." Demetrius drew a dagger, plunged it into one of the wood beams, yanked it free, and held it out to the soldier. "It would do him the most good right between these ribs." Demetrius pushed the point into Janus's rib cage, just hard enough to hurt. Janus impassively nodded. If he was frightened, it didn't show. Demetrius threw the dagger to the floor at Janus's feet.

"Now go! All of you! I want to be alone!"

The room emptied as the men raced each other to the door.

They dragged the injured man out the door.

Demetrius went to the window and threw it open. A cold breeze stunned him into sanity. He put his head in his hands. Maybe protecting his family would have been easier if he weren't king. But he wouldn't have a family if he weren't king, he reminded himself. Laparlana had been attracted to him because of his power. What would happen if he no longer had power? Would she leave? The thought struck him for the first time. After all, Dunbar's wife left after Dunbar lost the throne. Why did Dunbar want her in the first place? Her reputation alone was enough to scare off most decent men. But not Dunbar. Demetrius shook his head. What if Laparlana didn't really love him? The thought was like torture. He pushed it away. Of course she loved him; she was the mother of his child. But he was willing to kill for power. Surely a woman would marry for power. No, it wasn't true. Demetrius kicked a stool across the room. He was tired; that was it. He wasn't thinking clearly. She loved him. She had to.

He ran out of the room. He had to see her. He couldn't wait. He had to prove to himself she loved him.

THE HUT

Vayorn stirred. Searing whiteness stabbed the backs of his closed eyes. He squinched them tighter shut. What felt like a couple of minutes passed, and he slowly opened them. Sunlight poured in from an open window and pushed itself through gaps in the thatching above him. A piece of straw floated down and landed on Vayorn's nose. He sneezed. It blew back into the air. Through his bleared vision, the room looked gray and green. He tried to focus. *Not underwater, am I?* His head turned. *No, not underwater, but why can't I see? Where am I? Have to move!* His mind went back to the ship; what if it happened again? Would he recover? He got better the first time, but this was different; something felt wrong. Was it just his head aching, or did every item in the room resemble a dagger? Even the pieces of straw and rays of light were dagger-shaped. Maybe the green haze around him was just a storm coming. He jerked a shoulder off the bed. *Not again. Please, not again.* It was almost as if his body ended below his neck; there was no feeling past his shoulders. *What's wrong with me? What happened? Deng, my head. Where am I?*

He forced himself to move again; searing pain tore his arm. A groan escaped his parched lips; now he realized how dry they were. *Need water.*

"Don't try to move, sonny."

Vayorn's eyes shot open. A shadow stood in the doorway, blotting out the light. Something glinted from its right hand.

He has a sword. A green tinge passed over Vayorn's eyes.

Suddenly the figure was a giant copper blade, speeding closer. Vayorn struggled. It was about to touch him. He screamed.

A cold sensation chilled Vayorn's head and rang in his ears. His vision cleared. A kind face peered over him, an almost pitying look in its eyes. Vayorn tensed.

"Who are you?"

The man gasped. It almost seemed like he choked for an instant, before he whispered, "'Metrius?" Vayorn inched away.

The man cleared his throat. "Call me Dunbar."

Vayorn nodded and looked away. *So his name's the same as Father's.* He realized that he hadn't thought of his father in months. A slight thorn of guilt pricked him. *How could I forget him for so long?* What if he stopped thinking about his parents? He couldn't; where would his reason for revenge go if he did? He had to stay angry, to kill Demetrius. He looked up at the man. A tender look shone in his eyes: pity. That was the only explanation. He felt bad for Vayorn. How dare he. *How did I get like this again? Why?* Vayorn forced himself to sit up, feeling rushed back into his limbs, burning like hot water on frostbitten skin. He gritted his teeth. It passed quickly, but for an instant, he was sure he would lose consciousness. He swung his legs to the floor and stood. They wavered and tried to go out from under him. His chest slammed against the bed as he caught himself and waved Dunbar off. One foot slid forward. Carefully, he transferred weight to his other leg.

His ankle bent, and he fell. Dunbar pulled him to his feet and sat him down again.

"What am I supposed to call you, son? Gotta have a name, although *son*'ll do just fine most of the time."

Vayorn looked away. *Should be angry. I deserve more respect. But almost agree with him—kinda nice being called son. Sure beats boy. Why's he being so nice?* Blackeye had been too nice because the plan all along had been to kill Vayorn. *What makes this Dunbar fellow any different? Don't want him knowing who I am. At least not yet. But lots of people're named Vayorn. Don't want him just calling me son, like he's my dad. But it would be kind'a nice to have someone be my dad, even if it was pretend.*

"Vayorn," he mumbled. The man caught his breath. For an instant, something wet shone at the corners of his eyes.

"And the child's name is Agöri. It can't be," the man said, more to himself than Vayorn. *Agöri!*

Vayorn grabbed the man's arm. "The child you said, he's alive? He's here?"

"Yes, yes, calm down. He's outside playing."

Unsupervised? What if something happens to him? "Call him in."

The man stood. Vayorn's mind raced. *How's he alive? It was going to kill him. Dunbar must've rescued him. But why? He's not big enough to be worth selling. No one saves a life for no reason. Maybe he thinks Agöri'll be a better slave if he's raised as one.* His fists clenched. *Have to get away. Have to find a safe place. Before Demetrius finds me.* His heart began to hammer. *What if he finds out where I am? What if Dunbar's a spy? Gotta be a hefty reward for my capture. What if I can't get away in time? Can't leave Agöri. Who knows what'll happen to him.*

The patter of feet across the floor. Vayorn swiveled his head just as Agöri hurled himself into Vayorn's lap.

"See man? Named Dunbar. Look!" Agöri held up a ring on a chain. A rollicking laugh bounced around the room. Dunbar shook his head, still laughing.

*****

Dunbar tried not to stare. The boys were named Vayorn and Agöri; his sons had been nicknamed Vayorn and Agöri. Dunbar couldn't help but believe that this was no mere coincidence. Perhaps this was even a second chance.

Like plunging into cold water, looking at the older one sent chills down Dunbar's spine. Dunbar had hoped he would resemble Liesel, or Father, but he didn't. He didn't even resemble Dunbar. The boy's face, his eyes, his glare—all seemed to be the ghost of

Demetrius's younger self. It was almost frightening how strong the resemblance was.

Ah, but the little one. That tiny face provided all the comfort Vayorn's lacked. The child was, without a shadow of doubt, Dunbar's child. The nose, the pert grin—he reminded Dunbar so much of himself at that age. The little one's face was Dunbar's face. Except for the eyes. The eyes were Liesel's.

Dunbar tried to hold back tears, but as he listened to the boys talk, he found it harder and harder to be calm. They were his sons. He could feel it. Dunbar resisted the urge to run up to them and embrace them; he couldn't see Vayorn taking that very well. The only thing Vayorn had said to him all day was "We need to get to Lord Fangar." After Dunbar offered to lead them to Canjon, the boy coldly ignored Dunbar.

All evening, Dunbar had been studying the older one. A scar ran along the boy's right cheek. Dunbar shook his head. It was impossible. But there was no other explanation. He knew where that scar came from. He left the two and stood in the doorway, hiding his face. At least the scar became the boy, although it didn't heal like Dunbar had hoped it would. Ivaylo had been, what, two, when he got it? No, he was taken away before then; he was about eighteen months. Dunbar left him in the garden outside their hut for a minute and went in to grab a blanket to shield the child from the sun with. When he came back out, the baby was on the ground screaming, with a deep gash across one cheek. Dunbar never figured out how Ivaylo had gotten cut. None of his tools were within reach of the child. Freak accident? Perhaps. But there were enemies on the island. Allies of Demetrius. It was on purpose, Dunbar was sure.

Giggling wrenched his head back to the room. Vayorn was tickling the little one. Dunbar listened harder; it was almost too quiet to hear, but Vayorn was chuckling softly, almost as if he were afraid of laughing loud enough for Dunbar to hear. Dunbar looked away. Should he tell the boys who he was? He tried to imagine how Vayorn would respond. It wasn't hard to picture: an angry outburst, blame thrown on Dunbar for failing him, stony silence, and then the boy would leave. He would never cross paths with Dunbar again. Dunbar's second chance would be over before it began. He would lose the boys again; Vayorn would never leave the child behind, and this time they would be gone forever. Already he could see how strong Demetrius's personality was in Vayorn, so familiar, so alarmingly familiar. No, it was too risky. Better to allow Vayorn to trust him, perhaps become friends with him, and then come clean. If only he'd been able to do something. If only he'd watched the child more closely. Guilt filled him again. Not only did he lose Vayorn; he allowed Agöri to be kidnapped too. He was a failure. A miserable failure as a father. Father would never have allowed that to happen to Dunbar or Demetrius. Dunbar slumped to the ground. *If only Father were here. If Father were here, Demetrius would never have betrayed Dunbar. Dunbar's boys would have grown up with a father.*

He reached for Father's ring. It was gone. His breath caught for an instant. It couldn't be gone. He jerked his pockets inside out, flinging items onto the threshold. Nothing.

Nausea tightened his stomach. How did he lose it? Where?

His teeth gritted together. He ripped his coat off and shook it. Nothing.

Agöri ran past. Something bounced from a chain on the child's neck, capturing the firelight and throwing it at Dunbar. "Agöri?" The child paused. "Could you come over here?"

Agöri ran up. "You look sick, like puke sick. You eat something bad? Oh no, we ate it too. We be puke sick too?"

Dunbar exhaled suddenly and began laughing. His chest heaved like he'd been running. There it was. He hadn't lost it.

"What's that?" Dunbar gestured to the ring. He tried not to sound like he was laughing.

A crooked grin stretched across the child's face. "I borrow it." The last half of the child's sentence spurted between giggles.

"With permission? It looks a little important to just…borrow." Dunbar gently took it off the child's neck.

A heavy sigh came from across the room. Dunbar looked up. His eyes met Vayorn's. The loneliness in that empty gaze stabbed Dunbar. Then the boy rolled his eyes, crossed his arms, and turned his back to Dunbar, acting as if he found everyone in the room stupid.

Finally, the fire died down, and the boys were asleep in the bunk bed at the end of the room. But Dunbar still sat in the doorway, unable to sleep.

"Dunbar!" Liesel frantically gripped Dunbar's hand. Her body shook. Dunbar swallowed his panic, but it rose up his throat again. The baby should've come out by now. It had been three hours. Liesel screamed. Another contraction wracked her frame. Her nails dug into Dunbar's wrist. He winced but kept quiet. The contraction ended. She was still for a moment. He tucked her hair behind her ear. Sweat drenched her forehead and body. Her bloodshot eyes darted around the room, their whites showing like a frightened animal's. Dunbar held his breath. She had to be alright. She'd given birth twice before. But maybe this time was different. Maybe something was wrong with the child. Maybe it was backward. Maybe its cord was wrapped around its neck. What if it came out dead? Dunbar held her as she tensed, and her shoulders jerked.

"Come, don't you want to catch your child?" the midwife said. Dunbar looked up. That meant it was almost over. What if he dropped the baby? He'd never done anything like catch a baby before. But he stood and went to the end of the bed.

Dunbar chuckled. He still remembered the warmth as Ivaylo slid out into his waiting arms. He still remembered the way Leisel caressed the baby's face, the small sounds Ivaylo made as he nursed for the first time. If only that time had lasted. If only they had always kept him. But on the other hand, perhaps it was for the best that the child was taken. At least that way, he didn't have to watch his mother struggle through nine years of imprisonment and another birth, before finally throwing up her hands and walking out. What the boy didn't know couldn't hurt him. At least Dunbar could preserve some respect for Liesel in the boy's mind if the boy never knew what kind of woman she was. As far as the boy would ever know, she was dead; unfaithfulness was something Dunbar could never accuse Liesel of, whether it was true or not. He loved her too much to say that.

A snore echoed from the bottom bunk; Dunbar stifled a laugh. Even as a baby, Vayorn's snores had been loud enough to wake the dead, so Dunbar had always joked with Liesel. Now it sounded like a sleeping dragon.

Dunbar looked down at the ground. It was funny, really, that the only name the older one thought he had was his baby nickname. A smile appeared on Dunbar's face for a split second. It had been Ivaylo's favorite sound to make. *Vayo* was everything's name. Food was *vayo*, nap was *vayo*, daddy was *vayo*, even the boys were *vayo*. So Leisel began affectionately calling the baby Vayorn, and the rest of the family followed suit.

Dunbar sighed. If only Liesel would return, permanently.

SOLDIERS

"Well, isn't this a fine catch." Janus leaned off his horse. Arple curled into herself, trying to be as small as possible. Why hadn't she just listened to Apran? Her palms clammed over. Reddish in the moonlight, Arple watched heat rising off the soldiers around her. It gradually faded to silver as it cooled, high in the trees. Rough debris blew against her skin from an immense man, standing just behind Janus. His tattoo-spattered neck glowed just slightly in the moonlight. A month's worth of filth and tobacco emanated from the man in a green haze. Arple almost wished it was day; sunlight hurt, but it was better than being able to see smells bouncing off the moon's beams.

Her gaze riveted to the green haze. A queasy feeling tumbled around her stomach. She set her mouth in a wobbly line, and her knuckles whitened around the reins as she willed herself to remain calm.

Her mind raced. Should she fight? Run? Well, fighting really wasn't an option. She avoided looking at the sword in Janus's hand. What did it feel like to be stabbed? She shuddered. Why resist? It would be pointless and probably get her killed.

Janus ran a hand along her horse's flank. "Fine animal," he muttered.

The horse shied away from his touch. Arple laid a hand on it and whispered, "Stay calm. We'll be alright. Everything will be alright…"

A frenzied hope entered her mind. Perhaps if she gave him the horse, he would let her go. It seemed like a fair trade. She began to get out of her saddle. If she just handed him the reins, turned, and ran, maybe he wouldn't catch her. Being lost was better than slavery. She couldn't fight, but she could run.

But what would Maria do? Arple paused. Maria would never run. Even with all the odds against her, she would fight. With her blade at Janus's throat, she would be threatening to run him through if he didn't move out of her way. It would be no idle threat either; Maria was scary when she was protecting her family—or herself. Arple groaned. Why couldn't she be more like Maria? So much for growing up. So much for being the brave, capable adult Uncle Ilmari called her. She was still the same scared little girl she had always been. She was nothing like Maria. She never would be. She would always be afraid. Uncle Ilmari lied. She couldn't take care of herself.

With one foot removed from a stirrup, she tried to speak. Her voice squeaked like a rusty door hinge. "I'll give you my horse. Just please, sir, don't hurt me." Her feet were on the ground now with her back turned partly away from the man. Maybe getting down was a bad idea. She was within range of his sword. Again, the thought crossed her mind. What did it feel like to be stabbed? Would she die right away? Suddenly, she saw Maria in her mind, dagger drawn, resisting Janus to the very last of her strength.

Arple laid a shaky hand on her dagger hilt. If Maria could fight, she could. But just as she drew her dagger, the tip of a sword hooked it, barely brushing the top of her hand. She looked down. It was gone. Before she had time to think, a sword tip swung down to her neck.

Her scream froze in her chest. It was over. They would leave her here, and Apran would find her perhaps hours later. Perhaps after the Madaraks found her. She tilted her chin away from the point.

"Ah, buy your life with a horse? Intelligent creature. Almost human." He turned to the smelly one.

"It thinks we want to trade, poor thing. Don't you think it's more practical to just take the horse and it?"

Arple's heart fought inside her chest, like the wings of a caged bird against bars. The trade was like a stupid joke. Of course, Janus didn't have to trade to get the horse; he could just take it.

A man grabbed her wrists and pinned her arms behind her back. He began forcing her forward.

"Janus!" Surprise filled her. Was that her voice? But it was so strong. "You know to whom you owe your life. I saved you." She dug her feet into the ground. "If you saved me, and then I had you enslaved? You would vow to kill me." The man twisted her arm. She tried to keep talking. "Don't do this. Don't risk it. Your life is at stake if you take me. Ahhh!" She dropped to the ground holding her arm. Feeling sick, she tried not to cry. Every time she bent her elbow, fire shot up her arm. A heavy boot slammed her to her stomach, weighing her to the ground.

A soldier spoke up, "Well, in that case, take'er. I'm just about sick of ol' Janus the troll."

Janus stiffened. He reached into one pocket and slowly turned to face the soldier. "Just about sick of me, ey? Well, they say every sickness has a cure." He drew his fist out of his pocket. Small bars of copper lined his knuckles. Arple winced as it sped toward the man.

A thud, and the man crumpled to the ground. Someone bent over him. Janus turned back to the man pinning Arple.

"Guard it. The master's wife wants a pet. We'll keep it with us till we join his majesty again."

Arple stiffened. Pet? It? As if she was an animal. Father would never stand for this, for her to become some rich lady's pet. She would be treated like a well-bred dog, fed, cared for, and humiliated. She knew all too well what happened when a Saynasaf was made a slave. Hadn't she already lost most of her friends to Xíran slavers?

The man yanked her up and began tying her wrists. She struggled. He threw her to the ground and tied her ankles. The men around her laughed. Antikish words flew around her, mixed with coarse jesting in Common Tongue. Her cheeks burned.

"throw 'er again. Maybe she'll bounce!"

"I'll catch 'er!"

Laughter rang out.

Someone came up beside Janus. He gestured to the figure of the man, still motionless on the ground.

"Dead?" Janus spoke as if he were just asking what time it was. Arple's jaw tightened. How dare he treat life and death so lightly.

The men were still jesting.

A bright flash of orange lit the night. The talking died down. Arple strained, trying to loosen the cords a little. The ropes dug into her skin.

Another flash. Her horse reared. Janus flew over her head and planted himself in the saddle. Webs dropped from the sky, tangling around the arms and legs of the men, trapping them like flies in a spiderweb. Janus dodged one. More fire. Screaming filled the air. Arple tried to free herself.

Flames leaped from tree to tree, surrounding them in a blazing wheel. Above them, a dark silhouette dived in circles.

Arple looked to her left. In the sudden light, she could see clearly.

A tear slowly formed in her eye.

The still form was so close she could almost touch it. He didn't even look like he was sixteen yet. Maybe closer to fourteen, or even twelve. The childish face was pale, with blood dried along its mouth. The chest was still and breathless. A waxlike sheen sat over the lifeless cheeks and forehead. A small sword hung around his waist, so clean it looked like he had never used it. Around his wrist hung a small leather bracelet with a tiny portrait on a chip of wood dangling from it. Arple looked closer. An old woman, her hair graying, her figure portly, a kindly smile across her face, shone from the picture. With the painful realization it must be the dead child's mother, Arple looked away. He was only a boy. And he was dead. Janus killed him. And Janus didn't even seem sorry. A mother would never see her child again. Arple suddenly saw a small grave on a hill outside her town and heard her mother's desperate wailing. She saw the infant face, sweet eyes forever closed, the little hands never to reach for things again, the little voice never to learn its first words.

"'tis a dragon!"

Arple's eyes focused. The fire was closer. Panic seized her. She was still tied. What if she couldn't get out? But Mother needed her. Mother couldn't lose another child. She writhed on the ground, franticly trying to pull her hands free.

"Dragons don't exi—"

"Don't tell me it's not one! I knows a dragon when I sees one!"

Janus slashed the web off himself. "All of you, run! Leave the creature to the beast!" He kicked his heels in, spurred the horse through the flames, and disappeared.

"Help! Someone, he—" Arple choked on the smoke and curled into a coughing ball, trying to breathe. A hot tongue leaped up, speeding toward her. The snap and crackle of pine needle burning rang out, almost under her ear. Orange light surrounded her, suddenly blotting out everything. She closed her eyes.

A web wrapped around her. Almost before she could blink, she was lying on the ground, outside the flames. Something shook the earth behind her. The rope around her wrists and ankles loosened.

"Mistress ride Apran. Much hurry!"

Relief filled her. Of course, it was Apran. What other creature threw webs and spouted fire? Feeling prickled back into her limbs as she staggered to her feet. She dragged herself onto his shell.

Her weary limbs sank against the icelike surface. The soft feathers fluffed against her fingers. She curled her hands shut. A web rose around her and secured her to Apran. As they rose, she went limp, still gasping for air. The din of soldiers faded.

The fire fell away from her as a gentle breeze rollicked around her head and wiped the traces of darkness and filth from her skin.

She idly stared at one of her hands. The smoke and scent of soldiers hung around it in red and green blotches. A dark gray circle surrounded it where the rope had been. Slowly, like a rag making a dirty window shine again, the wind began to make her pale skin glow. The healthy silver of cleanness glistened in the moonlight. A small trail of discolored air faded off her skin, till she was as spotless as if she had risen out of the ocean.

She lay against Apran's shell, almost asleep, still trying to wake her dulled senses. Far below her, she felt hooves and feet, thundering off into the trees.

Even thousands of feet in the air, Arple could still see heat rising from the forest. Something glowed golden. Something else wasn't really glowing, but a blue stream of heat came up off it like smoke.

The high sound of night birds made ripples in the air. A wolf's mournful howl made a circle pattern up into the sky.

Her back straightened. It was a perfect night, almost. If the moon were a little less bright, she could see even more. But it was better than a full moon. Full moons hid everything, not to mention their horrible heat. But anything was better than full sunlight. So by most standards, tonight was perfect.

She raised her arms out to her sides, winglike. The soft satin of a cool breeze wrapped around them like delicate cloth. A deep sigh escaped her. She was alive. She didn't know where they were going, but she was alive.

But the flames seared into her mind, something she would never forget: a child's lifeless form, helplessness, and death so near she could feel it.

It was over though. She was safe.

The air rushed against her side, propelled in great gusts. She turned her head. A dark shadow swept alongside them. Its wings were almost as wide as Apran was from nose to tail. The silken feathers glowed a gentle lavender over the deep gray of plumage and down. The regal head was held proudly upright, turning in complete circles as it hunted the forest floor. Its talons, tucked up into its underbelly, clenched and unclenched patiently. As the sky clouded over, Arple admired the designs along its back, now crystal clear. Triangular in shape, they spread from one wing to the other, lengthening to edge each feather on the tips of the wings. It rose into the sky, high above Arple. A feather floated down on the breeze. She leaned out and caught it.

It was soft, softer than it looked. Delicately, she fondled it and turned it around in her palm. She couldn't help but marvel at how lovely it was. She opened a small bag at her waist and placed the feather securely inside.

Apran soared lower. A shining band of light cut through the trees, splitting the forest in half. It was the Rzeka River. Arple sighed. Especially from up high, it was so beautiful. How cold it must be, how clean. Moving water was never dirty. At this time of night, it would be perfect. Just a short swim, surely they had time for that. It wouldn't take long, and the moon was gone now; shriveling would be quick and near painless. Arple could almost feel the water against her scales, against her fin.

Suddenly, her dream crossed her mind. "Do you know what direction Vayorn went?" Her voice shook.

"Better! Know place! Apran much search till he find smell in cottage!"

Arple nodded, not daring to hope. Smell. What if Apran was tracking the wrong scent? Any person could smell like Vayorn. What if Apran led them to a total stranger? By then, Vayorn's trail would be cold, almost untraceable. And there would be nothing left of him. The Madaraks and wolves would see to that. She was too late. By now Vayorn was long dead.

Something hot rolled down her cheeks. She raised a hand to her face. Tears poured over it. How long had she been crying? Now she realized her chest was heaving. Suddenly aware of how sore she was, a small moan parted her lips. Her wrists and ankles burned. The bruise on her back ached. Her arm throbbed. Every muscle in her body sagged, unable to hold her upright. She dropped her head into Apran's feathers.

The dead child flared up in her mind again. No one cared, not even enough to bury him properly. And they were just going to let her die too.

Vayorn was dead. If only he had listened to her.

Her shoulders shook. The world was so cruel. Why couldn't she have stayed a child?

Her eyes closed. She fell asleep.

STONES

Demetrius leaned back in his chair. His head reeled. The empty tankard in his hand swirled.

"Barmaid!"

A girl ran up.

"Fill-thiz-gain." He paused. Her face…

Her eyes turned black. She grew about three inches, and wrinkles appeared beside her eyes. Her voice began to change. Suddenly, she was Mother. There he was again, the high walls of the ballroom rising around him. Dunbar waltzed by, so graceful, with a giggling girl on his shoulder. Demetrius turned to his partner and tried to smile. She looked away, curling her nose in disgust. Their feet tangled. Demetrius tried to move his feet, stumbled, and fell into the girl. She dropped to the ground. He offered her his hand.

As if he was offering her poison, she hit it away and stood. They resumed the dancing position. The bare tips of her fingers hovered in Demetrius's palm, as if she was afraid to give him her whole hand.

"Demetrius! How do you suppose to learn standing around like that? Idiot! Move your legs. Right, left. No! Left, clumsy ox!" Mother came over, her large frame shaking with each step, like a walrus on land.

Demetrius looked down, trying to watch his feet. Wasn't it already enough that she thought he was stupid? Why did he have to learn dancing anyway? It wasn't like he would ever dance when he was an adult; all the girls liked Dunbar, not him. So what was the point? He could hear Father in the other room, arguing with Lord Faron, his adviser. Demetrius gritted his teeth. What he wouldn't give to be in there, instead of out here with stupid Dunbar. Why did Mother make him be around Dunbar anyway? If she'd just drop insisting on Demetrius's dancing, he wouldn't have to be around little Goody Two-boots at all.

"Right! Left! Stupid donkey!" Mother grabbed him by the shoulder and pulled his head up by his hair. "You don't look at your feet when you dance. Look at her."

Demetrius raised his head to meet the girl's frown. She shuddered and looked like she wanted to vomit. He tripped.

"Stupid! You ugly, weak meedchen of a son! I'm ashamed of you!"

Demetrius stiffened. He knew what would happen. His mother would call Dunbar. Soon, the only person dancing with the girls would be Dunbar. And Demetrius? Forgotten as usual. Dunbar would show off "proper" dancing, and Demetrius would be ridiculed, if they remembered he existed at all.

His fist balled. No. Not this time.

He turned to Mother. She began to summon Dunbar over.

Demetrius pulled back his fist. One blow to the temple. That's all it would take to end this nightmare. He screamed. Mother turned.

He swung.

The maidservant fell to the floor at Demetrius's feet.

He blinked rapidly, confused. Where was Mother? Where'd Dunbar go? Soldiers sat on benches and stools all around him, fuzzy outlines, almost as if the room was full of smoke. Demetrius stared blankly. A sick feeling punched him in the gut. He hadn't imagined it all, had he? He flew up. The table overturned. Ale sloshed across the floor. His bench broke in half against the edge of the next table. His heart pounded in his head, so loud it was the only thing he could hear. He tried to walk to the door. No matter where he pointed himself, something was in his way. His shins knocked against a bench. He stumbled against a tall person.

Someone grabbed him by the back of the collar and one arm and dragged him out the door. Vaguely he saw the water trough in front of him.

A firm hand on his neck shoved his head underwater. He struggled. "I'm fine! I'm—" Another heavy shove. "Stop—" His mouth filled with water. He began shivering. "I'm sober, alri—" His ears rang as water rushed around them again.

Finally, the person stopped. Demetrius took a shaky breath. His mind cleared. He ran his hands through his hair, staring at the mess all over his shirt. Was that vomit? Why was there blood on his sleeves? What happened? He sank back on his heels. If he didn't hit Mother, who did he hit? The girl? The men thought he was insane. Maybe he was. A shiver ran down his spine. Insane.

Someone cleared her throat behind him. He turned. Laparlana was drying her hands on a towel. "Had enough to drink yet?" Her caustic tone stung.

Demetrius hung his head. "Didn't mean to get so drunk."

"The girl is injured. Why did you hit her?" Laparlana stared at the ground.

Demetrius shrugged. He couldn't explain what happened. She couldn't expect him to. And even if he tried, there was no way she would understand.

He laid a hand on her arm. "I'm sorry, alright? I won't do it again."

She shook him off. "You said that last time too. And the time before that. And the time before that."

"This time I mean it."

"Sure, you do." Laparlana yanked Demetrius to his feet, threw the towel in his face, and walked away.

Demetrius slumped on the edge of the trough. What happened to him? Fear wrapped around him like the skeletal arms of a dead tree. What if it happened but next time, he accidentally hit Laparlana? What if there was a knife in his hand next time? What if it happened while he was holding their child? He bent his head into his lap.

His chest tightened. He tried to fight the images crossing his mind. Almost like a fever dream, they were too real to be mere fears.

They were more like premonitions. His wife, lying on the floor in a broken heap, perhaps injured, perhaps killed. His child running from him, afraid. The pressure inside his head built. His chest constricted till he wanted to scream.

Something ripped into his leg. He looked down. His hands, curling till they looked like claws, had ripped through his pants. As he lifted them up, five raw scratches throbbed on his right leg.

A groan escaped his chest. All this time, he'd been protecting Laparlana from Vayorn. But the real danger had been so close to her, so close to her child, so close to him. The real danger was him. He clawed his leg again. It was one thing to protect her from others, but how did he protect her from himself?

He stood, seized a rock, and threw it as far as he could. Something bellowed. He threw another rock. It screamed again. The door opened. The screaming continued.

"Fangar? You're screaming. Is everything alright? Why are you still screaming?"

Demetrius turned to face the person in the doorway, a stone in each hand. The screaming rose to a howl. His chest ached. His breath became short.

The person backed away, turned, and ran.

A SILVER DAGGER

Vayorn sank to the ground. His sword and sword belt lay against the log behind him, dull-colored now that the sun had left the sky. Dunbar and Agöri would be back any minute. They'd been gone for hours.

Vayorn stared at the edges of the clearing. The trees were just beginning to turn light lavender. *How is dusk so beautiful? Never noticed it before.* He smiled slightly. *Maybe it's because every other dusk, I've been running from something.* He looked at his shoes. Muck and dirt caked their edges. His legs ached. *Gach, I'm tired. Wish I'd gotten better sooner. Four days in bed sure didn't do me any favors.* He observed the thick scar along his arm again. *Whatever he gave me, sure healed me quick.* His tongue tingled just remembering the stuff. It was like vinegar, but yellow and faintly skunky. *At least it did the trick. I'm out of bed.* He looked behind them. Even with a whole day's travel, the forest looked exactly the same as outside the cottage.

Dunbar and Agöri were close now; Vayorn could hear Agöri. Almost silently, he chuckled. *Gotta be the loudest thing on the lower continent.* He folded his legs, leaned back against a log, and surveyed his work. *Not bad.* The fire was roaring, and he'd managed to drag a few fallen trees over to sit against. His stomach growled. *Hope they got something.*

Suddenly, Agöri tumbled onto the log beside Vayorn. Dunbar came around to the other side of the fire.

"Did good, sonny." Dunbar sat down with a small groan and rubbed his lower back. "Not twenty anymore, I guess. Better start sending you young people to find food." He chuckled.

"Find anything?" Vayorn asked.

A smile pushed up the wrinkles by Dunbar's eyes. "Know how to skin a pheasant?" He pulled four plump birds out of his hunting bag. Vayorn nodded. As they worked, Vayorn kept the corner of his eye on Agöri. *Look away for three seconds, and he's up a tree or down a badger hole or who-knows-where.* He realized he was smiling. His mouth drooped to a neutral expression. Weak.

Dunbar's other bag was lying by a log, partway opened, across the fire from them. Dunbar's back was turned to it.

Slowly, Agöri sneaked over to the bag and began digging. Vayorn decided to ignore him. *Technically, he's not my responsibility. Not like he's actually my brother. But he'd better not steal anything.* Vayorn pinched his lips together. *I was never as bad as he is when I was little.*

Time seemed to creep by as the fire slowly got brighter. It was warm against the side of Vayorn's neck. He realized he wasn't worrying about anything. *Should be worrying. Who knows when Demetrius'll catch up with us.* But for some reason, it didn't feel as concerning as Vayorn thought it should. He was breathing easily, almost not paying attention to the bird he was cutting. Beside him, he heard Dunbar working through his two birds. What felt different about him? Maybe it was just that he was kind? No. Ilmari was kind. *But didn't feel the way Dunbar does.* The closest thing he could compare it to was sitting in front of a fire with Badurad: familiar, safe. The way he imagined a family would feel, with brothers and a father. He sighed. *Good old Bad'rad. Maybe should've taken him with me. Things were getting bad. How come I haven't thought of him for so long? Miss him. What if Demetrius sold the outdwellers?* He knew Demetrius was talking about "purging" the outdweller section just before he left. His fist balled. *If he did, he's as good as dead.* Vayorn quietly examined his knife. *Wouldn't take much bigger knife than this. Just a quick stab. Deng, could even hide one this size in my sleeve.* He exhaled. How did someone get like Demetrius? He had heard stories of Demetrius being young, handsome even, but those stories were the same as

Father's stories: fables. *He's always gonna be a skin-and-bones monster in my mind.*

Dunbar handed him a pair of sharpened sticks to spit the finished birds on.

Vayorn toyed with the knife. "Can I keep this?"

Dunbar nodded. Vayorn spitted his birds and laid them with Dunbar's.

As they sizzled over the fire, Vayorn folded his arms on top of his knees and rested his head in them. *Almost like being asleep. Can't remember being this happy, ever.* He sighed. The meat smelled so good. Something aromatic drifted from off the birds. Vayorn watched small pinches of spices fall from Dunbar's fingers. Sage, garlic, onions… He caught his breath. *It's Mama Yanya's recipe.* The back of his throat began to ache. He closed his eyes and tried to block out the memories.

Remembering hurt too much. *Stupid.* He looked at Agöri. *Someday, he's gonna die too, and you're not gonna be able to help him either. That's why you don't get attached to people. You're better off alone. You don't need parents. You don't need siblings.*

He stared at the flames, not really listening to Dunbar and Agöri's chatter. Time seemed to slow its pace too, as if it was enjoying the quiet as much as they were. Vayorn imagined shapes in the flames. If he looked closely, they almost looked like a palace. His palace. *No slaves, just paid help. Won't pay with money. Land, food perhaps. Lodging maybe. Don't want to live anywhere near Tarshal. Ever. Maybe build in Nacion. Or conquer a palace. Heard it's pretty over there, not too cold, not too hot, lots of land.*

Dunbar's voice interrupted his daydreaming. "Agöri, child? What have you got in your pockets? It's odd, but my bag's half empty. Imagine that."

Vayorn looked up. Agöri was falling off a log laughing, his pockets and shirt bulging. How did he do it? He rubbed his temples. Five minutes. He couldn't behave for five minutes? He stood and waved Agöri over to him. Dunbar followed.

"Okay, what did you steal?" Vayorn realized he sounded like Demetrius did when he gave a scolding. He changed his tone.

"Just give it all back, okay?"

"Might have something, might not," Agöri said. His smile seemed to reach his ears.

Vayorn groaned and began emptying Agöri's pockets. *Five minutes peace. Can't he just sit—calmly—for five minutes? But no, he just has to steal, from the one person who hasn't tried to kill us. Real clever, Agöri, real clever.*

Agöri protested, "Only borrow!" Vayorn kept emptying the filled pockets. "Give back!" Vayorn moved a handful of items out of Agöri's reach. "Pretty!" Agöri jumped after Vayorn's hand.

Behind him, Vayorn could hear Dunbar belly-laughing.

Something struck him about Dunbar's laughter; it was kind. He wasn't making fun of Agöri. He was just genuinely amused. *Genuine.* That was the word. *How's he so kind all the time? Deng. Really do wish he was my father.*

Agöri kept yelling, "No!" Vayorn grabbed another handful of items. "That mine now!" Vayorn tossed a golden cup to Dunbar before Agöri could grab it again. "Stop it!" Vayorn pulled Agöri away from the pile growing on the ground. "Shiny!" Agöri dived after another item. Vayorn caught him and removed one final bag from Agöri's pocket. "Uh-oh!"

Agöri grinned sheepishly as Vayorn held up the money pouch.

"Umm, only borrow?" Agöri smiled. Vayorn sighed and handed it to the breathless Dunbar, laughing so hard now tears were rolling down his cheeks.

"You…little…thief! Come here!" Dunbar gasped between roars. A tingle ran up Vayorn's spine. That laugh. He had heard it before, somewhere. *It was familiar. Where've I heard that laugh? Do I know him?* His smile faded. *Why is he so familiar?* The dozens of guests Demetrius brought into the palace crossed Vayorn's mind. *Was that where I saw him?*

What if he's taking us to Demetrius? He turned away from Dunbar and, without thinking about it, laid a hand on the knife, now stowed safely in a small leather scabbard on his left forearm.

He watched Dunbar pull Agöri over and ruffle Agöri's hair playfully.

"You, little child, are something else," Dunbar said.

"What else?" Agöri cocked his head.

Dunbar started laughing again.

Vayorn explained. "It's a figure of speech."

A confused look crossed Agöri's face. Vayorn tried not to seem troubled, but the nagging doubt stayed at the back of his mind. Could he trust Dunbar?

The rest of the evening passed slowly. The night lost its beauty. The fire didn't seem comforting anymore. Vayorn tried to be civil, but Dunbar's niceness was aggravating, and Agöri's antics were just annoying. By the end of supper, neither of them were talking to him.

Late that night, the fire dwindled to embers, and the sounds of deep sleep rose from Agöri and Dunbar, but Vayorn still sat up. *Deng. Everything stays away from me tonight, including sleep.* His eyes burned. He drew the small knife and fingered it in the dark, running his hand along the pointed silver blade and the small handle. Useful. The handle fit in his palm perfectly, as if it was made for his grip. It was light and practical, the most perfect weapon for assassination Vayorn could think of. *Dunbar uses these to skin birds?* He shook his head. A shaft of moonlight suddenly broke through the clouds and hit the blade. It seemed to glow. Vayorn stared at it. It was perfect. A smile began to form on Vayorn's lips. He imagined pummeling his old master to the ground, pinning him, and then performing the final act of revenge. He sighed, already anticipating the satisfaction he would feel. A silver dagger for a copper one. Seemed like a fair trade. All it would take is a quick jab to the neck in the middle of the night. And he'd be dead.

"Someday, Demetrius, I'll dance on your dead body," he realized he was thinking out loud. He glanced over at Dunbar and Agöri. Still, their backs heaved with deep, slumbering breaths. He leaned back against the log and stared at the slowly appearing sky above him, still toying with the dagger.

THE EMPTY HUT

Arple sank to the ground. It was his. The sleeve was torn and bloody; perhaps her dream had been partly right. But he was alive. Apran had already found his trail. That meant someone had rescued him. She turned the sleeve in her hand. Maybe, if he was close, she could still feel him. She held it away from the light, near the darkest corner of the room. Gradually, the edges began to glow red. She closed her eyes. It began to feel warm in her hands. The noises around her intensified. She pushed her ears past the walls around her. For an instant, the walls constricted like a tight shoe then suddenly gave way. Something dark and heavy in the east weighed down on her. A storm? How different they felt on land. To the west, the land shook lightly, like the surface of water when birds land on it. She heard light footsteps: deer. But no matter how hard she listened, nothing sounded or felt like humans. In a sense, it was relieving. That meant the soldiers were long gone. But it was also frightening. Vayorn was too far away to feel. Anything could be happening to him.

She opened her eyes. The room felt darker than it had earlier. Was something near? Or perhaps it was merely that the sun had changed positions. She rose and stood in the doorway.

A heavy east wind folded her in its arms.

Turning to face east, she stared at a black wall, slowly forming like the ranks of an immense army, already covering half the sky.

About a mile off, she could feel rain hitting the leaves and forest floor. The air rushed deep into her lungs as she filled them. Her skin tingled, almost as if she was in water. The air seemed to pulse with heat, as if the center of the storm was a great black furnace, boiling over onto the land below. A sharp line split the hills under the storm's edge, where one side was golden in the afternoon light and the other was dark black, as if the sun no longer existed.

Apran wasn't close. Arple didn't hear him. But maybe that was because he wasn't flying. He was probably going to wait out the storm. She found herself wishing he would hurry up. If he got hurt again, she would never know.

This morning, she didn't think he was well enough to carry her, but he insisted. They had been laid up for four days, but Arple thought it should have been at least six; getting attacked by a giant eagle was no joke. Apran wasn't fully recovered, but he could fly short distances if he rested frequently. It made for slow traveling; the trip to the hut should have only taken an hour. It took all day.

And now Apran was out there, still injured, determined to track Vayorn.

Arple wrapped her arms around herself, shuddering. Somehow, being attacked by a giant eagle was worse than being attacked by soldiers. Giant eagles hunted for sport, or so Uncle Ilmari had always told her. Now she believed it. It could have gone after any other creature, but it stalked her and Apran for an entire day. Finally, at sunset, it attacked.

Arple closed her eyes. Someone was coming.

She backed inside the hut. Maybe they hadn't seen her yet. The hut looked abandoned; there was no good reason for them to come in. She sank into the darkest corner of the room, behind a waist-high pile of clay pots and dishes. As if she was picking up a rat, she pinched a dirty shirt between two fingers and flung it away from her. Her nose curled. It was amazing, the level of filth some people could stand. From her hiding place, she could see the whole hut.

Disheveled furniture lay at haphazard angles around the room, covered in dirt, old bits of food, and greenish stains. Arple grimaced. The smell of vomit was strong in the air.

No matter where she looked, nothing was even close to tidy. if a woman had lived here, it would have at least been organized, even if it was filthy. The thought was comforting; it meant Vayorn didn't have an opportunity to fall in love with someone else while he was here.

She turned her head to the left. A small window let in the wind. Trying to be quiet, she moved a foot. Maybe she could close it; if it was open, whatever was out there could see inside. A pebble rolled under her foot. She winced. Too loud. Besides, there was no door, so closing the window wouldn't be any use.

The person outside was getting closer. She lay flat on the ground. Now it was so close she could feel its breathing. She closed her eyes. Was that a second heartbeat? Trying to be as small as possible, she shrank behind the pile. It came closer.

Something landed beside the first thing and entered the hut. The floor vibrated under its feet. Arple looked up. It was coming right toward her hiding spot.

She sprang to her feet and backed away.

Her foot tangled in the pile. She spun, flew backward, skidded into the mound, and found herself face up on a pile of broken dishes.

Someone grabbed her. She screamed. Was it soldiers? Bandits? Slavers? She picked up a pot. It was close enough to hit now. Her arm rose and swung down, angling the pot for the thing's head. It ducked. She swung again. A strong hand gripped her wrist. She seized another pot.

"Child! It's me."

She paused. Recognition released the tension in her muscles. The pots crashed to the ground.

"Uncle Ilmari!" She hugged him.

"Little one, what's happened to you? Your heart is racing." He lifted one of her wrists and examined the scratches from the eagle's talons. "What happened?"

"What are you doing here? How did you find me? Oh, I'm so glad you're here." Arple realized she was crying.

"Child, child. It's alright. Just breathe." He sniffed. "You smell like smoke. What happened?"

As quickly as she could, Arple told him about the last four days. She told him about her dream, the soldiers, the dead child, the fire, and Apran rescuing her. She told him about the eagle, being grounded as Apran healed, and how Apran was still gone. She spoke rapidly, and Uncle Ilmari had to ask her to speak slower several times. By the end, she was panting. "How did you get here so quickly?" Arple asked.

"Apran's not the only Varul who can carry humans. Alcaeus brought me."

"Alcaeus?"

Something barked behind her. A Varul twice Apran's size squished its head through the narrow doorway.

"Alcaeus," it said, "is pleased to meet master niece. He already greeted other Varul. Other Varul found trail. Alcaeus thinks we should follow Apran. Come?"

BLACK DOG TAVERN

"Well, better wake Vayorn up. Sun's about to rise." Dunbar stirred the fire back into life. He stretched his back, trying to loosen the knots in it. He winced. The young ones didn't know how lucky they were to be young. They'd traveled for two days, but neither of the boys had complained once about sleeping on the ground. It was amazing how resilient children were.

A few minutes passed. He heard Agöri rummaging through his bag again. He turned. Agöri was wearing a small metal bucket over his head; it was so large all Dunbar could see was Agöri's neck. Suddenly, a small "aha" came from inside the bucket, and Agöri pulled it off. Dunbar watched him look from the bucket, to Vayorn, then back to the bucket. Pretending he wasn't watching, Dunbar folded his cloak, still keeping an eye on Agöri.

Agöri tiptoed over to Vayorn and slid the bucket on top of Vayorn's head, so softly Vayorn didn't stir.

Giggling, Agöri ran off. He came back a few seconds later with a stick, trying so hard not to laugh his face was red. Dunbar could see his shoulders shaking as a few giggles escaped.

Agöri raised the stick high above his head. Dunbar choked back a chuckle as he caught the look in Agöri's eyes. They shone as if he was absolutely thrilled with himself.

Dunbar stifled another laugh as Agöri swung it down on the bucket with a resounding *bang!*

Vayorn flew up, swearing. The bucket sailed across the campsite and barely missed Dunbar. Vayorn threw his shoe at Agöri. Agöri ducked it and slid behind Dunbar.

Still swearing, Vayorn rubbed his head.

"Agöri, what time is it? Ah, think you gave me a migraine…," he muttered.

"Wake-up time!" Agöri fell on the ground giggling. Laughing so hard it hurt, Dunbar held his sides. This was going to be a good day.

*****

Vayorn stared at the sign. Was it just his mind, or was that a shadow above him? In the dim torchlight, he thought he could make out two red eyes if he stared hard enough. The hair on the back of his neck prickled. He turned away, trying to convince himself he was just imagining it. A shiver ran up his spine. As much he concentrated on Dunbar and Agöri, he could still feel its eyes on him. *How do you know you're not imagining it?*

The sign swung wildly. Vayorn jumped. The shadow was gone. He tried to reason with his hammering heart, but every sound made his skin crawl, even Agöri's breathing. Just the wind. *What's wrong with me? Just my imagination. Probably the shadows from Dunbar's torch.*

Something brushed Vayorn's neck. He yelped. Dunbar turned and gave him a funny look. "Anything the matter?"

Vayorn's hands were clammy. He shook his head. *Just an animal. Probably a bat or something.* He lifted one sleeve a little, then the other. Goose bumps covered his arms.

Pretending he was cold, he wrapped them around himself. *Deng. There's not even wind. Too quiet.*

He shivered. *Some inn. Looks like a jail. Why's Dunbar taking us here? What's wrong with sleeping outside?* He studied the building. Most inns were welcoming, but this one looked more like it was built to keep people out than bring people in. The large door was studded with iron and barred till it looked like a solid sheet of metal. *Good luck to anyone trying to get through that thing.* A small slit at eye level was covered with wood, like the peephole of a dungeon door. There was only one window, barely the width of Vayorn's head. A knot tightened in the pit of his stomach. *Why don't I hear anything? No inn's that quiet.* Sometimes a faint sound came from behind the door, but it was so vague Vayorn was almost sure he was imagining it.

Looks like a prison. Like a sudden blow to the back of the head, a thought struck him. It did look like a prison. Too much like a prison. His eyes widened and darted from Dunbar to the building and back again. A sick feeling twisted his stomach. *He's selling us out.* Vayorn's fist balled. *Deng, I should've gone with my gut feeling. Knew he was too nice.*

He slid his hand up into his sleeve and fingered the dagger.

Whatever I have to do, won't be a slave again. Better off dead.

As he shifted his weight from one leg to the other, something tapped his hip. He looked down. The sword swinging from his scabbard caught the light. Slowly, he moved his hand to rest on the hilt, with his eyes still glued to Dunbar as if he were staring at a snake.

I'll kill him if I have to. He glanced into the darkness behind them. *What if I grab Agöri and run? Can we get away before Dunbar calls soldiers? If we do get away, where do we go?* The scar along his forearm throbbed. *What if those terror-bird things come again? They'll kill us.* His head snapped back to Dunbar. The copper dagger glinted in his mind. *Can't stay here either. Have to get out. We'll die either way. Least if we run, we'll die free.*

Dunbar's fist rang out against the door. *Bang! Bang! Bang!* Something shuffled inside. *Too late now. Need to buy time.* He laid a hand on Agöri's shoulder and loosened his sword. *If I stab Dunbar, he can't call soldiers. We'll have time to run.* Vayorn drew his sword, wincing as the metal ground against the sheath. He peered up, expecting to feel Dunbar's sword against his throat. But Dunbar's back was still turned. Agöri tried to say something. Vayorn pinched him. Someone inside was talking. *Gach! Running out of time.*

He raised his sword, picked a spot on Dunbar's back, and lunged. Dunbar sidestepped and seized Vayorn's wrist around the joint. Vayorn struggled. His teeth clenched as Dunbar dug his fingers steadily into the soft spot on the inside of Vayorn's wrist. Vayorn's grip on the sword began to loosen. With a cry, he opened his hand. The sword hit the ground. His wrist throbbed. He kicked Dunbar, turned, and ran. Someone tackled him to the ground. His head hit something, and his vision blurred.

He opened his eyes. *What happened?* He realized Dunbar was behind him, pinning his arms.

"What do you think you're doing?" Dunbar shook him lightly.

"Let go!" Vayorn wrenched out of Dunbar's grip and stood in the shadows by the door.

"What's going on?" Dunbar asked. Vayorn tensed. *Why'd I do that? What if he kills me? Should've run when I had the chance.*

He closed his eyes. *What does it feel like to die? Wish he'd just kill me already. Maybe I'll die right away. Probably not.* It wasn't likely. He'd seen enough executions to know a person didn't die when they were stabbed; they began dying. But unless someone ended their misery, they lay on the ground in agony, slowly bleeding out. There was a screech as Dunbar drew his sword. Vayorn pressed his back against the wall. A few minutes passed in silence. Then he realized something; he was still on his feet. He opened one eye. Dunbar was standing in front of him. Vayorn opened both eyes as he looked down. Dunbar's sword lay on top of his own, on the ground, and Dunbar's hands were empty. Vayorn let out a sigh he didn't realize he'd been holding. *He's not going to kill me? Why?*

Vayorn shook his head. *Don't understand.*

Dunbar laid a hand on Vayorn's shoulder. "It's alright. I won't hurt you. I promise."

Shouldn't believe him. Why do I believe him? Vayorn avoided Dunbar's gaze. For the first time in years, he couldn't force himself to look angry. Weak.

Dunbar looked away. Vayorn composed himself. *Why'd I let myself do that? Now he thinks I'm weak.*

Dunbar knocked on the door again. They waited.

The slot opened. Vayorn blinked as a ray of light blinded him. When his eyes adjusted, he saw a small lantern hovering next to a pair of eyes in the opening.

"Business?" the voice on the other side of the door said. Vayorn gritted his teeth. *Sounds like a grindstone. Least he speaks Common Tongue.*

Dunbar stepped in front of Vayorn and Agöri. "Travelers on business. We need food and lodging."

Even with a door between them, Vayorn could sense scorn in the other man's tone. "A man and two children on business? *Ja pierdolę!* Only foolish men lie to Adrean. That's me! How I know you not be Xiran or Antikish slaver, eh? How I know children aren't slaves?"

So it isn't a prison after all. Just a stupid innkeeper. What the gach was wrong with me? Dunbar's had plenty of chances to run me through. But he hasn't. I gave him the perfect reason to. But he didn't. Why can't I trust him? If he wanted to kill me, he could've killed me long before now. Don't really have to reason to not trust him at this point.

Vayorn spoke up, still avoiding Dunbar. "He's our father. Squirt over here just started his apprenticeship to me and Dad. I've been half partner for about a year now. Started when I was nine. Satisfy you?"

"Name this family trade," the innkeeper pried.

Vayorn opened and closed his mouth several times. *What do I say?*

Dunbar answered, "I and my sons are apothecaries. We're traveling up to the high country to complete the older one's training and begin the little one's."

"Why high country?"

"Because if they're going to be any good as healers, they need to learn to survive and find food when there's not a town nearby."

"Prove this story."

"See, here are my tools." Dunbar held up a bag. *Same stuff he used to heal me. Is he an apothecary for real?*

"Sadly, I cannot buy food with medicine. If your sons want to learn survival, stay in woods." The slot began to close.

"Wait!" Dunbar rested his hand in it.

"Move fingers or I chop off!" The man waved a butcher knife threateningly in front of the opening. Vayorn winced. Great.

He's never gonna let us in.

Dunbar removed his hand. "Alright. I don't suppose you need gold all that bad anyway." He bounced his money bag from one hand to the other, right in front of the opening. The coins jangled musically against each other. Dunbar turned and gestured to Vayorn and Agöri to pretend they were leaving.

The door flew open. "Gold, did you say? We don't see much of that coin 'round here. Show Adrean."

Dunbar held out a palmful of coins, moving his hand so they would catch the light. Vayorn heard a sharp intake of breath from the black shape in the doorway.

"Please, enter, welcome to the Black Dog Tavern." The innkeeper stepped aside to let them in. Vayorn followed Dunbar inside, still feeling ashamed. *I tried to attack him? What's wrong with me? He should've killed me.*

Something stirred in the corner of the room. A low voice whispered, "Get Janus." Vayorn didn't hear it.

MIDNIGHT

Dunbar leaned against the wall. The room was silent, almost tomb-like. He looked down at Ivaylo. The boys had been asleep for hours, but Dunbar was still awake. He sighed. The last time he'd felt like this was the night Leisel left. A small smile tried to flicker to life on his face. Ah, Liesel. What would she think of their sons? She would be pleased with Agöri, and a night ago, Dunbar thought she would be pleased with Ivaylo too. But not after tonight. Dunbar looked down.

Ivaylo's face was peaceful—so peaceful it was almost unrecognizable. Dunbar shook his head. Somehow, Ivaylo could do what he did and still sleep.

Dunbar tried to understand his son, but after tonight, he didn't want to. The look in the boy's eyes outside the inn—Dunbar had seen it before. He kicked a pile of rags. Ivaylo should have been Demetrius's son; he was more like Demetrius than he would ever be like Dunbar. If only Ivaylo were less of a disappointment. And the close call only made the feeling worse. Ivaylo was nothing like the firstborn Dunbar had dreamed of. If Ivaylo looked a little more like Leisel, or Father, perhaps that would compensate. Perhaps that would make his strange behavior more excusable. Dunbar shuddered. It would seem more understandable if Dunbar had done something to frighten the boy, but he hadn't. He couldn't remember saying one thing that was even remotely threatening.

The moonlight glinted off their swords, hidden underneath Dunbar's bag. Did the boy actually mean to kill him? Dunbar didn't want to believe it, any more than he wanted to believe Demetrius was capable of betrayal. But like it was with Demetrius, every excuse Dunbar made for Ivaylo seemed shallow.

Dunbar didn't know how long Ivaylo had been planning to attack him; it seemed like a spur-of-the-moment mistake, but he couldn't be sure. What if the boy had tried it while Dunbar was asleep? Dunbar winced. Perhaps it was merely an accident. Ivaylo seemed ashamed after it, but he could just be pretending.

Dunbar sank to the ground. He'd expected the boy to be rough, mean even, but dangerous? He sighed. Always too late. How did he not see it? Over the past few days, Ivaylo's evasive attitude had been annoying, but it never once crossed Dunbar's mind that he could actually be dangerous. After the first day, Dunbar chalked the boy's strange behavior up to adolescence. After all, most boys went through a rough stage. It was normal. But now, looking back, Dunbar realized it wasn't so normal. Even at his worst, Dunbar never acted the way Ivaylo did. He shook his head.

Blind. The same way he'd been blind to the truth about Leisel.

No matter what Ivaylo did, he struck Dunbar as inadequate; was it really so hard to make civil conversation? Apparently, Ivaylo thought so. When he did break his silence, he swore or said something so crass it wasn't funny, even when he seemed like he was a good mood. But most of the time, he just sat there with that glare on his face, not saying a word. Sometimes, it felt like he wasn't even listening. Dunbar groaned. Ivaylo was too much like Demetrius.

He slipped over to Ivaylo and looked down. The boy was sleeping with the knife in his hand. Slowly, Dunbar bent closer. Perhaps, if he was quiet enough, he could take it. Last night, he'd regretted giving it to the boy, even before they'd finished eating, but now he couldn't sleep until he knew Ivaylo didn't have a weapon. When Ivaylo had asked to keep it last night, Dunbar hadn't thought anything of it; it was a nice knife. Most boys would give their right arm to own something like that. So once again believing Ivaylo was no different from himself as a boy, Dunbar gave it to him. When he handed it over to

Ivaylo, he'd expected Ivaylo to act like any other boy: admire it a little, say thank you, maybe try the blade against a piece of wood. But that wasn't what Ivaylo did.

Dunbar tried not to stare, but there was something disturbing about the way Ivaylo handled the knife, when he thought no one was looking. The sick fascination in the boy's eyes as he stared at the blade, it wasn't healthy. Dunbar pounded his fist against the wall. How had he been so blind? He'd seen the look in Ivaylo's eyes, the way they seemed to darken. It was almost as if Ivaylo was transformed into Demetrius. His smile was almost insane, a look Dunbar had only ever seen in one other person. But still, Dunbar ignored the way it made his skin crawl.

He began removing the knife from the boy's hand.

Ivaylo's eyes shot open. Dunbar jolted.

"It's okay. Take it. I'm not asleep yet." Ivaylo's voice was changed—so changed it could've come from a different person entirely. Suddenly, he didn't seem dangerous anymore. Dunbar stared at the tear tracks on the boy's cheeks. Carefully, he touched Ivaylo's shoulder. Would Ivaylo get angry? Blow up or, seemingly impossible, speak to Dunbar?

Ivaylo sat up.

The look in the boy's eyes was like the look in a lost child's: hurt, scared, pleading, but not angry. Dunbar rose to go.

Ivaylo started to say something then stopped. Dunbar paused.

It almost seemed like the boy wanted him to stay. He set the knife on the ground and sat. "You alright?"

Ivaylo took a deep breath. His face clouded over. Dunbar tensed. Maybe that was the wrong question.

A few minutes passed. Dunbar watched Ivaylo's face contort somewhere between rage and panic. The boy's back was rigid, and Dunbar watched his clenched fists warily. Dunbar inched away as he began to get up.

Ivaylo dropped to the ground, back slumped, eyes closed. "No," he whispered, "I'm not."

Dunbar nodded, about to prompt Ivaylo to keep talking.

The door flew open.

THE BROKEN WINDOW

The door flew open. The knife clattered on the floor as Dunbar dropped it and sprang for his bag. Vayorn crawled his fingers toward the handle.

"Show yourself!" Dunbar said; his back tensed. Something was coming through the doorway. Vayorn's fingers closed around the knife. He sheathed it and scrambled to his feet. Agöri sat up. His voice was sleepy. "What going—"

"You will come with us quietly. No fighting, or there will be consequences. I place you all under arrest in the name of Fangar Demetrius."

Dunbar backed away from the opening, hands empty.

Soldiers filed into the room and made an iron wall in front of the door. Someone in a dark cloak gestured to the pile of Dunbar's things. A second later, a soldier passed a sword to Janus. Vayorn's eyes widened. *Where'd he get a sword like that? Why was it familiar?* It looked almost like the sword in Vayorn's dream. He shook himself. That was impossible.

The dark cloak wove its way to the front of the soldiers. As it moved, something clinked under the fabric. A thick hand swept back the hood. Moonlight hit Janus's face, falling into the wrinkles and scars patterning it. Vayorn backed away. *What's he doing here?*

Vayorn pulled Agöri up. *Could we jump out the window in time?*

Dunbar pushed Vayorn and Agöri behind him till their backs were against the window. Vayorn's heart started racing. *What's he doing?*

A layer of frost bit his fingertips as his hands brushed against the window. *We could break it. Cold glass breaks easy.* One of the men moved a little. His sword caught the light. Vayorn winced. *Those things gotta hurt.* Clawlike barbs lined the blade. He tried to stay calm. *Does Dunbar have a plan?*

Dunbar glanced over his shoulder and caught Vayorn's attention. He gestured for Vayorn to look down; Vayorn followed his gaze. Dunbar's hand was behind his back. It opened and closed a few times slowly. He nudged Vayorn and closed his fist. One finger rose. Two. Vayorn realized he was counting down. *Ready when he hits five.* Vayorn's legs bent. Three. Do whatever he does. Four. Five.

"Run!" Dunbar swung around. His hand hit Vayorn. Vayorn flew backward.

"Jump!" Shards of glass flew around Vayorn. He wrapped his arms around Agöri. For an instant, nothing happened.

Then they plummeted.

Gach. This is gonna hurt. Vayorn closed his eyes.

He hit the ground. Past the middle of his back, nothing hurt; nothing felt anything at all. He lay there, trying to force feeling into his legs. Agöri got up.

Someone shook him. "Get up! They're coming!"

Vayorn staggered to his legs. Fire rushed through them. He tried to run.

Clop-clop-clop. Vayorn glanced over his shoulder. *Gach! They have horses.*

"Dunbar!" Vayorn pointed.

Dunbar looked back. His eyes widened. "Gach! Come on!" He made a sharp turn and plunged into the trees.

Vayorn kept as close to Dunbar as he could. Agöri's cold hand stayed latched to Vayorn's arm, as if it was frozen there. Without a lantern, even Dunbar was a dim shape, almost the same color as the shadows around him. But the darkness only seemed to amplify the sounds pursuing them. Branches snapped and underbrush crackled behind them. Horses' hooves drummed the ground. A voice bellowed. The sounds were getting louder; now Vayorn could pick up the voice's orders.

"They're gaining on us!" he yelled.

"This way!" Dunbar slid to a stop. Vayorn stumbled as Dunbar's shoulder shoved him to the right. Agöri's nails dug into Vayorn's arm.

"Go! I'll distract them!" Dunbar's voice was panicked. "Go!"

"We're not leaving you." Vayorn grabbed Dunbar's arm and pulled him in the direction Dunbar had pointed.

Branches whipped across Vayorn's legs. His face stung as the needles on the trees in front of him pricked him. Like running into a porcupine. Something jabbed his side. He jerked away from it. *How much time?* The sounds were too close now. Agöri whimpered.

"Vayorn, look!"

Vayorn glanced back. Lights flared up behind them. *Can't outrun them.* A branch slapped him across the face. *Have time to climb a tree?* He glanced back. The men were so close he could hear them breathing. *No time.* His chest burned. He tried to take a deep breath.

An arrow grazed his head. Another sliced his collarbone. *Have to warn.* He ran harder.

"They're shooting at—" Pain exploded in his arm. He shoved Agöri forward. "Keep running!"

He pressed a hand against his arm. An arrow shaft met his touch. *Have to run.* He staggered.

Something hit him. He collapsed. His leg burned like it was on fire. Liquid trickled down it. His head sank onto his knee. He groaned. Dunbar ran back and slung him across his shoulders.

Vayorn's head swung as Dunbar ran. He gritted his teeth. Every jounce twinged a cry out of him. He squeezed his eyes shut.

Can't go much longer. Vayorn felt consciousness slipping.

Dunbar stumbled. Vayorn flew forward and rolled. Fresh pain burned his leg. He reached down. Most of the arrow shaft was gone, except for a jagged end not much longer than his little finger. He couldn't feel the iron head. *Deng, that's deep.* He tried to stand. Dunbar ran over.

"Are you alright?"

Vayorn nodded. *Think I'll puke if I try to talk.* He smiled weakly. His leg throbbed as if it had a heartbeat of its own.

Agöri ran up. "Blood?" His voice shook as he stared at Vayorn's leg.

"We're trapped." Dunbar jerked his head toward the cliffs around them, walling them in on three sides. There was nowhere to run. Vayorn dropped to his hands and knees.

"Oi! Found them."

Vayorn craned his head. Armor clinked as the soldiers circled them. *Won't die lying down.* He tried to stand. Dunbar slid an arm around him and held him up as Vayorn's knees collapsed. Agöri hid behind Dunbar's knees.

Janus kicked his horse forward. His glance bounced off Vayorn and landed on Dunbar. "Give us the boys. They'll die, no way around it, but I can assure you, I'll be more humane than Demetrius. They'll die right away. Surely that's better than a long death. I would offer to dispatch you just as quickly, but sadly, Fangar Demetrius wants you alive."

Vayorn stiffened. *But why Dunbar? He's just an apothecary. Janus is making a mistake.*

"No! Leave these two alone. I'm the one Demetrius wants." Vayorn pushed words out. "Take me, not them."

Janus started laughing. "You think you're that important? Don't you know who Dunbar is? Oh, so he hasn't told you." Vayorn tried to hide his confusion. "Well, if he had, you would know he's far more valuable than you. Ask me why."

"Why."

"Isn't a father worth more than his son? Ah, confused again. Here's the truth, and it's not pretty. Your father never died. He's alive—at least till we hand him over to Demetrius."

Vayorn stared. *My father…* He shook his head and tried to force his tangled mind to think. Suddenly, it dawned on him. His legs swayed. *Dunbar's my father? He never told me. Why didn't he ever tell me?* He dropped to the ground. Agöri ran up to him.

Janus turned to Dunbar again. "So? I don't have all night. A quick and painless death for the boys, here and now. That, or we let Demetrius torture them to death. You choose. Just give them to us."

"Vayorn, still have your knife?" Dunbar whispered.

Vayorn nodded and handed it to him. His head spun. *Why did he leave me? Did he ever even try to rescue me? Didn't he care?*

Dunbar stepped in front of Vayorn and Agöri. "Kill me first," he said, but Vayorn didn't hear him. *Did he know what was happening to me? Or did he just not care?*

"What was that?" Janus asked.

"I said, kill me first."

"That could be arranged." Janus drew a sword and moved Dunbar out of the way with its tip. "I promise their deaths will be near painless." Janus turned to a soldier. "You, do your job." He gestured to the man's crossbow. The man nodded, loaded an arrow, raised his bow, and pointed it at Agöri.

He pressed the lever. The arrow released.

Vayorn bent over Agöri and steeled himself, waiting for it to hit him. *Wonder how many arrows it takes to kill someone? What if it goes through me and hits him anyway?* He closed his eyes.

Someone groaned. Vayorn lifted his head. Dunbar crumpled to his knees in front of them. The tip of an arrow protruded from the back of his thigh, so close Vayorn could touch it. Agöri whimpered.

The bowstring creaked again.

Vayorn pulled Agöri close.

Another arrow hit Dunbar. He dropped to his side. Vayorn glanced up. The bowman's eyes met his. Vayorn held his gaze. The hard look in the soldier's eyes softened. Vayorn realized the "man" was no older than he was. The boy lowered his bow for a moment. Janus elbowed him.

The bow creaked again.

THE ARROW

Red haze drifted up below Arple in pillars. Her eyes followed them to the ground. Someone was groaning. The air moved as something fell.

She squinted, forcing her gaze through the water-like murk. Only one thing made heat that strong: blood. Lots of it. Her eyes focused. Vayorn lay on the ground curled in a ball. Heat rose from his leg in a thick stream. Someone groaned. A man was stretched out in the dirt, an arrow protruding from his torso. The end of another stuck out of his leg. He was motionless.

Fear clawed at her throat. She realized Vayorn wasn't moving either. Was she too late?

Something creaked. She turned her head.

The tip of an arrow glinted as a large hand loaded it into a crossbow and pulled the string tight. The hand raised it and aimed it over the limp figure on the ground, straight for Vayorn's chest.

Vayorn lifted his head; she paused, frightened suddenly by the look in his eyes. The only thing in them was pain, dimming their light till she almost couldn't recognize him. They were like the broken windows of an abandoned building; lifeless. As the arrow slid into position, they seemed almost eager for death. A tear burned Arple's cheek. What had he been through? Purple circles rimmed his eyes along his cheekbones and faded into a thick layer of filth, broken only by small streaks of blood.

He smiled slightly, a weak, powerless smile. A smile that frightened Arple. She shivered. He bent over, and his arms tightened around something. Arple caught a glimpse of Agöri's head before Vayorn hid him.

"I have to save him!"

"Mistress! Not safe!"

"I don't care! Down!"

She kicked Apran into a dive. Her skin burned as she hit the cloudy air. Her teeth gritted. She dived lower till Vayorn was close enough she could hear his breaths.

Her gaze fixed on the bow. The heat trail rising from it turned gray as the man's finger landed on the trigger. Panicked, she kicked Apran. Maybe if she got close enough, she could take the arrow.

The bowstring quivered as the arrow flew.

She screamed. Helplessness overwhelmed her. As if she'd been punched in the stomach, she doubled over, still screaming.

There was nothing she could do.

Vayorn turned his head. Their eyes met.

For an instant, life filled his eyes. He whispered, "Take care of Ag—"

The arrow hit him.

Its feather protruded from deep inside his chest, just under his shoulder. He slumped sideways and fell. His breaths became shallow, and his shoulders shook as each gasp rushed out. Arple fought back fear.

"Go!" She gripped Apran tightly as he went lower.

"Mistress say when, Apran much-fire on iron-people." His shell began to warm underneath her. She winced. Heat wrapped around her legs and arms.

She waited till they were feet above the archer. "Now!" Fire exploded, drilling deep into the dirt. Smoke mixed with the blood in the air till Arple couldn't see. She leaned tighter into Apran's shell. Something cold hit her hand. She glanced over. Uncle Ilmari pressed a sword pommel into it.

"Go. We'll take the soldiers. Save him. Up ALCEUS!" He disappeared into the smoke. Another blast split the fog. She twined her hands into Apran's feathers and pulled left.

She felt something running. Someone screamed. Singed skin and hair filled the air. Arple's stomach lurched.

"See anything?"

"Apran see everything. Does mistress not?"

Arple coughed. "There's too much in the air."

"Apran find Vayorn!"

Arple kept her eyes closed as smoke filled them. She could feel shards of metal and filth as fire consumed the world below her.

Her eyes opened. There he was. Even from here, she could feel him struggling to get up.

They landed. She ran over. Somehow, Vayorn had gotten to his knees and was trying to stand. She grabbed his arm and made him sit. He was shaking, and his shirt reeked of blood.

Agöri stood next to him, staring so hard he wasn't blinking.

His face was pale where it wasn't smeared with black. Arple reached out to the child. He didn't move. It was like he didn't see her. She touched him. His stunned posture didn't change. She tried to get his attention. "I need you to help me."

Agöri stood like he was frozen. She spoke louder, "You need to help me, or he'll die!"

"I-I'm fine," Vayorn whispered, "it's just…a tiny…wound. Don't wor-worry."

Arple realized she was crying. "You're hurt. How can you say you're fine?"

"I'm fi—" Vayorn's lips paled for an instant. His eyes bleared. Arple tried to stay calm.

His shoulders jerked. His eyes focused again, "Arple…" His voice was so quiet Arple felt it more than she heard it.

"I'm listening."

"If…if I don't make it, you have to take care of Agöri. Promise me you will." He caught her eyes and stared into them. Arple felt his breath against her cheek as he leaned forward hesitantly. As he raised one hand and brushed her hair out of her face, he winced.

"I didn't think the engagement thing was for real. Never took it seriously. Till now. I love you, wish I'd stayed with you." His hand dropped and landed on her arm; his eyes dulled again. Arple felt him fighting for consciousness. His fingers dug into her wrist. He tensed. She stared in horror as heat stopped rising from him. As his other hand grew colder, she grabbed it.

"No!" Desperate, she raised it to her cheek. It was almost like ice.

Suddenly, his grip on her arm released. His hand opened. He fell forward. Arple caught him before he hit the ground and laid his head in her lap.

"No! Wake up! Say something!" Arple looked into his face.

His eyes were closed. Frantic, she listened for breathing. Silence.

"Vayorn!" She realized she was screaming. His shoulders jerked again. A single breath. A long pause. Another. She cradled him in her arms. Her shoulders shook. "Please…you have to live…please." She tried to breathe. Snot ran down into her mouth and stuck to her hair. She gasped as sobs choked her.

A tiny hand touched her shoulder. She turned her head to meet Agöri's empty stare. He didn't say anything, didn't move. Arple hugged him; his gaze stayed on Vayorn.

Arple stared at the arrow in Vayorn's chest, suddenly realizing she had to do something. Should she pull it out? But Vayorn would only bleed more. Should she wait for Uncle Ilmari? She watched Vayorn's chest, her dread growing. It was barely moving. What would Maria do? She groaned. She had to do something. But what if what she did only made it worse?

Uncle Ilmari ran up behind her. "I'll deal with him. The other man needs help."

"But I have to stay here—" Arple tried to see through her tears.

"Do what I tell you. The man needs you. You know what to do. The arrow in his stomach isn't deep. He must have been moving when he took it. Leave the one in his leg. It's stopping the bleeding right now. Go, I'll take care of Vayorn." He ripped his shirt in strips and started tugging on the arrow as he spoke. Each yank brought Vayorn's chest off the ground.

Arple turned away; she didn't want to see Vayorn bleed more.

THE CHALICE

"No! You have to leave!" Demetrius put the bedpost between himself and Laparlana. His hands itched as blood dried on them. Something moved in the corner of the room. He glanced over. The messenger was waking up.

A shudder ran down Demetrius's spine. He looked away; the boy's face was so disfigured it didn't even look human anymore. Still tightly gripping a sword, Demetrius's hand ached. Fear nagged at the back of his mind. What if next time, he hurt Laparlana? Near tears, he shrank away from her. All he wanted was to hold her, ask her forgiveness, but what if he accidentally hurt her? He didn't know what was worse: what he did or not remembering doing it. It was like he'd been asleep, fuzzy, blurry, like a vague nightmare. But it was worse than anything he'd ever felt, coming to himself, and seeing the mutilated mess under his hands, realizing the horror of what he was doing. The boy's arms, legs, and torso were slashed so deep the bone was showing. It was like sitting in a pool of water as he bled. The smell of vomit hung in the air; Demetrius's stomach tried to come up his throat. What if next time it wasn't just another soldier?

"Please!" Demetrius yanked his hand away as Laparlana tried to grab it.

"You're not safe with me. Trust me. Leave." He held the sword point out. She dodged left. He swung it to follow her. What if she didn't listen? Could she protect herself from him if it happened again? Demetrius's eyes wandered down to her swollen belly. No, she couldn't protect herself. Not now. If it happened, he'd kill her. He backed away. She had to listen.

Her eyes narrowed. A stubborn look settled in them as she folded her arms.

"No." She tried to go around the blade.

Demetrius swung around behind her with his back to the door.

"Stop." His voice shook. What if she didn't leave in time? She stepped forward. He backed up.

"Knock it off." Laparlana sidestepped, and her hand brushed Demetrius's arm. She wasn't backing down; she never did when she was in this mood. Demetrius had to begrudgingly admire her. Even six months pregnant, she was agile. A sly look crossed her face. Demetrius's stomach fell.

"Whatever you're thinking, stop thinking it."

She smiled and threw herself at him, straight for the sword. Desperate, he tossed it behind him before she could hit it, pushed her away, jumped the bed, and stood by the window on the other end of the room, opposite the door.

Laparlana huffed. She seemed like she was about to throw herself at him again.

"No, don't touch me."

Laparlana came forward and paused about three steps in front of him. Her jaw set. She placed her hands on either side of her belly. "You aren't dangerous."

"But this is the sixth time this week. Don't you see? You have to leave."

"Yes. I see. I see a man who doesn't care enough about his wife to listen to her." She gestured to a pile of empty bottles on the floor.

Demetrius looked down. Did she actually think he didn't care? Her words stung like salt in an open wound. He studied his shoe, unable to meet her gaze. "I love you. That's why you need to leave."

"Oh, a strange kind of love your love is. Every night, it's the same." Her voice rose. Demetrius tried to interrupt her. "Let me finish! You say one drink, but you mean ten. You say it's an accident, but somehow you get blind raging *drunk* every night. I'm done. You need to stop."

Demetrius started to panic. Done? What did she mean, done? She still loved him, right?

"I try!" He realized he was yelling.

Demetrius groaned. Why didn't she understand? He couldn't help it; he was too far gone. He'd tried stopping, so many times, but it never lasted. How did she not see? Another thought struck him. What if she did see but she just didn't care?

"If I could stop, I would. We've been running for eight days. I need a distraction…" Demetrius's hand brushed an empty bottle on the windowsill. It fell. The metallic sound of shattered glass. He winced.

Laparlana glared at the pieces on the floor. "You can, you just won't!"

"You don't get it! I can't!"

"Silence," Laparlana cut Demetrius off.

She lifted an empty chalice off the floor. "Don't tell me I don't understand." Her voice was quiet now, as if she was remembering. "I had a cup like this. But I always chose brandy. Never liked wine that much. It took me years, years, Demetrius, to stop. And I did worse, far worse than you've ever done, when I was drunk." She threw it across the room.

Demetrius was confused for a second. What did she mean?

Then he realized it; she did understand. He looked away. Why hadn't she ever told him? Would it have been easier to listen to her advice if he'd known?

"Let me get this off me." He gestured to the dried blood on his hands. "You have to leave."

"No, I have to take care of you." Laparlana shifted her weight to one foot.

"Please, just listen."

Laparlana reached out. "No, it's your turn to listen. Whether you think so or not, you need my help."

Demetrius shied away from her touch. *Why was she so persistent?*

She grabbed his arm and pulled him close.

"Aren't you afraid?"

"I've been your wife for more than a year. Nothing you do scares me anymore." She ran a hand across his face and grimaced. "You got it all over you."

He felt sick. Got what all over him? He rubbed his cheek. Bits of vomit came loose. He bent double and realized he was emptying his stomach again.

Laparlana waited till he was finished. "Come on." She pulled him to the door. "I thought this might happen again. There's a warm bath waiting in our room."

She began moving him down the hallway, keeping him on the unlit side of the corridor. When they passed other guests, she stood so that Demetrius was covered by her shadow. He shook his head. Why was she shielding him? He didn't have any dignity left, not after a week like this.

As they passed Demetrius's bodyguard Burkhart, she whispered something to the man. Grateful, Demetrius watched him nonchalantly make his way to the room they'd just left, seeming to be consumed in thought. Burkhart paused till the hallway was empty, then disappeared inside the room.

A few seconds later, he came out carrying the messenger and sped down the hall toward the back stairway. The boy's head lolled as Burkhart silently passed them. Demetrius shuddered. How was he supposed to get Laparlana to leave? She had to go, while she was safe. What if she didn't?

A KISS

Dunbar groaned. He tried to move. Pain seared his side. Someone's hands tightened around his shoulders, pinning him down. Panic rushed through his veins. He thrashed. Someone grabbed his ankles.

A faint voice. Then another, deeper sound. Dunbar struggled to clear his mind. The only clear sensation in the muddled jumble of his thoughts was pain. Even the hands on his arms and legs were fuzzy, as if he were only imagining them.

A face bleared into focus over him. The voice was clear for an instant. Now he was certain he was dreaming. That couldn't be Antarulra. She didn't know where he was. But it was like her face. Someone was speaking. Dunbar couldn't force his mind to focus long enough to understand. But the tone was comforting.

The voice kept up a steady rhythm, like the trickle of a creek. "It's alright, dear. Just let me get this out. You've been in worse. Remember that time Demetrius tried to have you assassinated? I didn't think you'd make it. This is just a scratch compared to that. Stop squirming. I'm almost done. The arrowhead's deep."

"Vayorn," Dunbar managed. Slowly, his mind began to clear. He looked to his left. It was like being plunged into some demented fever dream. He saw Vayorn lying on the ground behind him, an arrow deep in his chest. Dunbar tried to sit up.

Pain stabbed his leg. He blacked out.

When sound came to his ears again, a different voice was talking. "He'll be alright, won't he?"

"If we get him to my hut. The arrow was deep. But don't worry. Your Vayorn's strong. He'll make it, if I have anything to do with it."

"Why do you help us?" A man's voice now.

"I spent fifteen years thinking I'd never see the boys again. Do you think I'd just leave them now? Besides, their mother would want me to help them. Let's load them."

Dunbar stared as Antarulra's face hovered over him again. He went limp, feeling suddenly like a small child. He tried to form words. It seemed like his whole body was on fire. He almost wished he would pass out again. At least that way, he wouldn't feel anything.

A different face replaced Antarulra's. It was strange, more like a fish's than a human's. Dunbar tensed. It was getting closer. Perhaps he was hallucinating. He held a hand in front of his face. He watched the fingers wobble then change color. His head slammed against the ground as if a weight was tied to it. He started laughing.

"What's wrong with the man?"

"The man's name is Dunbar. It's just the medicine. It'll wear off in a few hours. It's kicking in now. In a few minutes, he'll be loopy enough he won't feel anything. Ilmari, can you take him on your animal? Good. I'll take the child, and Arple can take Vayorn."

"But your wings are so small. Surely you can't keep up with Varuls, especially carrying weight."

"I can manage just fine, thank you. Let's go."

Dunbar's eyes closed.

*****

Vayorn's body ached as if a giant hand were crushing his ribs into his backbone; his teeth clenched tight. Air sat in his lungs for an instant, ripped them apart like a knife, and whooshed out his open mouth. Another breath. Another.

A hand brushed his forehead, almost like ice, or cold, smooth marble. He parted his lips and tried to speak.

"Am I dead?" He winced. Was that his voice? He barely recognized it.

"No, you aren't dead."

Vayorn's stomach somersaulted. Excited warmth filled his body. Suddenly, he was sweaty. Arple? He opened his eyes.

She sat on the edge of the bed, half her face illuminated in the firelight from across the room. Her unbound hair flowed across the bed beside her like a curtain. Steam rose from the bowl in her hand. Vayorn's mouth watered. Food. She was whispering to him. He turned his head to look at her.

Suddenly, he forgot about being hungry. She was beautiful, even more than he remembered her being.

He forced his hand off the bed and rested it on her cheek. "You're here." He allowed the feeling to sink in. He realized he'd never expected to live, never expected to see her again. *She saved me. What made her do that? There was nothing in it for her.*

Arple paused. Vayorn realized she'd asked a question. He smiled and shrugged. She shook her head.

Deng. And I thought she was attractive at the engagement. How'd she get so much prettier? Her eyes sparkled like twin beams of starlight. Vayorn moved his gaze across her face, trying to memorize every tiny detail. She had a little blue freckle just under her right eye. When she smiled, the left corner of her mouth rose just a little. She giggled again. Her left frill shook in a cute, babyish way. Vayorn let his eyes rest on her lips. Suddenly he wanted to kiss her. *Would she let me?*

She was saying something, but Vayorn wasn't listening; he was still watching the way her mouth moved when she talked. *Deng, wish I could kiss her.* Her breath warmed his cheek. He realized her face was inches from his now. His breathing quickened.

She brushed a piece of hair out of his eyes.

He sat up and pulled her close.

Vayorn drew away from Arple. His face was wet with sweat. He could hear his heart racing, like the hooves of a horse on cobblestone. *Deng.* He reveled in the feeling for an instant.

The satisfaction that seemed to hit every one of his bones was almost like being in front of fire, but warmer.

Arple sat rigid, still looking shocked.

He waited for her to smile, perhaps lean in again or, if she'd never been kissed before, run off. He tried to look charming.

Arple took a deep breath. She didn't say anything, but her mouth softened into a small smile. She blushed and looked away. Vayorn waited for her to come in for another kiss. She didn't. *What's wrong? Most girls like it when I kiss them.* He tried to get her attention. She looked at him, touched his cheek, and began softly laughing. Across the room, a rocking chair creaked. Something bubbled over the fire. Arple stopped laughing, and looked away, as if she was embarrassed. *Just a kiss. Nothing to be so shy about. Why doesn't she want another?* Vayorn looked away and studied the blanket over his legs. A few minutes passed. He shifted and tried to look her in the eye again. Still silent, Arple began to rise. She paused, and sat down again.

"You kissed me?" she shook her head, pretending to be angry ."Deng, you've never been kissed?" He tried to make her laugh.

"Language! And yes."

Yikes. "Gach." Arple glared at him. "I don't talk like a peaceman." Vayorn tried to be funny but realized a second too late how sarcastic he sounded. *What's she expect? No one's perfect.*

"What's wrong with peacemen?" Arple bristled.

"What, you know one?" Vayorn cringed. *Why'd I say that?*

"I was raised by one." Arple sounded proud, as if being raised by a peaceman was the highest honor in the world.

"Oh…" Vayorn rubbed the back of his neck. *That's nothing to be proud of. Peacemen are weak.*

"Why did you kiss me?"

Vayorn bit his lip. *Deng.* He smiled a little, "I have to answer that?" he held her gaze.

Arple raised one eyebrow, waiting for him to continue.

He took a slow breath. *What do I say? Why is she asking this? Most girls don't act like this after a kiss.*

"Well, did you like it?" he asked.

"It was…shocking," Arple said hesitantly.

Shocking? What's she mean by shocking? Bad?

"Well…ah…most girls—"

"I'm not most girls. Wait…" Arple's eyes widened. Her jaw dropped. She turned to stare at Vayorn. "You've kissed other girls?" she snapped.

Vayorn shook his head. *What's wrong with her?* "I didn't mean that…"

"Then what exactly did you mean?"

"Just that, um…" Vayorn paused. *How do I explain?* He shrugged. "Well, I don't know."

Arple's brow furrowed. She placed her hands on her hips. "You've kissed other girls."

"You're being irrational. What's wrong with a kiss?"

Arple looked away from him, a hurt expression on her face. "So love, commitment, affection—it's, what, a game to you?"

Vayorn groaned. "It's not like that…"

"Then what is it like?"

"Just drop it already. Can't believe you're losing your gach over a kiss."

"Doesn't anything matter to you?"

Vayorn's head snapped up. She sounded disappointed, as if she'd expected better from him. *I am the way I am. Why won't she just understand already?*

"I didn't realize this was such a big deal to you."

"Leave me alone."

"I'm sorry, alright? I didn't know a kiss would make you mad."

Arple sighed. "It's alright. I don't know what I expected. After all, you're only an impulsive boy. Why would I expect you to act like a decent man?" She stood and walked away.

Vayorn threw his head back. *Women.*

THE SWORD

"Catch me!" Antarulra paused, arms out to her sides, eyes locked with Demetrius.
"Awww, come on, Demetrius, you're no fun."
"Chicken," she prodded. Demetrius lunged after her. Dunbar leaned against the fountain. How deluded could the boy be? She was no better than the dogs playing at their feet. Dunbar folded his arms. It was disgusting.

Demetrius wrapped his arms around her, barely missing her wings. She zipped upward just before they closed. He stared around himself as if he was looking for something on the ground. Dunbar let out a deep sigh. This had to end.

Antarulra dived down and bopped Demetrius's head with the tip of her wing. He reached up and dragged her down by a wrist. She pretended to struggle, but her eyes shone with almost human delight. Demetrius had both her wrists now.

Metri's face was happy, too happy. The boy rarely smiled, but when he did, Dunbar avoided looking at him. Even Mother had to admit Demetrius was by far the handsomer brother. Dunbar couldn't see why girls liked Demetrius so much, but it was maddening sometimes, the way they seemed to hang off his every scowl.

Antarulra whacked Demetrius again. He held on to her legs as she lurched into the air. His feet dangled above the ground. She struggled for a few seconds, then dropped into Demetrius's stomach, knocking him on his back underneath her.

He sat up. She was laughing now, and so was he. Dunbar squirmed. If only Liesel would look at him that way.

*****

Dunbar watched Ivaylo and Arple.

Their eyes shone, as if no one else existed but the two of them. In a subtle way Dunbar couldn't quite figure out, Vayorn seemed different. But as far as Dunbar could see, there was no obvious change.

Arple's cheek was resting in Vayorn's hand as if it had always belonged there. Dunbar tried to figure out what Vayorn saw in her. She was much like any other Saynasaf Dunbar had ever seen: fishlike features, scales on her face, frills. Nothing special. Nothing different. And yet Vayorn seemed attracted to her.

Dunbar sighed and looked away, suddenly uncomfortable. As much as he wanted to be happy for them, he couldn't help but feel it just wasn't natural for them to look at each other like that. Perhaps if Arple were a human girl, their affection for each other would seem more appealing, but she wasn't. She was a Saynasaf.

Vayorn laughed. Suddenly, Dunbar realized the change: Vayorn was smiling—a smile so shockingly different from what Dunbar was used to seeing it was almost unnerving. A smile like Leisel's, so beautiful it blotted out everything but happiness from his face. A sleepy droop around the corners of his eyes gave him an almost-childish look. Dunbar looked from his face to Agöri's, nestled in Antarulra's arms by the fire. They were almost identical. Arple giggled. He shifted his gaze back to them.

Dunbar shook his head. This had to stop.

*****

The pacing steps outside the door faded. Like the wind coming to a sudden stop, the silence ached in Demetrius's ears. Every drop of water falling from the ceiling rang like a bell against the floor.

In the bed beside him, Laparlana's breaths roared. Even Demetrius's own heart rang in his temples at the speed of war drums. Like a cold embrace, the darkness wrapped around him. In the coffin-like air, his worst fears seemed so real he could touch them. He tried to breathe and choked.

Light. That was what he needed. Light.

He slid out of the bed, shuddering as his bare feet met the ice-like floor. He reached across the bedside table. There was nothing.

Laparlana moaned. He slowly turned his head. Did he wake her up? He held his breath. She needed sleep. Even in the shadows, he could make out the sharp lines of her face; when had she gotten so thin? How long had it been since they started running? Demetrius shook his head. Too long. She was getting weak. He waited till her chest rose and fell slowly with deep breaths again. She was still asleep.

Demetrius staggered across the room, feeling for a candle.

Anxious worries ate away at him like worms inside an apple.

Why hadn't the soldiers come back yet? His hands hit a piece of paper—another death threat. He shuddered. How long would it be till they caught up? It seemed like no matter how hard he tried to shake them, they stuck to his trail like leeches. He bit his lip. Could Laparlana survive another flight through the hills? He found a candle. How much farther could they run? They'd run four days' journey from their last inn, but since Miasto? Twelve days. She didn't show it; Laparlana was too brave for her own good sometimes, but Demetrius knew she was often in pain. He saw the worried look in her eyes, when she thought no one was watching, and the way her bones seemed closer and closer to her skin each day. The baby hadn't started kicking yet; what if it was stillborn? But as much as that thought scared him, there was one thought that was even worse. Could Laparlana survive the birth? That was his worst fear. She was drained till Demetrius didn't recognize her sometimes. She had about four months till the baby was born; what could happen in four months? Demetrius ran his hand through his hair.

Why weren't the soldiers back yet? They were loyal, weren't they? He tried to reason with his fear.

Still, the nagging doubt wouldn't leave him. What if they turned him in? The lords weren't the only ones putting a price on his head. Men would do anything for gold; if there was one thing he'd learned from Father, it was that. Father hadn't cared much about reading or writing, but Father had ingrained history into Demetrius's head, with every dirty detail and dark secret that had been uncovered.

For an instant, Demetrius smiled. As a child, he could recite all thirty-four rulers of Antike since the beginning of the first age. He'd memorized every battle in all six civil wars; Mother was never impressed, but Father always was. Sometimes he would bring Demetrius in to recite for the lords; they never seemed to enjoy it as much as Father did.

Bang! Bang!

Demetrius jumped. Light burned his eyes. A dark shape blocked out a shadow in the doorway—Janus. The stench of smoke lifted off his ragged clothing and filled the room.

Laparlana sat up. She shielded her eyes and moaned.

"Wha-time-iz-it?" She rubbed her eyes.

Demetrius stepped between the light and Laparlana.

"We found them," Janus rasped. He held something out to Demetrius ...

*****

The sword glistened in Demetrius's hands, pulsing as if it were alive. His temples throbbed with fire. This was it. He looked down. The candlelight danced across the map, illuminating a red dot one day's journey away—so easy. So close. He could almost see Father's fingers around the pommel and hear the clank of metal against metal as Father carried it across the throne room. "This is yours, son. Use it wisely. Use it like a king. Use it like I would." Father had said that every time Demetrius touched it.

"I will," Demetrius whispered. *What would Father use it for? Justice. Did defending his family count? Yes.*

This wasn't the first time he'd held it; his earliest memories were of sitting in Father's lap during high court sessions, touching it and playing with the gems along its pommel, holding it sometimes when Father was able to supervise him.

It was beautiful.

He caressed the runes along the blade. At last.

Something creaked behind him; Laparlana grunted as she heaved herself out of the bed.

"Demetrius, are you alright?" Laparlana asked.

Demetrius nodded. He closed his eyes. The last time he'd held this sword was at Father's deathbed. He pinched his lips together, trying to stay calm. It had been so long since he'd thought about his promise to Father. Too long.

"You alright?" She glanced at the sword, then up into Demetrius's eyes.

Demetrius took a deep breath. "I was the last person Father spoke to before he died—" Demetrius choked. He steadied his breathing and tried to speak past the ache in his throat. "Sorry."

"I'm listening."

"You're the only person that knows this. Father made me promise I would rule, I would care for his people, as long as I had his sword. It was the last thing he said."

A strange look crossed Laparlana's face. She pressed a hand against her stomach.

"What's wrong?"

"Feel!" Her voice shook with excitement.

Demetrius laid his hand against her stomach. A small jerk.

Something pounded against his hand. The baby was kicking. Joy filled him for an instant. The child was alive.

Then a piece of paper fell to the floor.

Demetrius picked it up. The seal was unopened; how had it gotten in here? He couldn't remember receiving any messenger, and he hadn't left his room all day. The only people who had come in were Laparlana, Burkhardt, and a few servants. He opened it with shaking fingers. Laparlana's breath warmed his ear as she read over his shoulder.

To the usurper Demetrius Holger, second born of the Ancient House of Soturant:

Stop running. It is useless. You are found, and the only way to save your worthless life is to turn yourself in to us. We are easy to find; our spies are many. Do not run this time. It will not end well for the woman traveling with you.

Our spies say the woman with you is pregnant, but we've received no notice that you married. Therefore, we must assume she is your mistress, not your wife. As such, she will receive no mercy if we find her and will be charged with aiding and abetting a usurper and enemy of the people. We care not that she carries what we assume to be your child.

They will both be punished to the extremities of our law. There is nowhere she can hide.

You can avoid all this that we have threatened if you turn yourself in.

Consider carefully. She is a pretty woman, and it would be a shame to have to condemn her to certain punishments.

Signed,
The Sovereign Lords of Antike

Demetrius's chest tightened. His hand closed around the paper, smashing it. He gritted his teeth.

"I'll die before I let them do that," he said under his breath. There was only one choice. Vayorn and Dunbar had to be destroyed—quickly.

Laparlana leaned against him. The sword fell out of his hand. He dropped the letter, tilted her chin up, and kissed her, reveling in every tiny detail of her face. How had he thought she wasn't pretty when they first met? She was the most beautiful woman ever born.

Not because of her face or her figure. Because she was his.

He pulled away and led her to the bed. "Rest. You shouldn't be awake right now. Take care of our baby. That's the only thing you need to think about. I won't let anything happen to us."

He got her settled, turned, and slid out the door. Janus waited outside.

"Gather a detachment of men and saddle my horse."

"Your horse, milord?"

"I will make sure they're destroyed this time. I will see it with my own eyes."

THE RING

"Vayorn?" Dunbar touched the boy's shoulder. Ivaylo shook his hand off. Dunbar let a breath out slowly, trying to curb his exasperation. He wanted to speak calmly to the boy, but Ivaylo seemed to have a talent for provoking people. Dunbar didn't understand it; after all they'd been through, at the very least, Ivaylo could speak to him. It was almost like the boy enjoyed being angry. His frustration built. Ivaylo acted like he had a bone to pick with every person that walked by since the moment he woke up. He'd only been awake for twenty-four hours, and he already had every creature in the cabin angry with him. He still wasn't speaking to the female creature, whom Dunbar discovered was named Arple, and the only person he seemed to tolerate was Agöri.

Dunbar touched the boy's shoulder again.

"Leave." Ivaylo finally spoke, "Get away."

"Why?" Dunbar realized how harsh his tone was. He waited for Ivaylo to say something.

Silence.

"What did I do to deserve this?"

Suddenly, like a pile of dry brush bursting into flame, Ivaylo exploded, "You gaching left me! You lied! You could have told me! But you didn't! Did you even care? You knew where I was. You left me, when I needed you the most!"

"Left you?"

"Left me."

"I never left you. Not once. I gaching almost died for you. Explain."

"I'm not talking about last night. I'm talking about all the other nights in Tarshal you could've rescued me and…you…didn't"—Ivaylo's voice rose—"all the nights Demetrius got drunk…and beat the nearest breathing thing, me. All the nights I dreamed of someone, anyone, caring enough to help me. And no…one…did."

Ivaylo's words hit Dunbar like a load of rocks. Sick to his stomach, Dunbar slowly nodded. The boy had every right to be angry. Dunbar's fingers traveled up to Father's ring. A lifetime of failure. And he'd expected to just smooth it over in a week. If only he'd been honest. But he hadn't. And as much as he wanted to gloss over his mistakes, he knew he was a failure as a father.

But to hear Ivaylo say it out loud, Dunbar looked away. It was worse than any guilt he'd ever felt.

"I'm sorry."

Ivaylo turned his back.

*****

He lied. And all he can say is sorry? As if sorry fixes anything. Vayorn slammed his fist against his leg, right over the wound. He swore under his breath. *Wish I could walk. I'd take Agöri. They'd never see me again.* He glared at the wall beside him. *He left me. Did he care?*

The bed moved. He turned his head. Arple was sitting beside him. He looked away. *Last person in the world I wanna talk to right now.* She laid her hand on his knee.

"Vayorn, I know you're listening."

Vayorn turned his back.

She sighed. "I'm not going to apologize for getting angry. A kiss is a very sacred thing to my people, but you didn't know that. Your customs are different."

Vayorn slowly turned his head. *A kiss? Sacred? Please.*

"But I do need to apologize for yelling and insulting you. That was uncalled for."

Vayorn nodded curtly.

"You don't have to talk to me right now, but I just had to apologize. I'm sorry."

Vayorn pretended he didn't hear her and kept his gaze glued to the quilt over his legs. *Sorry—that's all anyone has to say. Sorry.* He waited for what felt like forever. *Maybe she'll just get up and leave.*

He looked again.

She was waiting, patiently, smiling as if they'd never fought. As she waited, her hand strayed to Vayorn's arm.

Antarulra came over. "Well, what secrets are we plotting with our heads so close together?" She carried a tray full of bandages, pots, and jars. Vayorn tensed. His wounds began throbbing.

"It's alright, it won't hurt as much this time." Antarulra moved Arple out of the way. "Go find something to do. We don't need every person in this cabin over here." She kept up a steady stream of talk as she began treating Vayorn's wounds. Vayorn knew he shouldn't trust her, but something about her put him at ease. Maybe it was the gentle way she spoke or her sense of humor, but she reminded him of Mama Yanya. He leaned back against the bed as she began pulling bandages away from his leg, trying to ignore the cold pain as air rushed into the gash. Antarulra kept working. He could hear Arple at the other end of the cabin singing to Agöri.

"We fought." He realized he was talking.

"Ah, so that's what happened. I expected it sooner or later." She opened a flask and began trickling golden liquid into Vayorn's leg.

"Expected it?" Vayorn looked away as pus oozed out and ran down to his ankle.

"Yes. She's your mate, your match. I knew it was bound to happen…this might hurt." She wiped away the mess and opened a bottle.

"How?" Vayorn braced himself as she poured brown acid into his wound.

"iI's just to clean it…I know it stings…I've seen enough young lovers to know when a pair is right." She rubbed cool salve in and rebandaged it with a clean fabric.

"Right? But…she's a Saynasaf." Vayorn turned so she could pull away the bandage on his shoulder.

"You're afraid of what people will say? Let's do your arm first…" She started unwrapping the cloth around his arm.

"No, it's not that. It's just…confusing, I guess."

"The best things in life are sometimes the most confusing."

Dunbar walked over. "Feeling better?"

Suddenly, Vayorn remembered he was angry at Dunbar.

NIGHT

The trees faded into the corners of his vision. His hands tightened around the reins. Their knuckles turned white. Even in the cold air, they sweated. His lips felt dry as he licked them. This was it. Victory, so close he could touch it.

The muted crunching of heavy footfalls in fresh snow crept beside him.

Demetrius examined his men. It was good. They were prepared. Each soldier's hand was empty, even of lanterns; Demetrius had decided against too much light. It would give them away. They had one chance. And one extra light could ruin it all.

Demetrius fought the urge to spur his horse into a gallop.

Already, the beat of his horse's hooves seemed too loud. Would Dunbar hear it? They had to move quieter.

Demetrius steadied his breathing, trying not to think about what was going to happen. He was afraid if he did, he'd go crazy with excitement. Any minute now. He reveled in a daydream as they got closer. The little hut in flames. His breathing quickened. Yes. The smell of death, of burning flesh. He forced himself to stay calm. His breath hissed between his clenched teeth. Dunbar would fall as he ran, a dozen arrows sticking out his chest, his neck, and his stomach. Demetrius rubbed his palms together. The chance of a lifetime.

Slosh. Slosh. Demetrius winced. Even the brine seemed too loud. Was it really necessary? Perhaps not. But without Dunbar and Vayorn's heads, the lords would never believe Demetrius. They needed proof. What if they didn't believe him anyway? Demetrius didn't want to think about what that meant.

A thought crossed his mind briefly: could he and Dunbar have ever been friends? It vanished just as quickly. No. Only rivals. Always rivals. The thought was depressing. As much as Demetrius didn't want to admit it, he wished things could have ended better after that argument, sixteen years ago.

The smell of woodsmoke was strong now, and there were tracks in the snow all around them. Tracks made by booted feet that weren't theirs. The hut was close. Demetrius unsheathed Father's sword. First Dunbar and Vayorn. Then every one of the nobles.

After tonight, the only heir would be Demetrius.

And if the nobles still refused to acknowledge his claim to the throne? All Antike would go to arms against them. They couldn't win. Not after tonight.

They broke through the trees. There it was.

*****

Vayorn caught Arple's eye and smiled apologetically. Arple smiled back. He'd been kinder to her this evening and even spoke to her for the first time since the kiss. She stood and pulled a chair beside his bed. The warm fire felt abrasive against her skin. She ignored it. Vayorn's face was almost healthy; his eyes were bright again, above the hollows under his cheekbones. The smell of warm soup drifted up from the tray in Arple's hands. She balanced it as she sat.

"Feeling better?" She helped him sit up, trying to sound cheerful. His face turned gray for an instant; Arple tightened her grip around his bicep. His eyes fluttered, as if he was about to pass out. She started to lay him down again.

He placed one hand on the bed and pushed into a sitting position. "I'm fine. Sick of lying down." He met Arple's eyes. "I didn't mean to stay mad at you."

"Pretty much all day." Arple lifted the cloth off the tray and passed the bowl to Vayorn. Soup dripped off his chin as he slurped it. Arple looked away; she was sure a pig had better table manners.

"Yeah"—*chomp*—"all day." His words were garbled in a mouthful of food.

"Want to talk about it?" Arple considered asking him to chew with his mouth shut. But he might get angry at her again. She tried to smile. "What?"

"The kiss."

"Ahhh!" Vayorn threw his hands up in frustration. A piece of half-chewed bread fell out of his mouth. Arple grimaced.

"Back to the kiss. What do you need to tell me?"

"Will you listen if I explain?"

"Yeah."

Arple paused. He was probably too busy eating to truly listen. But she could at least try to make him understand.

It was very hurtful to me, when you took that tone. Other girls? It felt like you didn't actually care about me; I was just one of them. A kiss is a very sacred thing to my people, like it's the highest, deepest, most powerful show of affection between betrothed couples. It's not a public thing…" She trailed off. There was nothing he knew that she could compare it to; Antike was too vulgar, too crude for there to be anything similar.

Vayorn took her hand, "Well, wish I'd met you sooner. Would've saved me a lot of time I wasted. You're not 'just one of them.' I love you. And that's what I meant when I kissed you." Suddenly, he winced. "Wanna talk about something…distract me?" he gestured to his shoulder. He passed the empty bowl to her and wiped his mouth along the back of his hand. Arple handed him a cloth.

"Like the way you're treating Dunbar?"

"What way?" he laughed.

Arple sighed.

Vayorn was still laughing.

"What?"

"Nothing. You're just cute when you're trying to argue."

"Oh." Arple tried to think of something to say. He was ruder than anyone she'd ever met. But that was because he was Antikish.

Dunbar walked by. Arple felt Vayorn stiffen.

"Alright, knock it off. Dunbar doesn't deserve this."

"This is the least he deserves," Vayorn mumbled. Suddenly his smile was gone.

"Listen to yourself! Do you think you're any better than him?"

Vayorn started to nod, still glaring at Dunbar's back.

"Are you perfect?"

"Um, of course not. But at least I didn't—"

"The way you're acting is any better than the way he acted?"

Vayorn looked away. Arple cupped his chin in her hand and turned his head to look into his eyes. "You demand perfection from him, me, Agöri, everyone. But you're worse to the people closest to you than anyone I've ever met."

Vayorn looked away again. His eyes were distant. "Do you even know what he did?"

"Tell me."

Vayorn sucked in a deep breath and began speaking.

Arple sat in silence, letting his words sink in. He looked worn-out, as if speaking had exhausted all his strength. The sober mood seemed to make the air heavy. Arple realized her hand was locked around Vayorn's and his hand was shaking. His anger seemed to rise off him like steam.

"I didn't know."

"Yeah." Vayorn's tone was short and sharp, suddenly empty of the good nature there had been in it all evening.

"That still doesn't excuse the childish way you're acting. I understand, your time in Tarshal was awful. It's nothing I would ever want someone I love to have to go through. But you could choose to see it differently. There was good in it. And it wasn't Dunbar's fault."

"He didn't try to stop it."

"It made you strong. Don't you see that?"

"No." Vayorn obviously did; he just wasn't admitting it. Arple huffed. Stubborn. That's what he was.

"You could though."

"Bullgach."

Dunbar suddenly came up behind Arple. His voice was thick. She realized he'd been listening; for how long, she didn't know. Maybe the whole conversation.

"I didn't know. I'm…I'm sorry. Please, blame me. I deserve it. But let me make amends. Let me fix my mistakes. Please, can't we start again? I don't deserve your forgiveness, but at the very least, would you let me show you how much I regret what I did?"

Vayorn's face softened. The hard lines gentled, and the anger left his eyes.

A stick broke. Arple closed her eyes.

"Something's coming." She listened harder, felt the earth shake under hooves, felt metal boots on the hard-packed ice.

She heard someone whisper, "That's the hut."

FIRE

Demetrius kneaded his knuckles into his palms, almost so eager he couldn't force himself to wait.

Not a single star shone; if anything, it felt like it was getting darker. The cold air dragged its fangs along Demetrius's neck. He shuddered. One sound, one crunching footfall in the snow, and this chance might be lost.

The silence rang in Demetrius's ears, as if it was straining to warn Dunbar.

A small slit of light traveled across the snow from underneath the door. The house was quiet, almost too quiet. What if Dunbar had already escaped? Demetrius shook his head.

There was no way. No one could have warned Dunbar.

"Take the house." Demetrius drew his sword. His hands stung as the cold sword pommel burned them. He closed his eyes, imagining the feeling of warm blood washing over them, Dunbar's blood.

*****

The floorboards rumbled. Vibrations traveled up Arple's legs like a thousand needles. She stumbled. Antarulra lifted her head. Their eyes met. Arple gulped; Antarulra felt it too. Something was getting close. Her legs shook as she tried to steady herself.

She turned to Vayorn. He sat pressed against the wall, his face the color of ash.

Suddenly, Antarulra burst into action. "Pack food, clothes, whatever you can!" Her voice split the tense silence.

Arple forced herself to move. She shoveled everything she could see into the bag. Dunbar brushed past her.

"They're coming!" Antarulra's wings beat against the ceiling as she lifted. Frantic bashing rang out. Pieces of straw and hard mud hit Arple. "It's frozen solid. We can't get out that way."

Desperation filled Arple. She realized she was out of breath. Arple's heart raced. Her body ached; was that fear? If it was, it was far stronger than anything she'd ever felt.

Vayorn groaned. She forced herself to stay calm. They couldn't get him out. Not quickly enough for him to escape.

The soldiers would kill him. Her body ached worse as memory threatened to swallow her. He was still wounded. He couldn't walk. He couldn't run. She moved faster. Where was Apran?

Bang! Bang! Smash! A piece of wood hit Arple. She turned.

Ilmari hit the wall with a fire poker again. The hole widened. He ripped one of the planks loose.

"Take Agöri!" Ilmari threw the child into Arple's arms. The tiny heart hammered, keeping time with Arple's.

Antarulra shoved them toward the hole. "Go!" She turned and began dragging Dunbar toward the hole.

Ilmari picked Vayorn up. Arple stumbled toward the opening.

*****

"Burn them out. But don't kill anyone." Demetrius's breath caught as the first torch flew.

This was it.

Flames lit the night sky.

*****

A brown pillar brushed her arms as a wooden chest burst into flame. Arple choked. Her head reeled. The ember-red curtain swept down onto the floor, swallowing everything it touched.

Each breath scorched her lungs. Red haze blurred her vision. Someone yanked Agöri from her.

"Wait!" She listened for someone to answer.

Suddenly, a wave of heat knocked her to the ground. She opened her eyes; it was coming closer. She could feel it. A tiny scream escaped as pain stabbed her body. She looked down; a small brown spot blistered on her arm and began to grow, reaching her elbow.

"Help!" She grabbed her throat as smoke choked her off.

*****

Demetrius's legs brushed the horse's side as he slid out of the saddle. A gust of wind rushed up his sleeves. He wrapped his cloak tighter. How was he not warm? He could feel the heat pulsing from the burning house, but he was shivering. He swore under his breath.

"Go around the back. Bring me anyone you find." He loosened his sword. This time, Dunbar would die.

*****

A vague voice filtered through the smoke. "Arple!"

Arple pushed herself up on one elbow. It was coming from her right. She dug her nails into the floor as she dragged herself toward it.

Her arms numbed. Fur-like ringing filled her ears. She reached her hands out, trying to feel any sensation. There was nothing. She realized she wasn't breathing. She gasped. Smoke flooded her eyes; her hand on the floor in front of her disappeared. She held her eyes shut. Long streaks of pain ran down her legs.

"Help!" Her arm gave out. Her head bounced against the floor. She moaned. Something fell behind her. Sparks caught on her hair. She rolled.

*****

Vayorn struggled. Someone shoved him, and he fell. The snow under his shoulder darkened. He tried to breathe. The metallic taste of blood filled his mouth. He eased a hand up to where the bandage had been; there was nothing. Nothing but warm liquid and the stinging pain of cold air against raw flesh. He clenched his jaw.

A set of firm hands wrenched his arms behind his back; he moaned.

Behind him, the blazing roof fell in. A scream pierced the air. *Arple!* He twisted himself around, trying to see the shimmer of her scales. *She's in there!*

"Arple!" *What if she doesn't get out?*

Another scream.

He threw himself down, tripped the man behind him, ripped a sword loose, elbowed the soldier in the face, and ran.

The edges of his vision splotched over. His blood-soaked shirt flapped against his torso as he ran. *Gach.* He gritted his teeth as he staggered. *Gonna bleed out.* The snow stung his bare feet. *What if I'm too late?* He forced his legs to work. Another scream.

*****

Demetrius straightened; this was it. Dunbar struggled as the soldiers pinned his arms tighter. A slow smile twisted Demetrius's lips. Could this get more satisfying? He nodded.

The men began tying Dunbar's arms to his sides. The ropes tightened. Dunbar moaned as someone shoved him to his knees.

"Kill me already." Dunbar raised his head and looked Demetrius squarely in the eye.

Demetrius's neck crawled. Why wasn't Dunbar afraid? He tried to meet Dunbar's confident, intense gaze. Suspicion filled him. Did Dunbar know something? Perhaps Dunbar had an escape plan after all.

Dunbar was still staring, with the beginning of an "I win, you lose" grin forming on his face. Demetrius backhanded him. Did he have to ruin this victory too? For once, couldn't Dunbar let him win?

Demetrius aimed a kick. It landed deep in Dunbar's stomach.

Dunbar doubled over, soundless. Demetrius kicked him again. Still silent. Again. Again. A small groan. Demetrius stepped back and aimed for Dunbar's face. A shriek split Demetrius's lungs. His foot met something. Dunbar bent into himself, blood pouring from his forehead.

Demetrius bent down to Dunbar's ear and whispered, "It's over. I win."

*****

Vayorn's knees knocked against the ground as he fell. His vision blurred.

Arple's faint voice broke through the fog inside his mind. "Keep calling!"

"Arple!" Vayorn pressed a hand to his shoulder. *What if I keep bleeding?*

The crunch of metal shoes on snow behind him. He rolled to his back. An axe blade sliced the air beside his ear. He forced his hand to close around the sword pommel. The axe blade rose into the air, arcing high above a helmeted head. It finished its circle, biting deep into Vayorn's shoulder.

Warm blood poured down his arm and ran over his numb fingers.

"Arple!" he managed. His arms shook. *Can't die yet. She's not safe.* He forced his sword into the man's torso. The edges of his vision turned black. He plunged deeper.

"Vayorn!"

"Arple!" His voice caught. *Can't die till she's safe.* He moaned as consciousness fled.

Suddenly, Arple's soft hand met his cheek.

"I'm here, I'm here." She laid her cheek against his. "You're bleeding!"

The sound of running feet. The last thing Vayorn saw was a raised sword tip, then Arple hurled her body over him.

*****

"I won't go soft on you this time," Demetrius muttered under his breath. He raised the sword and angled it for Dunbar's chest. His heart hammered. Father's sword reflected light into his eyes—from where, Demetrius didn't know, perhaps from itself, if that were possible—as if it were trying to blind him. Demetrius blinked hard. The light vanished.

Demetrius gestured to one of the men.

The man's fingers locked in Dunbar's hair and wrenched Dunbar's head back. Dunbar's exposed throat glistened with sweat, illuminated by the weak glimmer of the nearby lantern. He made a choking sound as Demetrius drew the sword back.

*****

Arple felt Vayorn's chest rise and fall beneath her. His blood stuck in her hair and along her arms, like black-red honey. She cradled his head.

Her skin tingled as the metal sword point hovered against her back. The man raised it.

Vayorn exhaled hard.

Arple's heart hammered. Time was running out.

She dived under the blade and reached for a knife at the man's waist; it came loose. She lunged for the man's throat. A burst of heat washed across her arms.

*****

Fire burned through his body and consumed all his senses. Vayorn moaned. Through the film over his vision, he saw someone fall. There was a guttural strangling sound, then silence…

*****

Arple stared at her hands; they were dyed such a deep copper they were almost sickening. The man lay at her feet, gasping. Blood rose from his throat. Vayorn lay on the other side of him, motionless.

Arple ran over. She laid a hand against Vayorn's neck, listening for a heartbeat. Her eyes closed as she focused. She had to hear something, anything. Silence. And he was still bleeding. Her shoulders shook. One heartbeat, just one, she silently begged him.

The ground shook. Something landed beside her. She stared as patches of white appeared in the copper over her hands: tears. Arple brought a hand to her face. It came away wet. Her shoulders convulsed.

"Mistress, command us," Alceus said.

She shook her head. He couldn't be dead.

*****

Sharp hands clawed into Demetrius's shoulders. He reached for the sword; something knocked it out of his reach.

Suddenly, his feet left the ground. He looked up into Antarulra's face.

He gritted his teeth against the bitter bile rising to fill his mouth. Her? Of all creatures? Then a thought struck him. What if she dropped him?

Sharp needles brushed his ankle; he looked down. The treetops lay at his feet like iron spikes, waiting to impale him.

"It's been a long time." His voice shook. Her grip loosened slightly.

"I've missed you…"

"Shut up," Antarulra snapped. She stared past him, avoiding his gaze.

He tried again, "I thought you were dead. That's what he told me."

"Still telling lies, after all these years."

"Please, A, I'm telling the truth."

"You haven't changed a bit." She loosened her grip more.

Demetrius tried to stay calm. "Please, don't…"

Antarulra began to let go.

"Deng, I've missed you." All the memories Demetrius had pushed back rushed over him: her cold hand on his, the warm feeling of their first kiss, her giggle. His chest tightened.

"I hate you. Do you think I miss you at all? I don't."

"What, you found your match?" Demetrius realized how caustic he sounded. She began to release her grip. He grabbed her arms. "Please! Don't!"

Jealousy transformed her voice. "I found my match, and he became a monster and is having a child with someone else."

"I'm sorry, A. If I'd known…"

"You did know! You stopped loving me and let him send me away!"

Demetrius's hand tingled as it brushed her wing. Did he stop loving Antarulra? Perhaps, if he hid it from Laparlana, he and Antarulra could… Suddenly, disgust filled him. Laparlana was his wife. How low had he really sunk, to think that he could buy his life at her expense? The back of his throat ached.

"A, I'm married."

"I'm dropping you. I hope you break your neck." Antarulra's arms suddenly disappeared.

"No! A! Antarulra! Please!" Demetrius plummeted.

*****

"Up that cliff!" Arple wrapped her arms around Vayorn's torso. Apran rose.

Apran landed in a small puff of snow. Arple dragged Vayorn onto the ground. He left a trail of blood behind him. Panic seized her. She laid her head against his chest. One dull heartbeat. Her hands flew. She had to get the wounds to close before he lost more blood. Perhaps even now it was too late.

Dunbar rolled, throwing himself into a pair of legs. Someone fell. He slammed his shoulders into the head as it hit the ground. His bound hands fumbled behind him for something sharp: a sword blade, an arrow tip, a piece of metal, anything.

His fingers moved across a blade; he began sawing the rope around his wrists against it.

The rope loosened. His heart raced.

Someone lunged for him. He dived, worked his hands to the front, and began to free himself.

A blade glinted on the snow: father's sword. He threw himself toward it.

The rest of the ropes fell to the ground as he cut them.

Movement behind him. He turned.

The tip of a sword brushed his chest.

He sidestepped. Iron clashed on iron as his sword rose. His temples throbbed.

He spun; his blade sank deep into flesh. He yanked it free.

Someone smashed into his back. His chest slammed against the ground. He forced air back into his lungs.

Suddenly, his mind melded with his limbs. His arms and legs danced with the ring of iron around him. Blood rushed over his hands.

He was on his feet again, beating out a steady tempo of metal against metal. A body fell against his legs; he jumped it and launched into the air. Another advance. A flash. Another body.

His hands chilled as the blood on them froze.

*****

Demetrius forced weight onto his leg. It seemed like every bone in his body was screaming. He pulled himself onto all fours. Suddenly he was on the ground again. He curled into a ball, trying to think past the giant hand crushing his body. He groaned. What if no one found him? Who would take care of Laparlana? He held his throbbing head in his hands. He couldn't die. Not like this.

CANJON

"Canjon..." Dunbar stifled a scream. His head spun. Someone's cold hands finished bandaging his leg. He dug his fingers into the saddle horn, trying to ignore the pain.

Ilmari's voice: "I'll sit behind him."

Dunbar blinked rapidly; his vision cleared.

Arple stood to his left, supporting Vayorn; Dunbar doubled over. Water swam across his vision.

Arple's voice: "You think it'll hold?"

Dunbar turned his head. Through the murk, it seemed like she was tying off a bandage around Vayorn's shoulder.

Antarulra secured Dunbar's waist to Alcaeus. "Yes, but we have to get them both to a safe place if they're going to recover." Her wing brushed Dunbar's face. He winced.

She tied Vayorn's limp body to Apran. "If he falls, he's dead. Hold onto him."

Arple mounted and leaned over Vayorn. Dunbar felt Ilmari steady him.

They rose into the air.

*****

He didn't know how many hours passed; he stopped keeping track after his body went numb. The icy air shook him like a dog shaking a rabbit. Even his ribs and back were beginning to lose feeling. He kept his eyes held shut, trying to grip consciousness for as long he could. How long did it take to freeze to death out here? He moaned. It was almost over; his mind was beginning to drift.

One word echoed through the murk inside his ears: Laparlana. He gritted his teeth. His mind fogged over. He forced it to stay clear for a second longer. Suddenly, a light flared up somewhere nearby.

A faint voice yelled, "Oi! I see someone!"

A blurry face swam above him. "Oi! You alright?"

Demetrius tried to speak.

The world around him went black.

*****

Vayorn opened his eyes. His heart raced. *Where am I?* Stone walls rose around him, bouncing back the light of a single candle. He tried to move. Something rustled. A face came into the light, her scales glinting like gold. He realized he was smiling.

Her soft hand brushed his cheek. He tilted his head toward it. *Arple? How?* He tried to speak.

"Don't. Just sleep. I'll still be here when you wake up."

The door opened. Uneven footsteps. Dunbar limped into view.

"Is he awake?"

"Yes."

The bed sank as Dunbar sat on it. "Are you awake enough to understand me?"

Vayorn nodded. There was something strange about Dunbar's voice. *Is he crying?* In the dim lighting, Vayorn couldn't tell.

"I need to know you forgive me. This is all my fault…" Dunbar trailed off.

Vayorn nodded and tried to speak; spots danced in front of his eyes. He gasped. *Gach.* He squeezed his eyes shut. His chest tightened. Arple's fingertips brushed his forehead. "Don't try to speak. Just don't. Try to breathe."

Vayorn moaned. His head felt like it was floating away from his body toward the ceiling.

"Hand me that," Arple said. Something made a scraping sound to his right.

"Drink…" Arple's arms leaned him into a sitting position. The rim of a cup brushed his lips. He swallowed. The dizziness passed. He opened his eyes. Dunbar was still sitting beside him.

"Is he alright?"

Arple nodded. "He's been doing this for a week. At least today he can understand us."

A week? Vayorn locked eyes with Arple, suddenly aware of the dark circles around her eyes. *How long's it been since she slept?*

Her hand brushed his as she laid him down again. "Antarulra said he'll live. But it could be months till he fully recovers."

The door opened again. Something ran across the floor and hurled itself onto the bed.

"He awake?"

"Yes, Agöri."

"It hurt him if I hug him?"

"Probably. But you can talk to him. Show him what you made."

"He talk?"

"Not yet. But he can hear you."

A tiny face came into the light. Agöri seemed older. *How old did he say he was? Looks at least twelve.* Another thought struck Vayorn. *Do I look older?* He sighed. *Wish I could ask for a mirror.*

A tiny book landed in his lap. Agöri held it so Vayorn could see it. Vayorn smiled, trying to muster up the strength to stay awake. Agöri kept talking, but Vayorn felt his mind beginning to fuzz over. *Have to stay awake.*

The heavy blanket over his legs rose to cover his shoulders. He thought Arple said something, but it was faint. His eyes closed. Silence…

*****

Dunbar rubbed his leg; the pain subsided. He ran his hands through his hair. Vayorn was so quiet. Perhaps the healer was right. Guilt hit him like a boulder. If only he'd done something, anything to prevent this. And if the boy did recover? His entire right arm would never regain its full strength. Dunbar lifted it and examined it. The skin around the bandages was bright pink—infection. If the healer had to amputate it... Dunbar shuddered. Vayorn might not survive the amputation. But worse, how would the boy react when they finally told him? Dunbar shuddered. He would have to tell the boy eventually; the infected blotches up and down the boy's forearm were darkening by the day. If gangrene set in, there would be no other option. Dunbar sighed. No matter what Antarulra said, no matter how many excuses she made for Dunbar, this was all Dunbar's fault. Every day of Vayorn's suffering, every cry of pain, Dunbar choked. He realized he was crying. His fingers tangled with Father's ring. A failure. Father had been right. That's all Dunbar would ever be.

As the hours passed, he watched the candle dwindle into nothingness till darkness consumed the room. He closed his eyes. Later, someone brought in another candle. The healer passed through; there was little change, he said, but part of the infection was starting to heal. Dunbar didn't know how much time passed—hours, days, weeks. Nothing mattered anymore. The healer came again and left looking a little more hopeful. At some point, someone brought in food; Dunbar left it untouched. The healer said two days had passed, and Dubar should get some sleep. Dunbar said nothing. Another few hours passed.

Suddenly, Vayorn's hand closed. His eyes opened.
"Dunbar?" he whispered. Dunbar leaned forward.
"Yes?"
"Where's Arple?"
"She had to get some sleep. She's been sleeping for two days."
"I'm not mad anymore. I want to be your son. I don't want to hate you."
Dunbar tried to steady his voice. The back of his throat ached as he forced words out, "I'm so glad." He looked away.
"Will I live?"

"Yes."

"Why's my shoulder hurt so much?" Vayorn's voice was stronger now.

Dunbar was silent. If only Vayorn hadn't asked. But perhaps the boy deserved the truth. He clenched his jaw. He couldn't tell the boy; he'd just have to make something up. Another lie? He examined the boy's pale face; how old was he? Sixteen? He looked older, far older. No, he couldn't tell the boy yet. It was too risky. He faked a lighthearted tone. "We had to stitch it back together. There was a cut about"—Dunbar gestured with his hands—"this deep into it. It was all the way down to the bone."

"Deng." Vayorn smiled proudly. Dunbar chuckled.

"We'll try to keep you entertained," Dunbar tried to joke.

Vayorn almost laughed. "You'd better. Gonna go gaching crazy if I have to stay in this bed for months."

Dunbar shook his head, trying to keep the mood light. "Then prepare to go crazy for months."

Vayorn's face fell for an instant. "We're not in…Tarshal, are we?"

"This is Canjon. My home."

Vayorn smiled. "I've never had a home."

"You do now."

"Where's Agöri?"

"Lessons."

"Lessons?" Vayorn laughed. "He's too smart to need lessons."

"Antarulra's retaking her position with enthusiasm," Dunbar laughed.

"Can I see him?"

The door flung open.

"Vayorn!" Agöri screamed, "You alive! You talking! Vaaayorn!" He jumped onto the bed. "Learned something. Wanna hear it?"

"Sure."

Agöri pulled himself up to full height, put on an important expression, and mimicked a refined accent. Dunbar heard Vayorn stifle a laugh.

Agöri began reciting. Dunbar realized he was reciting the rulers of Antike. His eyes widened. *How did the child remember all that?* The little voice went on. Finally, Agöri said, "Our grandfather, Rainulf, and Dunbar the First!" He collapsed onto the bed out of breath.

Vayorn started laughing, "I'm gonna be stuck here for a while. You gotta visit me every day, alright?"

Agöri nodded. "Promise!"

Vayorn was still talking. Dunbar pretended to listen. Perhaps the boy would recover… He seemed to take being bedridden well. And if his arm healed, all their problems would be solved. Dunbar studied the boy; something in him seemed changed. Suddenly, Vayorn's gaze locked on Dunbar. The tortured look Dunbar had come to expect from those eyes was gone.

They were peaceful.

Vayorn's eyes were happy, as if they had forgotten how to hate.

Dunbar leaned over and embraced his sons. Tears rolled down his face. Silently, he promised himself he would never lose them again.

ABOUT THE AUTHOR

H. A. Campbell thrives on the riches of epic tales, awe-inspiring lands, and cliff-hanger adventures. She drinks deeply of the beauty around her, often gazing at the dark mountain range she lives under when she lacks inspiration. Tolkien, Lewis, and George McDonald inspire her to reach for the deeper themes, the things that lay just under the surface of a character or a person. She hopes to inspire others similarly and to share the magic she has discovered in the worlds just beyond what we can touch, contained within the written page.